TAIPEI

Tao Lin is the author of the novels *Richard Yates* and *Eeeee Eee Eeee*, the novella *Shoplifting from American Apparel*, the story collection *Bed*, and the poetry collections *cognitive-behavioral therapy* and *you are a little bit happier than i am*. His work has been translated into twelve languages. He lives in Manhattan and is the founder and editor of Muumuu House.

ALSO BY TAO LIN

Richard Yates

Shoplifting from American Apparel

cognitive-behavioral therapy

Eeeee Eee Eeee

Bed

you are a little bit happier than i am

TAIPEI

A Novel

Tao Lin

VINTAGE CONTEMPORARIES
Vintage Books
A Division of Random House, Inc.
New York

A VINTAGE CONTEMPORARIES ORIGINAL, JUNE 2013

A portion of this work was previously published, in different form,
as "Relationship Story," in *Vice Magazine* (2011).

Library of Congress Cataloging-in-Publication Data
Lin, Tao
Taipei : a novel / Tao Lin.
pages cm
ISBN 978-0-307-95017-8
I. Title.
PS3612.I517T35 2013
813'.6—dc23   2013005675

Book design by Heather Kelly

Printed in the United States of America
10 9 8 7 6 5 4 3 2 1

TAIPEI

1

It began raining a little from a hazy, cloudless-seeming sky as Paul, 26, and Michelle, 21, walked toward Chelsea to attend a magazine-release party in an art gallery. Paul had resigned to not speaking and was beginning to feel more like he was "moving through the universe" than "walking on a sidewalk." He stared ahead with a mask-like expression, weakly trying to remember where he was one year ago, last November, more for something to do than because he wanted to know, though he was not incurious. Michelle, to his left, drifted in and out of his peripheral vision—far enough away for pedestrians to pass unknowingly between them—like a slow, amorphous flickering. Paul was thinking the word "somewhere," meditatively as both placeholder and ends, when Michelle asked if he was okay.

"Yes," said Paul automatically. As they entered a building, a few minutes later, he sort of glanced at Michelle and was surprised to see her grinning, then couldn't stop himself from grinning. Sometimes, during an argument, feeling like he'd been acting in a movie and the scene had ended, Paul would suddenly grin, causing Michelle to grin, and they'd be able to enjoy doing things together again, for one to forty hours, but that hadn't happened this time, partly because Michelle had grinned first. Paul looked away, slightly confused, and suppressed his grin. "What," he said in an unintentionally loud monotone, unsure what he felt exactly, and they entered a large, mundane elevator, whose door closed slowly.

"What," said Paul at a normal volume.

"Nothing," said Michelle still grinning a little.

"Why are you grinning?"

"No reason," said Michelle.

"What caused you to grin?"

"Nothing. Just life. The situation."

Entering the party, on the fifth floor, Paul realized he'd said vaguely negative things on the internet, at some point, about a person who was probably in attendance, so walked quickly to Jeremy—an easy-to-talk-to acquaintance—and asked what movies he'd seen recently. Michelle stood at a near distance—partly in view, then obscured, then fully in view—before approaching, with what seemed like a sly smile, to ask if Paul wanted a drink. Jeremy was calculating aloud the per-hour price of a two-part biopic on Che Guevara when Michelle returned with a beer. Paul thanked her and she moved away in an intermittent, curving, crab-like manner, seeming relaxed and disoriented. "She wants to be alone," thought Paul with some confusion. "Or she wants to let me be alone."

An hour later they were holding their third or fourth drinks, sitting on chairs in a dark corner, facing what seemed to Paul like one group of sixty to eighty friends. Loud, dancey, mostly electronic music—currently Michael Jackson— played from unseen speakers. Paul was staring at an area of torsos. In his previous relationships, he knew, he had experienced dissatisfaction, to some degree, as an empiri- cally backed enthusiasm for the future, because it implied the possibility of a more satisfying relationship with some- one he hadn't met; with Michelle, whom he felt closer to than his previous girlfriends—he'd told her this a few times, truthfully—dissatisfaction felt more like a personal failing, a direct indication of internal malfunctioning, which he should focus on privately correcting. Instead, he vaguely knew, he was waiting for Michelle, or some combination of Michelle and the world, to endure and overpower his negativity—to be the solution in which he would irreversibly, untraceably dis- solve. He sipped his wine, thinking about how Michael Jack- son had been using ten to forty Xanax per night, according to the internet, before he died last summer. Paul distractedly scooted his chair toward Michelle and, with unclear purpose, touched her shoulder, tentative and reckless as a child petting a large dog looking elsewhere. Expecting the bored expres- sion of ten minutes ago, when they'd looked at each other noncommittally as she returned to her chair with another drink, Paul was surprised by Michelle's severely, actively— almost seethingly—depressed expression. Michelle's face reddened antagonistically, in reflexive defense, it seemed, because then she appeared frustrated and a little confused, then shy and embarrassed. Paul asked if she wanted to leave soon. Michelle hesitated, then asked if that was what Paul wanted.

"I don't know. Are you hungry?"

"Not really. Are you?"

"I don't know," said Paul. "I would eat somewhere." One night, months ago, they had sat on a curb on Lafayette Street to continue an argument in a resting position. Paul had become distracted by Michelle's calm, intelligent demeanor and had begun to forget why they were arguing, even while speaking in an agitated voice, as he became fixated, with increasing appreciation, on how Michelle liked him enough to not simply leave and never see him again, which she could do—which anyone could always do, Paul had thought, suddenly intrigued by the concept of gratitude. "Do you want to eat at the Green Table?"

"If that's what you want," said Michelle.

"Okay. When do you want to leave?"

"After I finish this glass of wine."

"Okay," said Paul, and scooted his chair halfway to where it had been. "I'm going to introduce Kyle to someone. I'll be back in like five minutes."

Paul couldn't find Kyle, 19, or Kyle's girlfriend, Gabby, 28—his suitemates in an apartment off the Graham L train stop in Brooklyn—and was returning to Michelle when he realized he'd walked past Kyle, standing drunkenly alone in a dense area of people, as if at a concert. After some indecision, briefly motionless, Paul turned around and asked if Kyle wanted to meet Traci. Kyle nodded and followed Paul outside the gallery, to a wide hallway, where six people, including Traci—described earlier by Kyle as "really hot," by Paul as "her blog gets a lot of hits"—shook hands with one another. Paul grinned uncomfortably as he stared at one person, then another, thinking he had "absolutely nothing" to say, except maybe what he was currently thinking, which didn't seem appropriate and also kept changing. He noticed Michelle sitting alone, against a wall, around thirty feet away. The front of his head felt extraneous and suctioned as a plastic bag, stuck there in a wind, as he walked to her, aware she had probably seen him grinning at Traci, and asked if she wanted to go now.

"Do you?" said Michelle not standing.

"Yeah," said Paul looking toward the gallery.

"You can talk to Kyle more, if you want."

"I don't want to," said Paul.

"It seems like you do."

"I don't," said Paul, who viewed friends mostly as means to girlfriends, he knew, contrary to Michelle, who valued them as ends (they'd discussed this a few times and concluded, to some degree, that Paul had his writing, Michelle her friends). "I'm just going to say bye to him. I'll be right back." When he couldn't find Kyle in the hallway he walked robotically into the dark, crowded gallery thinking "lost in the world" in a precariously near-earnest tone. Kyle was standing with a group of people in a sideways manner that didn't clearly indicate if he knew them or not. He looked at Paul with an expression like he was thinking what to say, then like he was going to insult Paul, then less like he'd chosen to refrain than like he'd lost interest.

"I think Michelle feels like I'm not giving her enough attention," said Paul slowly.

"That's funny," said Kyle after a few seconds. "Because Gabby, after one of our parties, said you gave Michelle so much attention and were always next to her talking to her, but I'm always talking to someone else, and that I don't love her."

"What did you say?"

"That I love her and give her attention," said Kyle with a bored, self-loathing expression.

Paul couldn't find Michelle in the hallway, then turned a corner and saw her crouched on the floor, sixty to eighty feet away, discrepant and vulnerable, in the bright off-white corridor, as a rarely seen animal. Paul, walking self-consciously toward her, vaguely remembered a night, early in their relationship, when he somehow hadn't expected her to enlarge in his vision as he approached where she'd stood (looking down at a flyer, one leg slightly bent) in Think Coffee. The comical, bewildering fear—equally calming and surprising, amusing and foreboding—he'd felt as she rapidly and sort of ominously increased in size had characterized their first two months together. It had seemed like they would never fight, and the nothingness of the future had gained a framework-y somethingness that felt privately exciting, like entering a different family's house as a small child, or the beginning elaborations of a science-fiction conceit. Then, one night, in late April, after cooking and eating pasta together, Paul had complained—meekly, without looking at her face—that Michelle never helped wash dishes. Michelle stared at him silently a few seconds before her eyes became suddenly watery, the extra layer of translucence materializing like a shedding of something delicate. Paul stared back, weirdly entranced—he'd never seen her cry—before crawling across his wood floor, over his yoga mat, dizzy with emotion, to hug her and apologize. In May he began complaining once or twice a week (that certain things Michelle did were inconsiderate, that he felt neglected) and, by July, most days, was either visibly irritated or mutely, inscrutably despondent—as if he alone had a vast knowledge of horrible truths, which, he knew, he didn't—but could still feel good, to some degree, after coffee or alcohol or, when easily attainable, prescription drugs, most recently methadone, supplied by Michelle's friend who had fallen down stairs, which they'd ingested once every four to six days for five weeks, ending three weeks ago. One night, since then, Michelle had told Paul it seemed like he "hated" her and Paul, after around ten seconds, had cited a day they'd had fun together, then had grinned and said "no" illogically when Michelle correctly said they'd been on methadone that day.

"Why are you sitting so far away?"

"I'm waiting for you. You said you wanted to leave an hour ago."

Outside, on the sidewalk, Michelle walked quickly ahead with her hands in her jacket pockets, as if to better escape Paul with a more streamlined form, though also it was still raining. Paul asked what she wanted to do. "I don't know," she said. "I'm not hungry anymore."

They crossed 10th Avenue in a diagonal, not at an intersection, through headlights of a stopped taxi—two or three people were closing their umbrellas, getting in—onto the opposite sidewalk and continued downtown, bodies bent against the wind.

"Wait," said Paul. "Can we stop walking for a minute?"

They stopped, facing the same direction, on the sidewalk.

"What's wrong?" said Paul after a few seconds, slightly accusatorily.

"You've been ignoring me all night," said Michelle.

"I moved close to you and hugged you, when we were sitting."

"Once we got inside you walked away and started talking to other people."

"You walked away from me," said Paul. "I felt confused."

A deli worker standing under an awning was looking into some unspecific distance, honestly uninterested. "I've never felt you act this way before," said Michelle unsteadily, looking down, suddenly tired and scared, the protest of her having dispersed to something negotiable. For a few days, two or three months ago, she had considered studying abroad in Barcelona next spring, which would've meant four months apart. Paul thought of how they'd kept delaying buying plane tickets to visit his parents in Taiwan—in December, which was next month, he knew—as if in tacit understanding that their relationship wouldn't last that long. Paul felt himself trying to interpret the situation, as if there was a problem to be solved, but there didn't seem to be anything, or maybe there was, but he was three or four skill sets away from comprehension, like an amoeba trying to create a personal webpage using CSS.

"I'm just naturally losing interest," he finally said, a little improvisationally, and Michelle began quietly crying. "I didn't expect this at all," she said. "I've felt good about us the past two weeks. I thought we've been closer than we've ever been."

"I think I was affected by the study-abroad thing," said Paul nearly inaudibly, confused how she'd thought they'd been close the past two weeks.

"Go back to the party. I'll talk to you tomorrow."

"Wait. I don't think we should leave each other now."

"Have a good time with your friends," said Michelle sincerely.

"Wait. What friends?"

"We'll talk tomorrow," said Michelle.

"If we leave each other now it's over."

"It doesn't have to be like that."

"I only go to things to find a girlfriend," said Paul paraphrasing himself, and they stood not looking at each other, for one or two minutes, as rain from faraway places disappeared into their clothing and hair. Paul felt surprised by the friendly tone of his voice as he asked if Michelle wanted to eat dinner with him, in a restaurant.

"I don't want to talk to you right now," said Michelle.

"I don't want to be in a relationship where it's like this."

"I don't either," said Michelle.

"I'm going back if you don't want to do something."

"I want to go home. Good night."

"Okay," said Paul, and turned around, aware they hadn't parted like this before. He crossed 22nd Street and turned to cross 10th Avenue and saw Michelle disjunctively running and walking toward him, stopping at a red light with the posture of a depressed teenager. Paul thought of how she liked Nirvana a lot, and she crossed the street, slowing as she neared and stopping within arm's reach. "Paul," she said after a few seconds, and touched his upper arm, as if to offer a way back, through her, to some prior intimacy, from where they could tunnel carefully elsewhere, or to the same place, but with a kind of skill this time, having practiced once. Paul remained still, unsure what to say or think. Michelle lowered her hand to her side. "What are you doing?" she said, somewhat defensively.

"What do you mean?"

"Aren't you going back to the party?"

"Yeah. I said I was."

"Fine," said Michelle.

Paul felt passively committed to not moving.

"Why are you standing here?"

"You came back," said Paul feebly, and four to six people approached from the direction of the party. Michelle stepped into a soil-y area, lower and darker than the sidewalk, and leaned between spires on a metal fence, with her left profile—obscured by her long, dark hair—toward Paul, who stared dumbly at the gently convex curve of her back, thinking with theoretical detachment that he should console her and that maybe the discomfort of her forearms against the thin metal of the fence had created a location, accessible only to herself, toward which she could relocate, away from what she felt, in a kind of shrinking. "Do you—" said Paul, and coughed twice with his mouth closed. "Do you want to eat dinner with me somewhere?" Michelle turned toward him a little, moving her head to see through her hair. "What are you doing?" she said in a tired, distracted voice, and leaned back on the fence without waiting for an answer. After a vague amount of time Paul heard himself asking again if she wanted to eat dinner with him, at the Green Table, one of the few restaurants they wanted to but hadn't tried, then she was walking away, her long legs scissor-like in their little, orderly movements. It would take her thousands of steps to get anywhere, but she would get there easily, and when she arrived, in the present, it would seem like it had been a single movement that brought her there. Did existence ever seem worked for? One seemed simply to be here, less an accumulation of moments than a single arrangement continuously gifted from some inaccessible future.

As Michelle became smaller, then out of view, Paul distantly sensed the implication, from his previous thoughts, which he'd mostly forgotten, that the universe in its entirety was a message, to itself, to not feel bad—an ever-elaborating, languageless rhetoric against feeling bad—and he was troubled by this, suspecting that his thoughts and intentions, at some point, in April or May or years ago, in college or as a child, had been wrong, but he had continued in that wrongness, and was now distanced from some correct beginning to a degree that the universe (and himself, a part of the universe) was articulately against him.

In his tiredness and inattention these intuitions mani-fested in Paul as an uncomplicated feeling of bleakness—that he was in the center of something bad, whose confines were expanding, as he remained in the same place. Faintly he recognized in this a kind of humor, but mostly he was aware of the rain, continuous and everywhere as an incognizable information, as he crossed the magnified street, gleaming and blacker from wetness, to return to the party.

Michelle's absence in Taiwan was mentioned once, at din-ner with eight to twelve relatives, a week into Paul's visit, when Paul's father, 61, characteristically without prompt-ing or context, loudly joked that Paul's girlfriends always left him, then laughed in an uncontrollable-seeming, close-eyed, almost wincing manner. Paul's mother, 57, responded with aggravation that the opposite was true and that Paul's father shouldn't "lie recklessly," she said in Mandarin.

Paul hadn't seen his parents since they sold their house in Florida a year and a half ago and moved back to Taiwan, after almost thirty years in America, into a fourteenth-floor apartment, in a rapidly developing area of Taipei, with two guest rooms that his mother had repeatedly stressed were Paul's room and Paul's brother's room. Paul thought his par-ents looked the same, but he viewed his mother, who had been diagnosed as "prediabetic," a little differently, maybe as finally past middle age, though not yet elderly. Her emails, the past eight months, had frequently mentioned, as sort of asides, or reminders, to herself mostly, that she was using less sugar in her daily coffee, but really shouldn't be using any—her most emphasized message to her family, the past two decades, in Paul's view, was the importance of health to a happy life—though her doctor had said the amount she used was okay, and on days without sugar in her coffee, which was decaf, she felt "empty, like something is missing," she had said in one email.

When, one afternoon, Paul saw her putting sugar in her coffee, it seemed to them both like she'd been "caught" doing something wrong. She blushed and briefly focused self-consciously on stirring her coffee with a little spoon, then she looked at Paul and her mouth reflexively opened in an endearingly child-like, self-concious, almost mischievous display of guilt and shame and repentance that Paul recognized from the rare times he'd seen her do things she'd told him not to do, such as eat food that had fallen on the floor. After a grinning Paul obligatorily said something negative about sugar, that everyone, not only diabetics, should avoid it, his mother's expression resolved to the controlled, smirking, wryly satisfied demeanor of an adult who is slightly more amused than embarrassed to have been caught idly succumbing to a meager comfort that they've openly disapproved of for themselves and others. Paul unintentionally caught his mother using sugar two more times, the next two weeks, resulting in similar—but less intense—reactions and outcomes. The 24oz organic raw agave nectar he had mailed her, believing it was the safest sweetener for diabetics, had been opened but not used, it seemed, more than once or twice.

His fourth week in Taiwan, one more week than planned, his mother began encouraging him two or three times a day— with a slightly affected, strategic nonchalance, Paul felt—to move to Taiwan for one year to teach English. She mentioned Ernest Hemingway more than once while saying Paul would benefit, as a writer, from the interesting experience. Paul said he would benefit by being in America, where he could speak the language and maintain friendships and "do things," he said in Mandarin, visualizing himself on his back, on his yoga mat, with his MacBook on the inclined surface of his thighs, formed by bending his knees, looking at the internet. His parents encouraged him to stay a fifth week, which with some difficulty he decided against, thinking it "excessive," after which—his last few days in Taiwan—his mother began to stress that he should visit every December from now on, stating it as a fact, then making a noise meaning "right?" Paul's responses ranged from "maybe," to neutral-to-annoyed noises, to an explanation of why the more she pressured him the less influence she'd have on his decisions.

At the airport Paul's mother stayed with Paul until she wasn't allowed farther without a ticket. She pointed at her eyes and said they were watery. Paul was "required," she said in Mandarin with mock sternness, to visit next December.

In the terminal, sitting with eyes closed, Paul imagined moving alone to Taipei at an age like 51, when maybe he'd have cycled through enough friendships and relationships to not want more. Because his Mandarin wasn't fluent enough for conversations with strangers—and he wasn't close to his relatives, with whom attempts at communication were brief and non-advancing and often koan-like, ending usually with one person looking away, ostensibly for assistance, then leaving—he'd be preemptively estranged, secretly unfriendable. The unindividualized, shifting mass of everyone else would be a screen, distributed throughout the city, onto which he'd project the movie of his uninterrupted imagination. Because he'd appear to, and be able to pretend he was, but never actually be a part of the mass, maybe he'd gradually begin to feel a kind of needless intimacy, not unlike being in the same room as a significant other and feeling affection without touching or speaking. An earnest assembling of the backup life he'd sketched and constructed the blueprints and substructures for (during the average of six weeks per year, spread throughout his life, that he'd been in Taiwan) would begin, at some point, after which, months or years later, one morning, he would sense the independent organization of a second, itinerant consciousness—lured here by the new, unoccupied structures—toward which he'd begin sending the data of his sensory perception. The antlered, splashing, water-treading land animal of his first consciousness would sink to some lower region, in the lake of himself, where he would sometimes descend in sleep and experience its disintegrating particles—and furred pieces, brushing past—in dreams, as it disappeared into the pattern of the nearest functioning system.

On the plane, after a cup of black coffee, Paul thought of Taipei as a fifth season, or "otherworld," outside, or in equal contrast with, his increasingly familiar and self-consciously repetitive life in America, where it seemed like the seasons, connecting in right angles, for some misguided reason, had formed a square, sarcastically framing nothing—or been melded, Paul vaguely imagined, about an hour later, facedown on his arms on his dining tray, into a door-knocker, which a child, after twenty to thirty knocks, no longer expecting an answer, has continued using, in a kind of daze, distracted by the pointlessness of his activity, looking absently elsewhere, unaware when he will abruptly, idly stop.

2

Something staticky and paranormally ventilated about the air, which drifted through a half-open window, late one afternoon, caused a delicately waking Paul, clutching a pillow and drooling a little, to believe he was a small child in Florida, in a medium-size house, on or near winter break. He felt dimly excited, anticipating a hyperactive movement of his body into a standing position, then was mostly unconscious for a vague amount of time until becoming aware of what seemed to be a baffling non sequitur—and, briefly, in its mysterious approach from some eerie distance, like someone else's consciousness—before resolving plainly as a memory, of having already left Florida, at some point, to attend New York University. After a deadpan pause, during which the new information was accepted by default as recent, he casually believed it was autumn and he was in college, and as he felt that period's particular gloominess he sensed a concurrent assembling, at a specific distance inside himself, of dozens of once-intimate images, people, places, situations. With a sensation of easily and entirely abandoning a prior context, of having no memory, he focused, as an intrigued observer, on this assembling and was surprised by an urge, which he immediately knew he hadn't felt in months, or maybe years, to physically involve himself—by going outside and living each day patiently—in the ongoing, concrete occurrence of what he was passively, slowly remembering. But the emotion dispersed to a kind of nothingness—and its associated memories, like organs in a lifeless body, became rapidly indiscernible, dissembling by the metaphysical equivalent, if there was one, of entropy—as he realized, with some confusion and an oddly instinctual reluctance, blinking and discerning his new room, which after two months could still seem unfamiliar, that he was somewhere else, as a different person, in a much later year.

He kept his eyes pressurelessly closed and didn't move, wanting to return—without yet knowing who or what he was—to sleep, where he could intensify and prolong and explore what he residually felt and was uncontrollably forgetting, but was already alert, in concrete reality, to a degree that his stillness, on his queen-size mattress, felt like a kind of hiding. He stared at the backs of his eyelids with motionless eyeballs, slightly feigning not knowing what he was looking at—which also felt like a kind of hiding—and gradually discerned that he was in Brooklyn, on an aberrantly colder day in late March, in the two-person apartment, in a four-story house, where he had moved, a few weeks after returning from Taiwan, because Kyle and Gabby had wanted more space, to "save their relationship."

It was spring, not winter or autumn, Paul thought with some lingering confusion. He listened to the layered murmur of wind against leaves, familiarly and gently disorienting as a terrestrial sound track, reminding people of their own lives, then opened his MacBook—sideways, like a hardcover book—and looked at the internet, lying on his side, with his right ear pressed into his pillow, as if, unable to return to sleep, at least in position to hear what, in his absence, might be happening there.

That night—after leaving his room at dusk, then "working on things" in an underground computer lab in Bobst Library, as he did most days—Paul became "completely lost," he repeatedly thought, in a tundra-like area of Brooklyn for around twenty minutes before unexpectedly arriving at the arts space hosting the panel discussion, on the topic of self-publishing, he'd agreed to attend with his literary acquaintance Anton, 23, who was visiting from Norway. Paul began, at some point, during the ninety-minute discussion, to feel a mocking, sitcom-like conviction that, for him, "too many years had passed" since college—that without education's season-backed, elaborately subdivided, continuous structure, traceable numerically backward almost to birth, connecting a life in that direction, he was becoming isolated and unexplainable as one of those mysterious phenomena, contained within informational boxes, in picture-heavy books on natural history, which he would've felt scared, as a child, if he was alone in a dark room, to think about for too long. After the ninety-minute discussion, which seemed unanimously in favor of self-publishing, the audience was instructed, somewhat anticlimactically, to bring their folding chairs to another room and lean them against a wall, then Paul and Anton stood waiting for Juan, 24, an MFA student in fiction at NYU, who'd wanted to eat with them but was talking to an attractive woman.

"What should we do?" said Paul.

"I don't know," said Anton in a quiet monotone.

They decided to leave in three minutes, at 9:01. This was Paul's second or third social situation involving more than one person, excluding himself, since returning from Taiwan, two months ago. His only regular communication since his relationship with Michelle ended three and a half months ago was emails and Gmail chats with Charles, 25, who lived in Seattle with his girlfriend and who had sold most of his belongings, the past few months, in preparation to leave America indefinitely to travel alone in Mexico—and eventually South America—because he felt "alienated," he'd said.

"It's 9:04," said Anton.

"What should we do?"

"We could wait until 9:10."

"I don't know," said Paul grinning. "I don't know. Let's just leave now, I think." He didn't move for around ten seconds. "We should go," he said, and after a few seconds moved toward the exit, feeling slightly oxygen deprived.

"Hey," said Juan running. "Are you guys going to eat now?"

"Yeah," said Paul, and glanced, for some reason, at Anton, whose eyes, behind medium-thick lenses, appeared farther away but of higher resolution than the rest of his face.

"Sorry," said Juan looking at Anton.

"It's called Pacifico," said Paul outside. "The address is 97 Smith."

"I think Pacific is this way," said Juan.

"Pacifico," said Paul looking at Anton, who seemed to be grinning.

"This way," said Juan rolling his bike beside him.

"Wait," said Paul. "The restaurant is called Pacifico."

"I kept thinking it was on Pacific," said Juan with a serious expression.

"No," said Paul. "But it's probably near Pacific."

In Pacifico, a dungeon-like Mexican restaurant, Paul stared at his menu, waiting for his eyes to adjust in the diffuse lighting. He was aware of Anton and Juan, across the table, also holding and staring at menus. When their burritos arrived he noticed, with preemptively suppressed interpretation, that his, of the three, appeared slightly darkest. Then a large group of males from the panel discussion entered and seated themselves in a swarming and disorganized manner, which Paul experienced as a parody of surrounding a heterosexual, single male with a variety of ethnicities and ages of males.

While idly eating the salad-y remains of his burrito with a fork, around twenty minutes later, Paul became aware of himself analyzing when he should've left. He vaguely traced back the night and concluded he should've left when, on his way to the venue, he had been "completely lost." He allowed himself to consider earlier opportunities, mostly for something to do, and discerned after a brief sensation of helplessness—like if he'd divided 900 by itself and wanted the calculator to answer 494/494 or 63/63—that, in terms of leaving this social situation, he shouldn't have been born. He suppressed a grin, then channeled the impulse into the formation of what he thought of as a nervous smile and stood and mumbled "I'm going to sleep now" and "nice seeing you" until he was outside, where it was windy and cold.

21

He walked toward an F train station, aware of the strangeness of clouds at night—their enveloped flatness and dimensional vagueness, shifting and osmotic as some advanced form of gaseous amoeba—and remembered when he got lodged in an upside-down wood stool, as a small child, in Florida. His father had sawed off two rungs with an enormous, floppy, serrated blade while his mother, alternately grinning and intensely focused, careful not to allow her personal experience of the event impair its documentation, photographed them from different angles, sometimes directing their attention to the camera, like in a photo shoot.

The next two weeks Paul gradually began to view the five months until September, when his second novel would be published and he would go on a two-month book tour, as an "interim period," during which he would mostly be alone, "calmly organizing things," he said in an email to his mother. He had already been mostly alone, he knew, since returning from Taiwan, but in a vague way, often wondering if he should've gone to whatever social gathering. Now if he felt urges to socialize, to meet a romantic prospect, he would simply relocate them, without further consideration, beyond the "interim period," when he would be extremely social, he envisioned. Until then he would calmly focus on being productive in a low-level manner, finding to-do lists and unfinished projects in his Gmail account and further organizing, working on, or deleting them, for example.

In early April he got an email from Traci asking if she could email-interview him for a website. After a few emails Paul asked Traci, whom he now reasonably, he felt, viewed as a romantic prospect, if she wanted to meet for dinner. At an Asian fusion restaurant, which Traci had suggested, they talked for around fifteen minutes, during which Paul's interest steadily increased, before Traci mentioned living with her boyfriend. Paul was aware of the ice hockey game on the flat-screen TV attached to a wall, of the disparity between Thai food and ice hockey, as he slowly said "is, um, is it a studio apartment?"

Walking alone, to his room, an hour later, he realized he was deriving comfort from the existence, in his life, of a "backup prospect." There was a specific girl he liked who liked him back, but he couldn't remember who, it seemed. When he realized he'd been thinking of Anton, that he'd unconsciously de-gendered and abstracted Anton into a kind of silhouette, which he'd successfully presented to himself as a romantic prospect, he grinned uncontrollably for around thirty seconds, almost getting hit by a minivan when, rerouting to a darker street to better hide his face, he jogged somewhat recklessly across an intersection.

Paul felt more committed, after that, to viewing the time until September as an interim period, and didn't have an in-person conversation for more than a week, during which, to his own approval, he seemed to be settling, if precariously, with two days spent mostly eating, into a somewhat productive, loneliness-free routine. He remembered while peeling a banana one night that he had committed, months ago, to a reading in April—in three days, he learned from the internet, in a building near Times Square.

At the reading, after arriving ten minutes early by accident and talking to the organizer, then sitting alone and, to appear occupied, holding a pen and staring down at what he'd printed in the library—an account of his visit to Taiwan, four months ago—where he planned to return immediately after he and Frederick, an author in his early 40s, finished reading, Paul began to feel sleepy, in his seat. Yawning, he looked up and recognized Mitch, 26, a classmate from middle/ high school in Florida, where they had mutual friends but had never spoken to each other, that Paul could remember, approaching from a conspiratorially far distance, like an FBI agent but slower. Mitch had messaged on Facebook, a few weeks ago, that he might attend this reading.

"You look the same. What about me?"

"Taller," said Mitch seeming a little nervous.

"How can you tell? I'm sitting."

"The shape of your legs, and your body, I think. Something about your bone structure."

After the reading Lucie, 23, introduced herself and Amy, 23, and Daniel, 25, to Paul and Mitch, saying something about her and Amy's online magazine. Paul asked if they had business cards, not thinking they would. Amy, after encouragement from Lucie, reluctantly gave Paul a business card, seeming a little embarrassed. When Paul looked up from the business card, putting it in his back pocket, he was startled by the sudden appearance of Frederick smiling at him with his arm around Lucie in a manner that seemed calculated, but wasn't, Paul knew, to firmly establish they were "together." A bewildered-seeming, middle-aged woman with an Italian accent asked Paul something about agave nectar, wanting it for a diabetic friend, it seemed. Paul said he'd actually learned, a few months ago, that it raised blood sugar as intensely as sugar and that he'd mailed his mother unheated, unfiltered honey, which was the healthiest sweetener—for diabetics, or anyone—based on what he currently knew, which could be wrong, he also knew.

In a taxi to a party, forty minutes later, Paul imagined another him walking toward the library and, for a few seconds, visualizing the position and movement of two red dots through a silhouetted, aerial view of Manhattan, felt as imaginary, as mysterious and transitory and unfindable, as the other dot. He visualized the vibrating, squiggling, looping, arcing line representing the three-dimensional movement, plotted in a cubic grid, of the dot of himself, accounting for the different speed and direction of each vessel of which he was a passenger—taxi, Earth, solar system, Milky Way, etc. Adding a fourth dimension, representing time, he visualized the patterned scribbling shooting off in one direction, with a slight wobble, miles from where it was seconds ago. He imagined his trajectory as a vacuum-sealed tube, into which he'd arrived and through which—traveling alone in the vacuum-sealed tube of his own life—he'd be suctioned and from which he'd exit, as a successful delivery to some unimaginable recipient. Realizing this was only his concrete history, his public movement through space-time from birth to death, he briefly imagined being able to click on his trajectory to access his private experience, enlarging the dot of a coordinate until it could be explored like a planet.

At the party, which was mostly people in their 30s and 40s, Paul asked Amy an open-ended question about her parents. When she began, after a pause, to answer, he moved his phone from his pants pocket to his ear. "Hello," he said in a clear voice, and felt physically isolated, like he was wearing a motorcycle helmet, as he peripherally observed Amy moving her wine, almost spilling it, to her mouth.

"Just kidding," said Paul. "No one called me."

Amy had a glassy, disoriented expression.

"I don't have a phone call," said Paul.

"That was good," said Amy looking away.

"Just kidding," said Paul grinning weakly.

The rest of the party, after briefly talking to Lucie, who invited him and Mitch to a party next week at her apartment, Paul talked mostly to Daniel, who had enough money from selling marijuana in San Francisco that he hadn't had a job since moving here last autumn. Paul asked if Daniel liked drugs. Daniel said he liked "benzos" and opiates. Paul asked if he liked Rilo Kiley and he became quiet a few seconds, seeming worried, like he might not be able to answer, before saying "um, not really."

Paul went with Daniel, the next night, to a BBQ-themed party, where their main focus, soon after arriving, was on discerning how to leave tactfully, considering how much food they'd eaten and how little they were contributing to conversation, for a party at Kyle and Gabby's apartment. Standing in a kitchen, at one point, while Daniel was outside smoking, Paul felt like a shark whose eyes have protectively "glossed over" during a feeding frenzy, as he mechanically ate salad, cheese, a burger, apple pie, chips while vaguely focused on not doing anything to cause others to talk to him.

At Kyle and Gabby's apartment—his first time back since moving out—Paul uncharacteristically approached an intriguing, attractive stranger named Laura and asked her questions with a serious expression, standing at a maybe too-close distance, as if after an unskillful teleportation he didn't want to underscore by fixing. Laura was here with her friend Walter, who knew Gabby. Paul could see that Laura, who wasn't looking at him, didn't like his presence and was getting annoyed, but due to alcohol he felt unaffected by this information and kept asking questions, including her age and what college, if any, she attended, or had attended. As Laura's annoyance intensified to a slightly curious disbelief she became extra alert—focusing exclusively on Paul with a challenging, vigilant expression. She asked why he was asking so many questions.

"I'm not. I'm just trying to talk."

"Why are you interrogating me?"

"I'm just trying to have a conversation."

"What college did you go to?" said Laura accusatorily.

"New York University. How old are you?"

Laura walked away, somewhat aimlessly, into the room Paul crawled across the first time he saw Michelle cry—around a year ago, he realized. In the room now was a king-size bed, which occupied maybe 80 percent of its surface. Paul was sitting alone, at the snack table, thirty minutes later, when Laura approached with a bored expression, unaware of his presence until he stood and said "I highly recommend the Funyuns" in an exaggeratedly helpful voice, choosing Funyuns—corn in the shape and flavor of fried rings of onion—somewhat randomly from the eight to twelve snacks on the table.

"Oh, really?" said Laura reciprocating his tone.

"Let me help you," said Paul lifting the giant plastic red bowl toward Laura, who chose and bit a piece, then moved backward a little, with a playful expression, nodding and smiling, before turning around and walking away, reappearing around twenty minutes later at a near distance, moving directly, as if after a search, toward an inattentive Paul, seated in the same chair as earlier, not apparently doing anything. Before he could say anything about Funyuns, or form any thoughts, Laura had told him her full name, which she wanted him to memorize, quizzing him on it twice—crudely, functionally—before abruptly walking away.

Around midnight an aimlessly wandering Gabby, appearing lost in her own kitchen, stopped in front of Daniel and said "you have a nose ring," with a slightly confused expression to Daniel, who confirmed he did. Gabby, a foot and a half shorter than Daniel, stared up at him a few seconds before saying something that, Paul thought, conveyed she earnestly believed nose rings were objectively bad. She asked where Daniel was from and said "oh, that makes sense, then," appearing visibly less tense, when Daniel said San Francisco.

Paul, staring at Daniel's left profile, said "I just realized you look like Hugh Jackman."

"He looks like Richard Tuttle," said Gabby.

"I don't know who that is," said Daniel.

Gabby said Richard Tuttle was a famous artist. Daniel said when he was young his father only brought him to galleries and museums whenever they went anywhere. Paul heard someone say "sculptor." Someone who didn't know Daniel drunkenly said "he got the nose ring so people won't think he's Hugh Jackman" to Paul at close range. Gabby mentioned another artist Daniel didn't know and Paul began to sometimes say "you're too mainstream for us" in a loud, sarcastic voice while staring at Gabby—thinking that, by underscoring that he and Daniel were obviously too mainstream for her, he was sincerely complimenting her knowledge of the art world—who ignored him easily, with no indication of any awareness of his presence. When Gabby finally looked at him, seeming more confused than agitated, Paul sarcastically sustained a huge grin, which Gabby stared at blankly while appearing to be thinking, very slowly, due to alcohol, about what, if anything, she should do about what was happening. After around five seconds she walked away with a slight, momentary wobble. Kyle appeared around fifteen minutes later and said "leave" to Daniel, who was grinning about something else.

"Huh?" said Daniel.

"Leave," said Kyle.

"Are you serious?"

"Yes," said Kyle, and Paul realized, with a sensation of low-level epiphany, that Gabby, offended by the nose-ring encounter, must have forced Kyle to tell Daniel to leave. Paul said this aloud a few times, to seemingly no one, then asked why Kyle was "being mean." Daniel said he would leave after he finished his drink and Kyle said "that's fine" and walked away.

"Jesus," said Paul. "Gabby hates nose rings."

"I didn't think she was angry when we talked," said Daniel.

"You're probably benefiting this party the most out of anyone," said Paul. "You're standing in one place, occasionally saying something witty, causing people passing by to laugh. You're not even eating anything."

"I planned to go to another party anyway," said Daniel.

Almost half the party, thirty minutes later, was on the wide sidewalk outside the apartment building, grinning drunkenly or looking at one another with openly bored or neutral expressions, waiting for directions to the other party. Paul, who was grinning uncontrollably, had approached groups of acquaintances asking if they wanted to go to a different party while a cheerful-seeming Daniel, standing in place in the kitchen, sometimes assumed the role of an unruly tyrant, saying things like "get every single person" and "we aren't leaving until you get every person." Paul had wanted to tell Daniel he shouldn't want so much from life but couldn't remember the stock phrase for "don't want too much in life" and, after a long pause, had said "you shouldn't want so much in life." Mitch had repeatedly held shots of tequila toward Paul, who drank two and, at one point, entered the small room where

Kyle and Gabby slept and interrupted Gabby and Jeremy and Juan by asking if "anyone" wanted to go to "a different party," aware he was unaffected, due to alcohol, by Gabby's presence.

Someone said it probably wasn't a good idea to stand "in a giant mass blocking the entire sidewalk" in front of the party they'd just abandoned, and the group of twelve to fifteen people began walking in a direction, led vaguely by Daniel, who was talking into his phone. Laura slung an arm around Paul's shoulder and said "Paul" loudly and that she was going to slap him if the party wasn't good and asked for a cigarette. Paul said he didn't smoke and Laura walked away. After around ten blocks Daniel moved his phone away from his head and told Paul—and three or four other people within range—that they'd walked in the wrong direction. Paul said someone needed to make an announcement because the group, which wasn't stopping, was too large for information to spread naturally to itself. "We walked the wrong way," shouted Mitch. "Stop walking. We walked the wrong way."

People scattered a little, on the sidewalk, looking at their phones, seeming confused but surprisingly calm, except Laura's friend Walter, who was moving an unopened Red Bull Soda in arcs through the air, as if wielding it, while sometimes saying "what's the address of the party?" to seemingly no one, with an agitated expression, then abruptly walked away, followed by Laura.

"Wait," said Paul, and hit her shoulder with a chopping motion while intending to touch it lightly. Laura briefly turned only her head—she was frowning—while continuing to walk away. Paul went with Daniel and Mitch to the other party, which they found after around forty minutes, when everyone else had gone home, to bars, or sheepishly back to Kyle and Gabby's party.

•••

When Paul woke, the next afternoon, Laura, 28, had already friended and messaged him on Facebook. She had a MySpace page, as an unsigned rapper, with six songs, including one whose music video, in which she rubs pizza on her face and feeds pizza to her cat, Paul remembered feeling highly amused and impressed by when he first saw it, when it had "gone viral," to some degree, one or two years ago. In the library, that night, Paul discovered Gabby had defriended him on Facebook and was surprised that Kyle, his closest friend the past two years, except the nine months he was with Michelle, had also defriended him and that both had unfollowed him on Twitter.

The next night, outside Taco Chulo, a Mexican restaurant in Williamsburg, Laura apologized for being late and said she'd gotten lost on the walk from her apartment, eight blocks away. Paul asked if she wanted to eat at Lodge, which had "good chicken fingers," or Taco Chulo, as they'd previously agreed, and she seemed confused. In Taco Chulo a waiter said to sit "anywhere." Paul watched Laura move very slowly, in a kind of exploring, it seemed, as if through darkness, to arrive at a four-person table, where once seated, with a slightly desperate expression, not looking at Paul, she focused on signaling a waiter. Paul also focused on signaling a waiter. Laura ordered a margarita, then sometimes turned her head 90 degrees, to her right, to stare outside—at the sidewalk, or the quiet street—with a self-consciously worried expression, seeming disoriented and shy in a distinct, uncommon manner indicating to Paul an underlying sensation of "total yet failing" (as opposed to most people's "partial and successful") effort, in terms of the social interaction but, it would often affectingly seem, also generally, in terms of existing. Paul had gradually recognized this demeanor, the past few years, as characteristic, to some degree, of every person, maybe since middle school, with whom he'd been able to form a friendship or enter a relationship (or, it sometimes seemed, earnestly interact and not feel alienated or insane). After finishing a second margarita Laura became attentive and direct, like she'd been at the party, when she had been probably very drunk, Paul realized.

"You have a girlfriend?" said Laura, surprised.

"No," said Paul, confused. "Why?"

"You said 'my girlfriend.'"

Paul said he meant "ex-girlfriend." Laura said she'd thought he was "a Gaylord," because at the party he'd been surrounded by males, which someone had called his "fans." Paul said the party was "like, seventy percent males" and that he had always thought the word "Gaylord" had been invented by someone in middle school for derogatory purposes by combining "gay" and "lord." When he showed Laura prints of his art (which, according to StatCounter, she'd already seen on one of his websites), she seemed to reflexively feign seeing them for the first time: her eyes, upon sight, became and remained slightly unfocused and she made a noise indicating she was seeing something new, but when he asked if she'd seen them before she said "yeah," but seemed to continue feigning "no." Paul, endeared by her extreme and complicated helplessness, took back his art and focused conversation on other topics. They agreed to leave, but continued talking for around forty-five minutes, inviting each other to parties that weekend. Paul felt a kind of panic when they realized the parties were the same night and said "I don't know what to do" and "maybe they aren't on the same night." Laura said they could go to both parties—which seemed immediately obvious—and asked if Paul wanted to go to K&M, where her friend was DJ-ing. Paul carefully said he did, then went to the bathroom, thinking that for matters involving social interaction he shouldn't trust himself, at this time, after being mostly alone for around four months.

In K&M—empty except for the DJ, bartender, two other people—they each drank two shots of tequila and sat with glasses of beer in a booth, side by side, facing a giant screen showing *Half Baked* on mute with subtitles. Laura complimented Paul's hair and level of "casualness" and, going partially under the table, held a candle toward Paul's shoes— which from Paul's above-table perspective felt stationary and storage-oriented as shoe boxes—asking what brand they were.

"iPath," said Paul.

"I can't see. What are these?"

"iPath. The brand is iPath."

"I like them," said Laura.

"iPath," said Paul quietly.

Laura said her ex-boyfriend was in a band and used heroin and they already stopped seeing each other, but it was "ongoing," for example he asked her to a movie last week and she went and it was awkward. "I just wish he would disappear," she said in a sincere-seeming manner, staring at *Half Baked,* which Paul saw on her right eye as four to six pixels that sometimes changed colors. Laura said she didn't want to talk about her ex-boyfriend. Paul asked if she'd tried heroin and she said no, but liked painkillers, then nuzzled his shoulder with her head. When he said he had a headache and drugs in his room and asked if she wanted to go there, she seemed instantly distracted (as a reflexive tactic, Paul felt, to not appear too eager) and expressed indecision a few minutes, then said she also had a headache, then directly stated, more than once—in an openly and uncaringly, Paul felt with amusement, confirmation-seeking manner indicating her previous indecision was at least partly feigned—that she wanted to go to Paul's room to ingest his drugs.

Outside, after fifteen minutes of failing to get a taxi, they began walking purposelessly, both saying they didn't know the correct direction to Paul's apartment, maybe twenty blocks away. Paul's arms felt more tired, from signaling taxis, than "in five years, maybe," he estimated aloud. They got in a minivan taxi, which after a few minutes dropped them off near the center of a shadowy, tree-heavy intersection.

The address was correct, according to the street sign, but Paul didn't recognize anything, even after turning two full circles while dimly aware, in a detached manner reminding him of his drunkenness, that his behavior's dizzying effects might be counterproductive. He heard Laura, somewhat obligatorily, he thought, say she was scared, then said he was a little scared, then in a louder voice, as if correcting himself, said he was confused. His inability to recognize anything began to feel like a failure of imagination, an inability to process information creatively. His conscious, helpless, ongoing lack of recognition—his shrinking, increasingly vague context—seemed exactly and boringly like how it would feel to die, or to have died. He felt like he was disappearing. He was aware of having said "is there another Humboldt Street, or something," when he realized he was—already, without a feeling or memory of recognition—looking at the bronze gate, thirty to forty feet away, of the walkway to the four-story house in which, in an apartment on the second floor, he shared a bathroom and kitchen with Caroline, an administrative assistant at the New School with an MFA in poetry.

•••

In Paul's room Laura tried to identify some of his fifteen to twenty pills and tablets, mostly from Charles, who had mailed them before leaving for Mexico, with her phone but the internet wasn't working. Paul's MacBook, which he'd spilled iced coffee on, was in Kansas being affordably repaired. Laura swallowed two of what Paul knew was Tylenol 3. Paul swallowed a Percocet and, somewhat arbitrarily, he felt, three Advil, then turned off the light, saying it was hurting his headache.

Paul was aware, as they lay kissing in the dark on his mattress, of Laura petting his upper arm in a manner that seemed independent of their kissing (but, he dimly intuited, because they were of the same source, must be discernibly related, on some level, if only as contributors to some larger system). Laura wanted to continue kissing but couldn't breathe, she said, because her nose was stuffy. "I'm sorry, I don't want to be needy," she said a few minutes later. "But I can't sleep without noise, like a fan." Paul turned on the bathroom vent. Caroline turned it off a few minutes later. Paul turned it on and texted Caroline his situation and that he would pay five dollars to keep it on tonight.

Paul woke on his back, with uncomfortably warm feet, in a bright room, not immediately aware who or where he was, or how he had arrived. Most mornings, with decreasing frequency, probably only because the process was becoming unconscious, he wouldn't exactly know anything until three to twenty seconds of passive remembering, as if by unzipping a file—newroom.zip—into a PDF, showing his recent history and narrative context, which he'd delete after viewing, thinking that before he slept again he would have memorized this period of his life, but would keep newroom.zip, apparently not trusting himself.

February to November
relationship with Michelle

December
visited parents in Taiwan for first time since they
moved back

February
moved from Kyle and Gabby's apartment to new room

April
unconsciously viewed Anton as romantic prospect
met Laura at Kyle and Gabby's party

May to August
"interim period"

September/October
book tour

December
visit parents again?

Paul's father was 28 and Paul's mother was 24 when they alone (out of a combined fifteen to twenty-five siblings) left Taiwan for America. Paul was born in Virginia six years later, in 1983, when his brother was 7. Paul was 3 when the family moved to Apopka, a pastoral suburb near Orlando, Florida.

Paul cried the first day of preschool for around ten minutes after his mother, who was secretly watching and also crying, seemed to have left. It was their first time apart. Paul's mother watched as the principal cajoled Paul into interacting with his classmates, among whom he was well liked and popular, if a bit shy and "disengaged, sometimes," said one of the high school students who worked at the preschool, which was called the Discovery Center. Each day, after that, Paul cried less and transitioned more abruptly from crying to interacting with classmates, and by the middle of the second week he didn't cry anymore. At home, where mostly only Mandarin was spoken, Paul was loud and either slug-like or, his mother would say in English, "hyperactive," rarely walking to maneuver through the house, only crawling, rolling like a log, sprinting, hopping, or climbing across sofas, counters, tables, chairs, etc. in a game called "don't touch the ground." Whenever motionless and not asleep or sleepy, lying on carpet in sunlight, or in bed with eyes open, bristling with undirectionalized momentum, he would want to intensely sprint in all directions simultaneously, with one unit of striving, never stopping. He would blurrily anticipate this unimaginably worldward action, then burst off his bed to standing position, or make a loud noise and violently spasm, or jolt from the carpet into a sprint, flailing his arms, feeling always incompletely satisfied.

Paul's first grade teacher recommended he be placed in the English-as-second-language program, widely viewed as for "impaired" students, but Paul's mother kept him in the normal class. His second grade teacher recommended he be tested for the "gifted" program and he was admitted and began going every Friday to gifted, in which most of the twenty-five to thirty students, having begun in first grade, were already friends. Paul felt alone on Fridays, but not lonely or uncomfortable or anxious, only that he was in a new and challenging situation without assistance or consequence for failure—a feeling not unlike playing a difficult Nintendo game alone, with no instruction manual. Paul played chess one Friday with Barry, who suggested Paul's second move. Barry knew more about chess, so was being helpful, Paul thought, and did as suggested for his third move also, then watched an extremely happy Barry dash through the rectangular classroom telling groups of classmates he'd beaten Paul in a four-move checkmate. Paul told three classmates Barry had "tricked him," then returned to the floor and put the chess pieces away and, with a sensation of seeing a spider crawl out of view inside his room, felt himself reassimilating Barry into the world as a kind of robot-like presence he would always need to be careful around and would never comprehend. In third grade, one morning, Paul finished telling something to his friend Chris, who was strangely unresponsive for a few seconds, then with an exaggeratedly disgusted expression told Paul his breath smelled "horrible" and "brush your teeth," then turned 180 degrees, in his seat, to talk to someone else. Paul mechanically committed to always brushing his teeth and adjusted his view of Chris to include him, with Barry and 90 to 95 percent of people he'd met, as separate and unknowable.

In fourth grade, Paul spent two days with Lori, a second grader in his neighborhood. Lori kissed Paul's cheek in a tree, then in her room showed him a Mickey Mantle card from her father, who'd said Mickey Mantle had the record for most RBIs. Paul, who collected baseball cards, said Hank Aaron had the record for most RBIs. Lori said he was probably right, because he was really smart. At dusk, the next day, rollerblading on the longest street in the neighborhood, Lori said she needed to try harder than Paul to go the same speed, because her legs were shorter, which Paul thought was insightful.

Entering middle school, sixth to eighth grade, Paul wanted to play percussion like three of his friends, including his "best friend," Hunter, but his piano teacher said percussion would bore him, so he chose trumpet, which he disliked, but continued playing until the summer before high school, when he switched to percussion on the first day of "band camp," which was ten hours of practice every weekday for two weeks. During lunch break, that day, Paul was practicing alone by silently counting and sometimes tapping a cymbal with a soft-headed mallet when a senior percussionist, the section leader, began teasing him from across the room, saying he was "so cool" and something about his baggy jeans, which his skateboarding brother, at college in Philadelphia, had left in Florida. Paul was unable to think anything, except that he didn't know what to do, at all, so he committed to doing nothing, which the senior incorporated into his teasing by focusing on how Paul was "too cool" to react, continuing for maybe thirty seconds before commenting briefly on Paul's hair and leaving the room.

Believing that all the senior's friends and acquaintances, which included almost every person at band camp, now viewed his main effort in life as wanting to be "cool," which he did want, to some degree, but which now seemed impossible, Paul became increasingly, physically, exclusively critically, nearly continuously self-conscious, the next few days, in ways he hadn't been before—but probably had been in latent development since preschool—and which affected his musicianship. His middle school friends, including Hunter, among whom he'd been most fearless and at least equally competent at whatever sport or video game, watched him fail every day to play the simplest parts, usually tambourine or triangle, of each piece. The percussion instructor that year punished everyone with push-ups if one person, usually Paul, played something incorrectly more than once. Paul's friends—subtly, then openly, with confusion and frustration—began to express disbelief at Paul's inability to count to a number and hit a cowbell or cymbal. Paul was too embarrassed, by the end of the first week, to speak to his friends—all of whom seemed to have easily befriended the section leader and other upperclassmen—and by the second week had begun committing, in certain situations, to not speaking unless asked a question.

Two months into freshman year he had committed to not speaking in almost all situations. He felt ashamed and nervous around anyone who'd known him when he was popular and unself-conscious. When he heard laughter, before he could think or feel anything, his heart would already be beating like he'd sprinted twenty yards. As the beating slowly normalized he'd think of how his heart, unlike him, was safely contained, away from the world, behind bone and inside skin, held by muscles and arteries in its place, carefully off-center, as if to artfully assert itself as source and creator, having grown the chest to hide in and to muffle and absorb—and, later, after innovating the brain and face and limbs, to convert into productive behavior—its uncontrollable, indefensible, unexplainable, embarrassing squeezing of itself. To avoid awkwardness, and in respect of his apparent aversion to speaking, Paul's classmates stopped including him in conversations. The rare times he spoke—in classes where no one knew him, or when, without knowing why, for one to forty minutes, he'd become aggressively confident and spontaneous as he'd been in elementary/middle school, about which his friends poignantly would always seem genuinely excited—he'd feel "out of character," indicating he'd completed a transformation and was now, in a humorlessly surreal way, exactly what he didn't want to be and wished he wasn't.

He ate lunch alone, on benches far from the cafeteria, listening to music—his sort of refuge that was like a tunneling in his desolation toward a greater desolation, further from others and himself, closer to the shared source of everything—with portable CD players and earphones, feeling sorry for himself, or vaguely but deeply humbled, though mostly just silent and doomed. Sometimes, thinking of how among fifteen hundred classmates only two others, that he'd noticed, were as socially inept as he—a male in his grade, an obese male one grade lower—Paul would feel a blandly otherworldly excitement, like he must be in some bizarre and extended dream, or lost in the offscreen world of some fictional movie set in an adjacent county.

In Paul's sophomore or junior year he began to believe the only solution to his anxiety, low self-esteem, view of himself as unattractive, etc. would be for his mother to begin disciplining him on her own volition, without his prompting, as an unpredictable—and, maybe, to counter the previous fourteen or fifteen years of "overprotectiveness," unfair—entity, convincingly not unconditionally supportive. His mother would need to create rules and punishments exceeding Paul's expectations, to a degree that Paul would no longer feel in control. To do this, Paul believed, his mother would need to anticipate and preempt anything he might have considered, factoring in that—because Paul was thinking about this almost every day, and between the two of them was the source of this belief—he probably already expected, or had imagined, any rule or punishment she would be willing to instate or inflict, therefore she would need to consider rules and punishments that she would not think of herself as willing to instate or inflict. Paul tried to convey this in crying, shouting fights with his mother lasting up to four hours, sometimes five days a week. There was an inherent desperation to these fights, in that each time Paul, in frustration, told his mother how she could have punished him, in whatever previous situation, to make him feel not in control—to, he believed, help solve his social and psychological problems—it became complicatedly more difficult, in Paul's view, for his mother to successfully preempt his expectations the next time. Paul cried and shouted more than his mother, who only shouted maybe once or twice. Paul would scream if his mother was downstairs while he was upstairs, in his room, where some nights he would throw his electric pencil sharpener and textbooks—and, once, a six-inch cymbal—at his walls, creating holes, resulting in punishments, but never exceeding what, by imagining their possibilities, he'd already rendered unsurprising, predictable. The intensity of these fights maybe contributed to Paul's lungs collapsing spontaneously three times his senior year, when he was absent forty-seven days and in hospitals for around four weeks.

One night, standing in the doorway of his parents' bedroom, when his father was on a months-long business trip, crying while shouting at his mother, who was supine in bed, in the dark, Paul heard her softly and steadily crying, with her blanket up to her chin in a way that seemed child-like. Paul stopped shouting and stood sobbing quietly, dimly aware, as his face twitched and trembled, that he felt intensely embarrassed of himself from the perspective of any person, except his mother, he had ever met. He said he didn't know what he was talking about, or what he should do, that he was sorry and didn't want to complain or blame other people anymore, and felt an ambiguous relief, to have reached the end of a thing without resolution and, having tried hard, feeling allowed—and ready—to resign. He didn't stop blaming his mother, after that, but gradually they fought less—and, after each fight, when he would revert to his belief about discipline, he would apologize and reiterate he didn't want to blame anyone or complain—and, by the last month of senior year, had mostly stopped fighting.

On one of Paul's last days of high school he and Lori were both getting rides home from Hunter, who due to a difficulty in refusing requests from people who could see him—in elementary/middle school, whenever a mutual friend rang his doorbell, he and Paul would pretend no one was home—

sometimes spent ninety minutes driving classmates home after school. The past eight years, since Lori kissed Paul on the cheek, they'd spoken maybe three times (the day after they rollerbladed together she had begun hanging out with a boy with a "rattail" hairstyle), and the most intimate Paul had been with another girl was a ten-minute conversation, at an "away" high school football game, with another percussionist.

Lori repeatedly asked Paul why he wouldn't speak and, not receiving an answer, began provoking Paul to "say anything," seeming as committed to eliciting a response as Paul was to not responding. Lori was loudly asking, with genuine and undistracted and bemused curiosity, which Paul felt affection toward and admired, as he stared away from her, out his window, why he couldn't speak—and if he could just "make any noise"—when Hunter, who'd been talking to someone in the front passenger seat, sort of forced Lori to stop by aggressively asking about her current boyfriend. As he had consistently, the past eight to ten years, Paul felt endeared by Hunter, who used to be an equal, but now—and for the past three or four years—was like an overworked stepfather or sensitive uncle to Paul, the mentally disabled stepson or silent, troubling nephew.

Paul hadn't seen Laura since she slept over, five days ago, when he brought a mix CD and Ambien to her room, which was more than half occupied by a full-size bed. She offered him red wine she was drinking from a wineglass and typed "sex tiger woods" into Google and clicked dlisted.com. Adjacent to a photo of Tiger Woods, smiling on a golf course, were blocks of text, in which "Ambien sex haze" was in bold around ten times.

Laura typed "ambient" into Google.

"No," said Paul grinning. "That's the music, delete the *t*."

Laura laughed and typed "ambien and alcohol and klono-pin and" and grinned at Paul and, though she had a Klono-pin prescription, Paul knew, and was probably on Klonopin, said "just kidding" and deleted all but "ambien and alcohol." Every result, it seemed, warned strongly against combining Ambien and alcohol, but Laura said she drank "a lot," so it would be okay. Paul crawled onto her bed and touched her cat Jeffrey and, after a vague amount of time, became aware of a slight blurriness to his vision, like he was seeing from two perspectives in time, milliseconds apart, and that he felt vaguely sleepy and not nervous. He asked if Laura could turn off the light, which seemed uncomfortably bright. He felt confused, to some degree, by everything, but at a delay, as if continuously realizing past confusions, which could no lon-ger be resolved, so were not problems. They seemed to be watching a foreign movie off her computer, then Paul noticed the light was on and that they were lying against a mound of blankets, kissing lazily, with eyes closed and long pauses, maybe sometimes asleep. He became aware of his mix CD, of some of his favorite songs, sounding unpleasantly, almost nightmarishly, noise-like. Paul realized they were trying to undo his belt and weakly imagined what would happen if his jeans were removed and heard Laura say "we just met" from what seemed like a nearby, inaccessible distance and wondered if he was asleep, or dreaming, but knew he was awake, because he was moving physically. He was trying to remove Laura's clothing. He felt like he was trying to remove the surface of a glass bottle by pawing at it with oven mitts. He expressed confusion and Laura said "it's just a skirt . . . and tights" and stopped moving completely, it seemed, as Paul continued touching her strange outfit with hands that felt glossy and fingerless, suspecting at one point, with some sarcasm, that she was wearing a corset.

"It's been two hours, I think," said Paul after staring at his phone around ten seconds. "Jesus," he said, and sneezed.

Entering Lucie's party, an hour and a half later, Paul felt like if he wasn't careful he would fall in an out-of-control, top-heavy manner toward whomever he was greeting and hurt himself and multiple others by reflexively grabbing people and pulling them down with him in a continuing effort to remain standing. He realized he might be unconsciously hunching his back, to be nearer the floor, when Lucie, though four or five inches shorter, appeared to be above him as she thanked him for linking her magazine on his blog. Paul introduced Lucie and other people to Laura by saying "this is Laura" a few times without looking at anyone's face, while moving toward areas with less people. "Hey," said Paul, as he passed Mitch in a crowded space, and mumbled something about "going somewhere," which in combination with a peremptory nodding was meant to convey they would definitely talk at length, later tonight, since they hadn't seen each other in a long time—months, maybe.

In an empty kitchen, a few seconds later, Paul realized Mitch, who worked for Zipcar, had driven him and Laura—and others—to this party. Paul stared into a refrigerator, bent at his waist, waiting for himself, it seemed, to think or do something. "Trying to choose two beers," he thought after a vague amount of time, and chose two at random, then found Laura and went with her through a window, onto a fourth-story roof, where they passed a shadowy area, emanating the language-y noises and phantom heat of four to six people, to a higher area, where they were alone. Paul, dangling his legs briefly off the building, scooted backward, passively cooperative, as a distracted-seeming Laura pulled him away from the edge. They sat facing hundreds of the same type of four-story building, the expanse of which, in most directions, darkened dramatically, creating an illusion that one could see the Earth's curvature, until blurring, in the distance, into a texture. Sometimes, looking at a city, especially a gray or brown one, at night, Paul would intuitively view it as a small and irreducible thing that arrived one summer and rapidly grew, showing patterns of color on its expanding surface, then was discolored by autumn and removed of its exterior and deadened by winter, in preparation for regrowth, in spring, but was unable, in its form, to enter the natural cycle, so continued growing, in a manner as if faceless and skinless, through summer, autumn, etc., less in belligerence or tyranny, or with some abstruse knowledge of its own rightness, than as a stranded thing, sightless and uninstructed, with an objectless sort of yearning. Seeing the streets and bridges and sidewalks, while living inside a building, locked in a room, one could forget that it was all a single, alien, seeking entity.

Paul realized he and Laura had been staring into the distance—unaware of each other, it seemed—for maybe two or three minutes. He looked at her profile. Without moving her head, in a voice like she was still considering if this was true, she said Paul was "devious" for bringing her to a party where another girl liked him.

"What girl likes me?"

"Lucie," said Laura after a few seconds, still staring ahead, systematically reinterpreting her and Paul's prior interactions, it seemed, with this new information.

"Why do you think she likes me?"

"I can tell," said Laura, and lit a cigarette.

"She has a boyfriend," said Paul.

Laura said something seemingly unrelated about cooking.

"You should cook for me," said Paul distractedly.

"You won't like it—it'll be dense and unhealthy."

"I like pasta and lasagna," said Paul, and thought he heard Laura ask if his computer was in Canada and was nervous she might be confusing him for another person. "What computer?"

"You said your computer was getting fixed in Canada."

"Oh," said Paul. "Kansas, not Canada. Yeah, it's still there."

On their way back inside Paul and Laura passed the shadowy area, from where an unseen Amy said something implying Laura had stolen her cigarettes, using the word "cute" antagonistically. Paul had an urge to accelerate, but Laura, ahead of him, continued at her leisurely pace, maneuvering carefully through the window, into the kitchen.

Paul followed a slow-moving Laura through a long, dark, almost boomerang-shaped hallway, which felt briefly room-like, as they sort of lingered in it, or like it wanted to be a room, with furniture and guests, but maybe was shy and too afraid of causing disappointment, so impaired itself with two conspicuous openings to conventionally shaped rooms, a sort of recommendation against itself. Paul and Laura entered a large room of sofas and tables and eight to twelve people, including Daniel, who encouraged Paul to "test-drive" a foot-massage machine, which was on the floor, audibly bubbling hot water.

"Take off your shoes and socks," said Daniel.

"I don't want to use that," said Paul, and turned around and distractedly sat on a backless, deeply padded, uncomfortable seat, which yielded at least a foot from Paul's weight. Laura was ten feet away, in a throne-like chair, facing Paul, but not looking at him, or anyone, it seemed. Paul openly stared at her for around ten seconds, to no response, then moved chips and guacamole onto his lap (partly because he felt anxious about Laura seeming to refuse to look at him) and focused on steadily eating while repeatedly thinking "eating chips and guacamole." He looked at his hands, and felt his mouth and throat, doing what he was thinking, and felt vaguely confused. Was he instructing his brain? Or was he narrating what he saw and felt?

Laura seemed less distracted, but more worried, than before. Paul moved toward her with what felt like a precariously sustained gliding motion and sat against and above her, on the chair's sturdy armrest, in a comically awkward manner he hadn't foreseen and was preparing to reverse, by returning to his seat, when Laura lifted his arm and placed it ungently around her neck—maybe a little disappointed that she had to do it herself—where it remained, independent and heavy as a small boa constrictor, for a vague amount of time, during which Paul, remaining almost completely still, felt increasingly reluctant to move, or speak. At some point, maybe three minutes later, Paul asked if Laura wanted to go to the other party.

"Yes," she said.

Paul felt like parts of his and Laura's bodies, as they stood on the front stoop hugging tightly under one umbrella, waiting for Walter's car, were oppositely charged magnets covered with thick velvet. Paul crawled into Walter's car's backseat, spilling red wine; unable to find the cork, he wrapped the bottle in a plastic bag. He faced ahead, seated between two people, and realized no one had cared, or noticed, at all, it seemed, about the wine. Paul thought "I'm in hell" when people began to loudly mimic the guitar parts of the

Led Zeppelin playing from a tape deck, resulting mostly in demonic-sounding noises and a kind of metallic, nightmarish screeching. Paul couldn't discern if they did this regularly, or if it had just been improvised. "Ambien has a negative effect on music for me," he thought.

At Laura's friend's party Paul sat alone at the snacks table, eating crackers and drinking wine, sometimes with unfocused eyes. Then he was sitting on a mattress in a space-module-like bedroom, in which six to ten people, smoking marijuana, watched a video off a MacBook of obese people screaming in pain earnestly while exercising and being screamed at motivationally, in what seemed to be a grotesque parody, or something, of something. Paul felt strong aversion to the video, and also like he'd already experienced this exact situation—he remembered his aversion to the video and the way someone to his right was laughing—and wanted to ask if this already happened, but didn't know who to ask, then realized he wanted to ask himself. Around an hour later, after more crackers and wine, Paul thought he heard Laura drunkenly say something like "let him through, my new boyfriend," loud enough for probably ten to fifteen people to have heard, as she beckoned him to sit with her and her three closest friends, including Walter, on a four-seat sofa. Walter drove everyone on the sofa to Laura's apartment to smoke marijuana, around 3:30 a.m., when the party ended.

On the sidewalk, outside Laura's apartment, a heavily impaired Paul explained that in high school his lungs collapsed three times and one of the doctors said smoking marijuana would increase the chance of recurrence by 4,200 percent. Laura said he wouldn't have to smoke. Paul said the smoke would be in the air and that he was allergic to Laura's cat and had a horrible headache. He hugged Laura, then walked toward the Bedford L train station, half a block away.

•••

The next night Laura emailed that she wished Paul wasn't allergic to Jeffrey so he could be with her, in her room, listening to the rain. Paul asked if she wanted to eat dinner together tomorrow night. Laura said she felt like she missed him and "well, I guess I'll see you tomorrow," characteristically answering a question indirectly and ending an email casually.

Paul was aware he felt mysteriously less interested in her after reading that she felt like she missed him and realized he hadn't considered what a relationship between them would be like: probably not sustainable, at all, due to a mutual lack of strong interest. He was aware of not acknowledging her line about missing him in his response, which included a short list of restaurants he liked.

Paul met Laura the next night outside the clothing boutique in SoHo where she worked. "I think this is a bad idea, I always go home after work to nap," she said with a worried expression, walking slowly away from Paul, who signaled a taxi, which they exited fifteen blocks later at a deli, where they bought a 40oz and two bottles of beer.

Seated, in Angelica Kitchen, they looked at each other directly for the first time that night. Laura seemed anxious and tired. Paul said the restaurant was organic and vegan and Laura said she had been trying to eat better since meeting Paul, who grinned while saying "you've been trying to eat butter?" twice, during which Laura began to blush.

"I thought you said 'butter,'" said Paul grinning.

Laura looked at her hand touching a fork on the table.

"I thought you said you're trying to eat butter."

"Stop," said Laura moving the fork slowly toward herself.

"Stop what?"

"You're making fun of me, I think," said Laura looking at him tentatively.

"No, I'm not. I wouldn't do that."

Laura was motionless, looking at her lap with downcast eyes, like she was waiting for Paul to finish. Paul asked if she believed him and she didn't respond and he felt stranded and withering and asked again if she believed him, then quietly said "I honestly thought you said 'butter.' " He nervously moved a spoon to his lap and, aware they were both looking down, felt himself absorbing the irresolution of the butter misunderstanding as an irreversible damage. He asked if she wanted to leave, for a different restaurant maybe. Laura poured beer from the 40oz into Paul's glass, already 95 percent full, and said "let's just drink more, I just need to drink more" and apologized for "being like this."

"It's okay," said Paul. "I'm sorry about the butter thing."

Laura blushed and looked down by slowly moving her eyeballs. Paul apologized and said he wouldn't talk about it anymore and that he liked Laura's eyebrows, which were black, in contrast to her naturally blond hair. They talked tensely, with a few long pauses, about the difference between Scottish and Irish people and Paul began to worry about the rest of dinner, but after they finished the 40oz and mutely focused on their menus a few minutes they settled into a calm, polite, somewhat resigned manner of leisurely occupying each other. When their mashed potatoes, chili, cornbread, noodle soup arrived they talked less and Paul began to feel a little sleepy. Laura thanked him for showing her this restaurant, which she wanted to try lunch from soon.

Outside, on the sidewalk, Laura immediately walked toward the 1st Avenue L train station at an unleisurely pace, seeming less rushed than resolutely continuing with a prior, focused, unobstructed momentum. Paul realized, with some confusion, that he'd obliviously assumed they would do something together after dinner; more than once, as they waited for the bill, he'd considered suggesting they see a movie at a theater that was in the opposite direction they were currently walking. Laura was crossing streets and sidewalks at unconventional angles, as if across a field, in a diagonal, it seemed, to get there sooner. Paul wanted to stop moving and sit or lay on the sidewalk, partly as a juvenile tactic to interrupt Laura's departure.

On the train Laura became significantly more talkative and, it seemed, happier. Paul thought of how at every job he'd had, in movie theaters and libraries and restaurants, almost every employee, probably especially himself, would become predictably friendlier and more generous as closing time neared. At the Bedford station, before exiting the train, Laura apologized again and unsolicitedly said "maybe I'll feel better and come over later, in a few hours," which seemed to Paul like a non sequitur, or an extreme example of the "closing time" effect.

In his room, with the light on, Paul lay entirely beneath his blanket, aware that Michelle was the last person who'd affected him this cripplingly—to zero productivity, not even listening to music, motionless between his blanket and mattress like some packaged thing. He heard a ringing noise, or the memory of a ringing noise, which meant another of his limited number of nonregenerative hearing cells had died, though his room was nearly silent. He became aware of himself remembering a night when he and Michelle, alone in her mother's mansion-like house in Pittsburgh, made salad and pasta for dinner and sat facing each other, bisecting a long wood table like a converted canoe. Paul had begun to feel depressed without knowing why—maybe unconsciously intuiting what life would be like in a giant house with a significant other and a routine, how forty or fifty years, like windows on a computer screen, maximized on top of each other, could appear like a single year that would then need to be lived repeatedly, so that one felt both nearer and withheld from death—and within a few minutes was silent and visibly troubled, staring down at his salad. Michelle had asked what was wrong and Paul had said "nothing," then she'd asked again and he'd said he felt depressed, but didn't know why, then at some point she went upstairs, where Paul found her on her bed, in her room that seemed too big for one person, in a fetal position on her side—oval and exposed, on top of her sheets and blanket, as an egg. Paul dreamed something about his cube-shaped room being a storage facility in which he'd been placed by an entity that believed in his resale value. While in storage he could interact with others, look at the internet, go on a book tour, but if he damaged himself he would be moved to a garbage pile, on a different planet. He woke a few times, then remained awake, obstructed from sleep by his own grumpiness and discomfort, the main reasons he wanted to sleep.

He reached outside his blanket and pulled his MacBook "darkly," he felt, toward himself, like an octopus might. It was 12:52 a.m., almost three hours since leaving Angelica Kitchen. Laura, to Paul's surprise, had emailed twice—a few sentence fragments apologizing for her awkwardness at 11:43 p.m., a paragraph of elaboration at 12:05 a.m. Paul emailed that he understood and liked her and thought she was "cool." She responded, a few minutes later, seeming cheerful. After a few more emails she seemed almost "giddy." They committed—earnestly and enthusiastically, Paul felt—to get tattoos together tomorrow.

•••

Laura arrived around 4:30 p.m., seeming tired and distracted, with cheese and a bottle of wine and knitting materials in a plastic bag. Paul said they should go to Manhattan before night and Laura asked why and Paul said for tattoos. Laura said she wanted to stay inside to work on her set of a dozen "monster masks," which she wanted to use in a music video for one of her songs (and which, based on photos Paul had seen on the internet, she seemed to have been knitting for more than a year). They shared a Klonopin, and when it began to get dark outside Paul suggested a restaurant two blocks away, but Laura didn't want to go outside, so they ordered Chinese food—minnow-size pieces of slippery chicken in a shiny garlic sauce, six fortune cookies—and ate only a little, then shared an Ambien and sat, at a distance from each other, on Paul's mattress.

Paul patted the area beside him and Laura said "stop trying to make sexy time" in an earnest, slightly annoyed voice. Paul grinned and honestly said he wasn't and felt confused. Laura, who had finished most of the bottle of wine herself, lay curled in a corner of the mattress and was soon asleep. Paul absently looked at the internet a little, then woke, three hours later, around midnight, to Laura putting her things into her plastic bag. She was going home, she said, because she had to feed Jeffrey and had work in the morning.

The next night Paul was with Mitch and Matt—another classmate from Florida, one year ahead of Mitch and Paul, currently "on vacation" alone—at Barcade, a bar with dozens of arcade machines. After one beer Paul texted Laura "hi, how's it going" and interpreted her almost instantaneous response of "super" as her wanting to finish an undesirable task as quick as possible. Paul texted he was at Barcade with "high school friends" and if Laura wanted to come. Laura texted "I'm all out of quarters" after five minutes. Paul texted "I have some quarters for you" with a neutral expression and a cringing sensation, then showed Mitch and Matt the texts, saying he felt depressed. Matt's friend Lindsay (whom he was staying with while on vacation) arrived and everyone walked six blocks to a bar with outdoor Ping-Pong tables. Daniel arrived with his friend Fran, 22, whose intriguing gaze, Paul noticed with interest, seemed both disbelieving and transfixed in discernment, as if meticulously studying what she knew she was hallucinating. Paul looked at his phone—it had been more than an hour since he texted Laura that he had quarters and, as expected, she hadn't responded—and heard Daniel say "a Mexican place" and something about "six tacos" to Mitch.

"Eight tacos," said Paul absently.

"I said six tacos," said Daniel.

"Six tacos," said Paul. "Was it, like . . . a taco platter?"

"No. This place has small tacos."

"It wasn't a taco platter?"

"It wasn't a taco platter," said Daniel.

"I don't get it," said Paul without thinking.

"Bro," said Daniel grinning.

Paul asked Fran what she had eaten.

"Enchiladas," said Fran.

"I can never remember what those are," said Paul, and went to the bathroom. When he returned Lindsay invited everyone to her Cinco de Mayo party—in five days, at her apartment—then everyone, except Fran, who Daniel said was an undergrad at Columbia and had left to do homework, walked eight blocks to a bar called Harefield Road to meet a group of people Paul knew as acquaintances from his involvement in poetry. Seconds after sitting in the outdoor area Paul openly said "I want to comfort myself with food" without looking at anyone, in a relatively loud voice, with a bleak sensation of unsatisfying catharsis from having accurately, he felt, expressed himself. "I'm just going to eat whatever tonight," he said, and stood, asking if anyone knew about food options at this bar. Two acquaintances said there were, at this time, around 2:30 a.m., only paninis. One of Daniel's two suitemates, who said she'd written an article about Paul and reviewed books anonymously for *Kirkus*, went with him to order a panini. Paul asked if she liked a baseball book, which she mentioned having reviewed, and she talked without pause for what seemed like ten minutes, during which Paul, staring at her calmly, thought "she's definitely drunk" and "normally I would be interested in her, to some degree, but currently I'm obsessed with Laura" and "she seems maybe focused on not appearing drunk, which is maybe affecting her perception of time, of how long and off-topic and incomprehensible her answer has become." Paul carried his panini outside and "openly exchanged witty banter while feeling severely depressed," he thought while speaking to various acquaintances. One said she'd met Paul, when he lived with Shawn Olive, at least three times. Paul said he didn't recognize her, but also had forgotten that he'd once lived with Shawn Olive. He ate half his panini and said it was unsatisfying and left the bar and returned with Tate's cookies and Fig Newmans, which he offered to each person. He asked Lindsay what her roommate, whom she'd been talking about, was doing. Lindsay said "sleeping, watching TV, or smoking weed" and Paul said "we should go to your apartment," aware he was somewhat desperately, if maybe sarcastically, trying to direct his interest away from Laura, toward any girl he had not yet, but still could, meet tonight.

"This bar's special feature: 'paninis until really late,'" said Paul to a drunk-looking acquaintance on the way out.

• • •

In Lindsay's apartment's common room Paul sat eating Fig Newmans on one side of a five-seat sofa with Mitch and Daniel on the other side. Lindsay's roommate was sleeping. Paul was vaguely aware, as he reread texts from Laura, of people pressuring Matt to smoke marijuana. Matt was standing alone in a corner of the room—seeming in Paul's peripheral vision like a figure in a horror movie—saying things, as explanation for his choice not to smoke marijuana, about his grandfather's alcoholism. Paul half-unconsciously mumbled something—to himself, he felt—about feeling thirsty and within a few seconds Matt was standing above him asking if he wanted water. After bringing him a glass of water Matt asked if Paul wanted to use his MacBook to look at the internet. Paul felt endeared to a degree that—in combination with his distraught emotional state, and as he dwelled a few seconds on how Matt's behavior was like the opposite of pressuring someone to smoke marijuana—he felt like crying. Matt returned with a large MacBook from the room he was sleeping in while on vacation.

"Thank you," said Paul smiling.

"You're very welcome," said Matt.

"You're being really nice to me."

"You're the guest here," said Matt, and Paul gingerly asked if he "by chance" had an iPod cord, sensing he would enjoy further indulging an appreciative subject with his gratuitous helpfulness. Paul accepted Matt's iPod cord with a sensation, he felt, of daintiness, which remained as he transferred mostly pop-punk songs from Matt's MacBook to his iPod nano. Around 4:30 a.m., in his room, Paul bit a piece of a 150mg Seroquel and listened to songs he hadn't heard since high school, mostly the EP *Look Forward to Failure* by the Ataris. He woke at night fifteen hours later and, while showering, felt like he lived in a module attached to a spaceship far enough from any star to never experience daylight.

Three days later Paul exited the Graham L train station carrying beer and guacamole ingredients in a paper bag from Whole Foods for Lindsay's Cinco de Mayo party. Sitting cross-legged on the sidewalk against a Thai restaurant was a girl with dyed-black hair. As Paul approached she looked up knowingly with an innocent, wary gaze.

"Hi," said Paul. "Are you Fran?"

"Yeah," said Fran.

"I'm Paul."

"I know," said Fran, and slowly closed her notebook.

"Are you doing homework?"

"My friend's homework."

"Nice," said Paul staring transfixed at Fran's delicate and extreme gaze, like that of a skeleton with eyeballs, or a person with their face peeled off. Paul began talking—slowly, before accelerating to a normal speed—about how Daniel had sounded "really drunk" on the phone but had sent witty, insightful, elaborate texts of mostly long, elegant sentences. Fran said Daniel was like that when on Klonopin. Paul asked if he could have a Klonopin and Fran gave him one and looked to his left, where he was surprised to see Daniel standing in place, a few feet away, looking at Fran with the fixed, discerning, earnest gaze of a three-year-old processing information without considering utility or personal relevance. Paul asked Daniel how many Klonopin he had taken.

"Five," said Daniel.

"Jesus," said Paul.

• • •

When Paul entered the party, ahead of Daniel and Fran, Lindsay wreathed a plastic snake around his head and pulled him toward a hallway designated for photographs. Paul mumbled the word "bathroom" and walked away grinning into the kitchen, where Matt was standing alone, not apparently doing anything. Paul asked about his vacation. Matt said he drove a rental car without a plan to Maine and ate seafood in a restaurant alone, did other things alone. "It was really good," he said, and briefly displayed a haunted and irreducibly unenthusiastic expression before reaching for chips. Paul walked out of the kitchen and looked at Fran sitting alone on the sofa where he'd eaten Fig Newmans five days ago and returned to the kitchen and, while peripherally aware of a self-conscious Matt slowly creating guacamole, asked Daniel what he'd meant—in one of his dense, interesting texts—when he said he felt like there'd been "strange occurrences lately." Daniel said he read all of Paul's books last autumn while in San Francisco and told his friends he had a feeling that when he came to New York City he would meet Paul and they would become friends. Daniel was alert and expressionless as an advanced cyborg as he explained that he'd gone to Paul and Frederick's reading because Amy didn't want to be alone with Lucie and that none of them had known Paul was reading.

"I've felt similar things," said Paul. "Since Kyle's party, when I met Laura. Or, I mean, actually, the night before that, at the reading near Times Square, when we met."

"How do you feel about it?"

"About what?"

"It," said Daniel vaguely.

"It seems good. New things keep happening, which seems good. I just felt right now like it's going to end tonight."

"You're pessimistic about it," said Daniel as a neutral

observation, staring intensely at Paul with a serious, almost grim expression.

"We haven't referenced it until now."

"I'm sorry for talking about it and causing you to think it might end," said Daniel earnestly.

"It's okay," said Paul, a little confused. "Maybe it won't end. But I wonder if we need to make an effort, for it to continue."

"Well," said Daniel hesitantly. "Don't you think it just needs to happen naturally?"

"Yeah," said Paul.

"Well, then we wouldn't make an effort, then, huh?"

"I mean if we need to keep doing things, instead of staying inside," said Paul.

"You said you only go to like one party a month. But you're at almost every party."

"This isn't normal at all," said Paul. "Before we met I probably did less than one thing a month."

"Why do you think that is?"

"Probably because I met people I like."

Daniel hesitated. "What people?"

"You, Mitch, Laura . . . Amy," said Paul. "I'm going to the bathroom." When he returned Fran and Daniel were making guacamole energetically, with spoons and a mashing strategy, adding onion and cilantro and salsa and garlic powder, having apparently replaced Matt, who was very slowly, it seemed, moving a beer toward his mouth. Paul began eating guacamole as it was being made, with chips, to no discernible opposition. In a distracted voice, without looking at anyone, he asked if Daniel and Fran wanted to go to a "book party" tomorrow night at a bookstore in Greenpoint and they seemed interested. Fran gave everyone vodka shots. Matt moved into a position facing more people and, with an earnest but powerless attempt at enthusiasm, resulting in a a weak form of sarcasm, asked if everyone wanted to go to the roof.

On the fourth-story roof Paul said he wanted to run "really fast in a circle," vaguely aware and mostly unconcerned, though he knew he didn't want to die—less because he had an urge to live than because dying, like knitting or backgammon, seemed irrelevant to his life—that due to alcohol and Klonopin, in a moment of inattention, he could easily walk off the building. He collided with an unseen Fran—who seemed already confused, before this, standing alone in an arbitrary area of the roof—and felt intrigued by the binary manner that his movement was stopped, though how else, he vaguely realized, could something stop? He texted Laura, inviting her to "come eat Mexican food at a party," then went downstairs and indiscriminately moved refried beans, guacamole, three kinds of chips, cucumber, salsa, beef onto his plate until he had a roughly symmetrical mound of food, on top of which—on the way out of the kitchen, as a kind of afterthought—he added a fluffy, triangular wedge of cake. After carrying the Mayan-pyramid-shaped plate of food, with some difficulty, up the ladder, onto the roof, where he silently ate it all, he belligerently directed conversation toward Laura-related things, then said he felt cold and was going inside. He descended the ladder until his head was below the opening to the roof and tried to hear what Fran and Daniel—who remained outside smoking—were saying, while unaware of his presence, but couldn't, and also didn't know what could possibly be said that he would want to secretly hear, so returned inside the apartment and lay on his back on the sofa in the common room.

He woke to flash photography, then to Lindsay's voice, in another room, loudly saying "get out." Lindsay entered the common room and said, to a blearily waking Paul, something about "your friend" looking inside her purse, trying to steal her shoes. Paul stared blankly, a little embarrassed to have slept on his back, for an unknown amount of time, on the apartment's only sofa. He looked at his phone: no new texts. After saying "sorry" a few times to Lindsay, who seemed unsure if she felt negatively toward Paul, he put a half-eaten onion, beer bottles, other trash into his Whole Foods bag and descended stairs behind Daniel and Fran, who was quietly murmuring things vaguely in her defense. They decided to go to Legion, a bar, one and a half blocks away, with an outdoor area on the sidewalk.

"Were you trying to steal her shoes?" said Daniel.

"No, I wasn't," said Fran quietly. "Our shoes look the same."

"I'm asking because you've told me you like to steal things when you're drunk."

"I wasn't stealing her shoes," said Fran in a loud whisper.

They were walking toward Paul's room, after ten minutes in Legion, when it became known, in a manner that seemed sourceless, as if they realized simultaneously, that Fran had "accidentally," she then said, stolen a leather jacket, which she was wearing. They agreed it would be inconvenient for the owner to not have their phone, which was in the jacket, but continued walking and each tried on the jacket, which seemed to best fit Paul, who found two gigantic vitamins in one of its pockets. In his room he put the phone on the table beside his mattress and, saying he didn't want to be near it, sort of pushed it away. He opened his MacBook and played "Annoying Noise of Death" and saw that Daniel was calmly observing himself, in the full-length wall mirror, as he exercised with Caroline's five-pound weights that were usually on the floor in the kitchen. Fran said to put on Rilo Kiley. Paul said it was Rilo Kiley and, after a few motionless seconds, Fran slowly turned her head away to rotate her face, like a moon orbiting behind its planet, interestingly out of view. Paul grinned to himself as he lay on his back and propped up his head with a folded pillow, resting his MacBook against the front of his thighs, both knees bent. Daniel sat on the mattress in a position that a robot in a black comedy about a child with two fathers, one of whom was a robot, would assume to recite a bedtime story, looking at Paul however with a slightly, stoically puzzled expression. "When you asked me if I liked Rilo Kiley, the night we met, I thought you were joking," said Daniel.

"No," said Paul. "Why did you think that?"

"You're more earnest than I thought you'd be."

"I wouldn't joke about something like that."

"Like what?" said Daniel.

Paul said he wouldn't pretend he liked something, or make fun of liking something, or like something "ironically." Daniel sort of drifted away and began looking at Paul's books with a patient, scholarly demeanor—in continuation, Paul realized, of a calm inquisitiveness that had characterized most of his behavior tonight, probably due to the five Klonopin he'd ingested, though he was always inquisitive and would continue asking questions, in certain conversations, when others would've stopped, which Paul liked. Twenty minutes later Daniel was reading pages of different books and Paul was looking at methadone's Wikipedia page (". . . developed in Germany in 1937 . . . an acyclic analog of morphine or heroin . . .") when Fran returned from outside with cuts on her face and neck from a group of girls, she said, that called her a bitch and said she tried to steal shoes and attacked her, pushing her down. Daniel asked how the girls opened the gate to the house's walkway. Fran repeated, with a vaguely confused expression, that she was attacked. Paul, who hadn't realized she had left the room, asked how she reentered the gate without a key. Fran stared expectantly at Daniel with her child-like gaze, then quietly engaged herself in a solitary activity elsewhere in the room as Daniel and Paul began pondering the situation themselves, to no satisfying conclusion. Fran said she wanted to go dancing at Legion before it closed in less than an hour and Paul thought he saw her put a number of pills into her mouth in the stereotypically indiscriminate manner he'd previously seen only on TV or in movies. Fran and Daniel did yoga-like stretches on Paul's yoga mat and snorted two Adderall—crushed into a potion-y blue, faintly neon sand— off a pink piece of construction paper. Daniel briefly hugged a supine Paul, then stood at a distance as Fran lay flat on top of Paul with her head facedown to the right of his head. Fran didn't move for around forty seconds, during which, at one point, she murmured something that seemed significant but, muffled by the mattress, was not comprehensible. She rolled onto her back and Daniel pulled her to a standing position. Paul was surprised to feel moved in a calming, tearful manner—as if some long-term desire, requiring a tiring amount of effort, had been fulfilled—when, before leaving for Legion, both Daniel and Fran affected slightly friendlier demeanors (rounder eyes, higher-pitched voices, a sort of pleasantness of expression like minor face-lifts) to confirm meeting at the book party Paul mentioned earlier and had forgotten.

Paul realized after they left that he'd gotten what from elementary school through college he often most wanted— unambiguous indications of secure, mutual friendships—but was no longer important to him.

The book party, like algae, feeling its way elsewhere, moved slowly but persistently from the bookstore's basement to its first floor, to the sidewalk outside, converging finally with other groups at a corner bar, where Paul failed more than five times to recognize or remember the faces or names of recent to long-term acquaintances—and twice introduced people he'd already introduced to each other, including Daniel and Frederick, both of whom however either feigned having not met or had actually forgotten—but due to 2mg Klonopin remained poised, with a peaceful sensation of faultlessness, physiologically calm but mentally stimulated, throughout the night, as if beta testing the event by acting like an exaggerated version of himself, for others to practice against, before the real Paul, the only person without practice, was inserted for the actual event. Fran left for her apartment, which she shared with a low-level cocaine dealer majoring in something art related at Columbia, to prepare a kind of pasta, "with a lot of things in it," that was her specialty, it seemed. Paul and Daniel arrived ninety minutes later and Fran served a giant platter of cheese-covered, lasagna-like pasta—attractively browned in a mottled pattern of variations of crispiness—in small, colorful plastic bowls with buttered toast on which were thin slices of raw garlic. They ate all of it, then arranged themselves on Fran's three-seat sofa and watched *Drugstore Cowboy* on Daniel's MacBook. Paul was unable to discern the movie as coherent—he kept thinking the same scene, in a motel room, was replaying with minor variations—but was aware of sometimes commenting on the sound track, including that it was "really weird" and "unexpected."

Before becoming unconscious Paul was aware of a man wearing a cowboy hat being carried out of a drugstore by four people and of himself thinking that, if the people dragging the man were invisible, the man would look like he was gliding feetfirst on a horizontal waterslide, steadily ahead, with out-of-control limbs and a crazed, antagonistic expression, as if by experimentally self-directed telekinesis.

• • •

A week later Paul had organized plans to see *Trash Humpers* and was waiting for Fran and Daniel at the theater. He had first asked Laura, who seemed to be in a relationship with her ex-boyfriend—pictures had appeared on Facebook in which they looked happily reunited in what seemed to be a faux-expensive hotel—to see the movie and she'd said she wanted to but not tonight. Fran gave Paul six 10mg Adderall for her and Daniel's tickets and a disoriented-seeming Daniel, who had no money left, asked if Paul had any snacks. Paul gave Daniel a sugar-free Red Bull he got from a Red Bull–shaped car parked outside the library and Daniel drank it in one motion with a neutral expression.

"Fran said she'll pay you back if you give me one of the Adderall she gave you," whispered Daniel a few minutes into the movie. "I don't think I can stay awake without it." In the movie costumed actors made noises in parking lots and inside houses while destroying and/or "humping" inanimate objects. Paul woke, at one point, to Fran laughing loudly when no one else in the small, sold-out theater was laughing. When Paul wasn't asleep he felt distracted by a feeling that Daniel had eerily turned his head 90 degrees and was staring at him, but each time he looked Daniel was either asleep or looking at the screen. The last ten minutes of the movie Paul was peripherally aware of Daniel's unsupported head continually lolling in place and twitching to attention in a manner reminiscent of a middle/high school student struggling and repeatedly failing to remain awake in a morning class. Daniel seemed fully alert seconds after the movie ended. Paul asked how he slept despite Adderall and Red Bull.

"Susie-Q," said Daniel with a smirk-like grin indicating both earnest disapproval and a kind of fondness toward Seroquel and its intense, often uncomfortable tranquilizing effects—as if, believing Susie-Q wasn't malicious, he could forgive her every time she induced twelve hours of sleep followed by twelve to twenty-four hours of feeling lost and irritable, therefore she functioned, if inadvertently, as a teacher of forgiveness and acceptance and empathy, for which he was grateful.

They were the last three people, after the movie, to leave the theater. They stood on the sidewalk, unsure what to do next. Fran had planned to go to Coney Island tonight and stay until morning for her birthday, which was today—she'd created a Facebook listing, which Paul remembered seeing—but none of her friends wanted to go, because she didn't have any, she said. Paul said he also had no friends and that they should celebrate by "eating a lot of food."

At Lovin' Cup, a bar-restaurant with live music, Fran and Daniel ordered drinks, went outside to smoke. Paul laid the side of his head on his arms, on the table, and closed his eyes. He didn't feel connected by a traceable series of linked events to a source that had purposefully conveyed him, from elsewhere, into this world. He felt like a digression that had forgotten from what it digressed and was continuing ahead in a confused, choiceless searching. Fran and Daniel returned and ordered enchiladas, nachos. Paul ordered tequila, a salad, waffles with ice cream on top.

When the food arrived Paul ordered tater tots and more tequila. They ate silently in the loud bar. Paul felt he would need to scream, or exert an effort that would feel like he was screaming, to be heard. He was aware of Fran, to his left, quietly eating with her mouth near her plate, as if to hide something, or probably to reduce the distance to her enchiladas, which in Paul's peripheral vision appeared shapeless, almost invisible. After Fran left to "do homework," she said,

Paul and Daniel decided to try watching *Drugstore Cowboy* again, in Paul's room.

On the walk to Daniel's apartment, to get *Drugstore Cowboy*, dozens of elderly, similarly dressed Asian men were standing in a loosely organized row, like a string of Christmas lights, seeming bored but alert, on a wide sidewalk, across from Bar Matchless. Daniel asked one of them what movie they were in and the Asian man seemed confused, then said "Martin Scorsese" without an accent when Daniel asked again.

Around forty minutes later Paul said "that looks like the group of Asians . . . we saw earlier," realizing with amazement as he saw Bar Matchless that they had unwittingly walked to the same place.

Daniel's two suitemates were seated at a round, thin, foldable table on chairs Paul immediately viewed as "found on the street," talking to each other, it seemed, after returning from a concert. Except for a broom and what Daniel confirmed— grimly, Paul felt—was a giant plastic eggplant of unknown origin, there was nothing else in the common room.

Daniel's room had a dresser, mattress pad, wood chair, tiny desk. Within arm's reach, outside his window, was a brick wall covered with gradients of gray ash. Daniel showed Paul, who felt self-conscious and crowded, standing in place, a candle shaped like a lightbulb and said it was from his sister. Paul stared at it, unable to comprehend, in a way that made the behavior seem unreal, exactly why Daniel was showing it to him, with a feeling that he'd misheard, or not heard, something Daniel said a few seconds or minutes ago.

Paul woke sitting on his mattress with his back against a wall, beside Daniel, who seemed asleep and was also sitting. The room was palely lit by a cloudy, faintly pink morning. Paul's MacBook, in front of them, showed *Drugstore Cowboy*'s menu screen. Paul shifted a little—his right leg was numb—and Daniel began talking in a clear voice, as if he'd been awake a few minutes already. Daniel wanted to ingest Adderall instead of sleep. Paul, who couldn't remember if they'd watched the movie, distractedly asked what they would do "all day."

"What we normally do. Walk around. Fix my computer."

"I feel . . . sleepy," said Paul.

Daniel said something about Adderall.

"I feel like I'll still be sleepy," said Paul.

"You'll be awake, trust me."

"I'm not sure if I want to."

"I feel like you're eight years old or my girlfriend," said Daniel around five minutes later.

"I really don't know what I want to do," said Paul grinning.

An hour later, after each showering at his own apartment, they met and ingested Adderall and walked to Verb, a café without internet, where they drank iced coffee and ingested a little more Adderall, then went in an adjacent bookstore, where Daniel showed Paul a translated book of nonfiction with a similar cover—off-center black dot, white background—as Shawn Olive's poetry book.

"That's funny," said Paul grinning, and they got on the L train, then walked to the Apple store on Prince Street. Daniel's MacBook, which had files he needed for his job as a research assistant to an elderly ghostwriter (of sports autobiographies) who owed him $200, would require two weeks to be fixed. Daniel asked if Paul would go with him to Rhode Island, in three hours, to stay with Fran's family for a weekend. Paul declined, saying he hadn't been invited. Daniel said he confirmed last week but didn't want to go anymore and that, a few minutes ago, Fran texted she couldn't, against expectation, get any Oxycodone—without which it was going to be "unbearable," Daniel felt, for both himself and Fran, to be around Fran's family. Paul declined again, saying it seemed stressful. It began raining from a partly sunny sky, and they went in an Urban Outfitters. Daniel walked to a table of books and stood without looking at anything, like a tired child waiting for an overbearingly upbeat mother to finish shopping.

"You seem worried," said Paul.

"Sorry. I'm trying to think of an excuse to tell Fran."

It was sunny and cloudless, around twenty minutes later, when they sat side by side on a bench in Washington Square Park. Daniel swallowed something and mutely handed Paul a 20mg Adderall, which Paul swallowed. Two preadolescent girls ran around the fountain area repeatedly. Paul said he felt like he hadn't run as fast as possible in probably five or ten years. When the Adderall took effect Daniel began to praise Paul's writing without restraint or pause for twenty to thirty minutes and asked about Paul's IQ. Paul said it was either 139 or 154. Daniel was quiet a few seconds, then with a slightly troubled expression said his IQ was higher, seeming like he felt more complicatedly doomed, as a person, with this information. Paul said his mother always said that his and his brother's IQs were exactly the same, but sometimes also said she was required, as a parent, to say that.

Daniel said his sister had multiple doctorates, his parents and aunts and uncles were all high-level professors, but he was "not anything." Paul knew from previous conversations that Daniel, as a teenager, had been on months-long retreats to Buddhist monasteries, culminating in something like a year alone, when he turned 18, in India or Tibet. Daniel walked away to call Fran and Paul read a text from Laura asking if he wanted to see *Trash Humpers* tonight. Paul texted he already saw it, and they made plans to record a song in his room in two hours. Daniel returned and said he told Fran his computer had to be fixed today, or not for two weeks, and he needed it to do work, because he hadn't paid last month's rent, so wasn't going to Rhode Island, and that "she got really angry."

"I feel like you did the right thing . . . I mean . . . outside of being honest," said Paul grinning. "Your relationship with her is more accurate now."

"Your use of the word 'accurate' is interesting."

"She has a more accurate view of your view of her now probably," said Paul.

Laura arrived with Walter, whom Paul hadn't expected, two hours late and reacted to Paul's agitation, as they walked from the bronze gate to the house, with resentment and dismissiveness, then became a little apologetic in Paul's room, showing him texts she'd sent to Walter telling him to hurry.

"You can't blame me," said Walter, and chuckled. "I don't even know why I'm here. You suddenly just started texting me to drive you here."

"Now everyone is turning against me," said Laura smiling nervously, not looking at anyone. Paul asked Walter if it was true, as he'd thought he'd read on Gawker, that Detroit, where Walter was from, only had seven grocery stores. Walter laughed quietly and said that wasn't true and that Detroit was comparable, he felt, to Ann Arbor maybe. Paul said he was going to Ann Arbor in September, for his book tour, and asked what size it was, and was peripherally aware of Laura turning away, like she'd observed the interaction and concluded something, as she said "now you're going to ask Walter a lot of questions."

"It's like Berkeley," said Walter.

"It's that big?" said Paul in a dreamy voice, and moved, vaguely for privacy, from the mattress to the floor, where he texted Daniel and ingested a Klonopin, weakly thinking "it won't begin working until I won't need it as much anymore." Walter and Laura, who had brought a tambourine and a shaker, talked idly, a few feet from Paul, who thought Walter's grumpiness after leaving Kyle and Gabby's party, when he'd wielded a Red Bull Soda, now seemed endearing. Paul noticed Laura looking at his pile of construction paper and said she could have some if she wanted, and she focused self-consciously on wanting some, saying how she would use it and what colors she liked, seeming appreciative in an affectedly sincere manner—the genuine sincerity of a person who doesn't trust her natural behavior to appear sincere. Paul went outside and opened the bronze gate and laughed a little when Daniel said he should "grow an enormous afro without any warning" for his next author photo and they sat on the front stoop. The late-afternoon sky, in Paul's peripheral vision, panoramic and mostly unobstructed, appeared rural or suburban, more indicative of forests and fields and lakes—of nature's vast connections, through the air and the soil, to more of itself—than of outer space, which was mostly what Paul thought of when beneath an urban sky, even in daytime, especially in Manhattan, between certain buildings, framing sunless zones of upper atmosphere, as if inviting space down to deoxygenate a city block. Walter exited the house and mentioned a party in Chelsea and left. Laura exited a few minutes later, meekly holding her tambourine and shaker and some construction paper. "I see you 'got in on' the construction paper," said Paul in the sarcastic, playful voice he'd used to recommend Funyuns the night they met, but with a serious expression. "Good choices, in terms of colors. Good job."

"You said I could have some," said Laura hesitantly.

"I know," said Paul. "I'm glad you got some."

"Well, I'm going home now," said Laura with a shy expression, not looking at anyone.

At a party that night Paul met Taryn, a friend of Caroline and Shawn Olive's, and became gradually—almost unnoticeably—intrigued by their interactions. They rarely talked and never touched but remained, for some reason, near each other, as if one was the other's manager or personal assistant, but neither knew their role and could only study the other for clues, which they seemed to do, gazing at each other anthropomorphically, for seconds at a time, surprisingly without awkwardness, then she seemed to disappear and was quickly forgotten. Paul sat with strangers on a crowded staircase and drank a beer while looking at his phone, sometimes staring at its screen for ten to twenty seconds without thinking anything, before maneuvering through a crowded hallway into a medium-size room. Around twenty-five people were dancing to loud music with faces that seemed expressive in an emotionless, hidden, bone-ward manner—the faces of people with the ability to stop clutching the objects of themselves and allow their brains, like independent universes with unique and inconstant natural laws, to react, like trees to wind, with their bodies to music.

Paul walked directly to a two-seat sofa (golden brown and deeply padded as the upturned paw of an enormous stuffed animal) and lay on it, on his side, facing the room, and closed his eyes. After a blip of surprise, which disintegrated in some chemical system of Klonopin and Valium and alcohol instead of articulating into what would've startled Paul awake—that he'd fluently, with precision and total calm, entered a room of dozens of people and lain facing outward on a sofa—was asleep. When he woke, an unknown amount of time later—

between five and forty minutes, or longer—he observed neutrally that, though he was drooling a little and probably the only non-dancing person in the room, no one was looking at him, then moved toward the room's iPod with the goal-oriented, zombie-like calmness of a person who has woken at night thirsty and is walking to his refrigerator and changed the music to "Today" by the Smashing Pumpkins. Every person, it seemed, stopped dancing and appeared earnestly annoyed but—as if to avoid encouraging the behavior—didn't look at Paul or say anything and, when the music was changed back, resumed dancing, like nothing had happened.

In early June, after four more parties, two at which he similarly slept on sofas after walking mutely through rooms without looking at anyone, Paul began attending fewer social gatherings and ingesting more drugs, mostly with Daniel and Fran, or only Daniel, or sometimes alone, which seemed classically "not a good sign," he sometimes thought, initially with mild amusement, then as a neutral observation, finally as a meaningless placeholder. Due to his staggered benzodiazepine usage and lack of obligations or long-term projects and that he sometimes ingested Seroquel and slept twelve to sixteen hours (always waking, it seemed, at night, uncomfortable and disoriented and unsure what to do, usually returning to sleep) he had gradually become unaware of day-to-day or week-to-week changes in his life—and, when he thought of himself in terms of months and years, he still viewed himself as in an "interim period," which by definition, he felt, would end when his book tour began—so he viewed the trend, of fewer people and more drugs, as he might view a new waiter at Taco Chulo: "there, at some point," separate from him, not of his concern, beyond his ability or desire to track or control.

When he wanted to know what happened two days ago, or five hours ago, especially chronologically, he would sense an impasse, in the form of a toll, which hadn't been there before, payable by an amount of effort (not unlike that required in problem solving or essay writing) he increasingly felt unmotivated to exert. There were times when his memory, like an external hard drive that had been taken from him and hidden inside an unwieldy series of cardboard boxes, or placed at the end of a long and dark and messy corridor, required much more effort than he felt motivated to exert simply to locate, after which, he knew, more effort would be required to gain access. After two to five hours with no memory, some days, he would begin to view concrete reality as his memory—a place to explore idly, without concern, but somewhat pointlessly, aware that his actual existence was elsewhere, that he was, in a way, hiding here, away from where things actually happened, then were stored here, in his memory.

Having repeatedly learned from literature, poetry, philosophy, popular culture, his own experiences, most movies he'd seen, especially ones he liked, that it was desirable to "live in the present," "not dwell on the past," etc., he mostly viewed these new obstacles to his memory as friendly and, sometimes, momentarily believing in their viability as a form of Zen, exciting or at least interesting. Whenever he wanted to access his memory (usually to analyze or calmly replay a troubling or pleasant social interaction) and sensed the impasse, which he almost always did, to some degree, or that his memory was currently missing, as was increasingly the case, he would allow himself to stop wanting, with an ease, not unlike dropping a leaf or stick while outdoors, he hadn't felt before—and, partly because he'd quickly forget what he'd wanted, without a sensation of loss or worry, only an acknowledgment of a different distribution of consciousness than if he'd focused on assembling and sustaining a memory—and passively continue with his ongoing sensory perception of concrete reality.

In mid-June, one dark and rainy afternoon, Paul woke and rolled onto his side and opened his MacBook sideways. At some point, maybe twenty minutes after he'd begun refreshing Twitter, Tumblr, Facebook, Gmail in a continuous cycle—with an ongoing, affectless, humorless realization that his day "was over"—he noticed with confusion, having thought it was a.m., that it was 4:46 p.m. He slept until 8:30 p.m. and "worked on things" in the library until midnight and was two blocks from his room, carrying a mango and two cucumbers and a banana in a plastic bag, when Daniel texted "come hang out, Mitch bought a lot of coke."

Daniel and Mitch were outside a bar, discussing where to use the cocaine. Paul said Daniel looked "really tired" and asked if he needed some eggplant, in reference to a joke they had that Daniel was heavily dependent on eggplant and almost always suffering its withdrawal symptoms, which could be horrific. Daniel said he stayed up last night with Fran, currently sleeping, to celebrate, by eating brunch and buying drugs, that she'd quit her job she got three days ago waitressing in a Polish restaurant.

They crossed the street to Mitch's friend Harry's apartment, where Harry, whom Mitch had earlier given some cocaine for his birthday, was repeatedly trying to hug more than one person at a time while shouting what one would normally speak. Paul walked aimlessly, into a kitchen, where he stood in darkness at the sink peeling and eating his mango. He washed his hands and walked through the apartment's main room—two desktop computers and speakers on a corner table, four large windows overlooking Graham Avenue, ten to fifteen people hugging and shouting, two medium-size dogs—into an institutionally bright hallway, where he heard Daniel in a bathroom whose door wasn't fully closed. "It's me," said Paul, and pushed the door, against resistance, which relented when he said "it's Paul," revealing a vaguely familiar girl, who appeared extremely tired, sitting on a bathtub's outer edge, looking at Daniel and Mitch huddled on the floor around a toilet-seat lid with cocaine on it.

"You're doing it without me," said Paul in an exaggerated monotone.

"We thought you left," said Daniel.

"I wouldn't just leave," said Paul.

"Out of anyone I know you're probably most likely to just leave," said Daniel crushing cocaine with his debit card.

Paul looked at the girl, who shrugged.

Mitch, who was allergic to Harry's dogs, sneezed.

"Jesus, be careful," said Daniel quietly.

"He's sharing it with us," said Paul. "And all you can do is berate him."

"Bro," said Daniel, and seemed to grin at Paul a little.

At Legion, twenty minutes later, Paul was sitting alone on a padded seat, staring at an area of torsos that were beginning to seem face-like. He texted Daniel that he was going to Khim's to "stock up on eggplant" and walked six blocks to the large deli below Harry's apartment, feeling energetic and calm, listening to Rilo Kiley through earphones at a medium volume. He paid for an organic beef patty, two kombuchas, five bananas, alfalfa sprouts, arugula, hempseed oil, a red onion, ginger, toilet paper and carried two paper bags reinforced with plastic bags toward Legion. Harry approached on the sidewalk with a panic-like expression of uncommitted confusion and, staring ahead, passed with a sweating forehead like the person in *Go* who is abandoned by a friend in

an alleyway outside a rave while—due to too much ecstasy—
foaming at the mouth.

Mitch and Daniel, in the soundless distance, were outside
Legion. As Paul approached, crossing a street, Daniel entered
Legion. Mitch said they were openly snorting cocaine off a
table in the back room, because the bathroom line was too
long, when a security guard approached and Mitch threw the
bag of cocaine (which Daniel was currently trying to find)
under a table, or somewhere. They crossed the street, went
in White Castle, sat in a booth. Paul realized a poster said
"chicken rings" not "onion rings" and said it seemed "insane"
and speculated on the process that must be required of making the meat into a paste to mold into rings.

"I'm worried about Daniel," said Mitch.

"He has a warrant for his arrest in Colorado, I think," said
Paul.

"Jesus," said Mitch.

"It's probably better if he goes to jail instead of you. He's
unemployed and in debt to like five people. He has a seventy-
dollar tab with me. I think he needs six hundred dollars in
one week for overdue rent. You have a real job and a nice
apartment. If he goes to jail I'll relinquish his tab."

Mitch was fidgeting a little.

"We can make a blog about him and mail him letters,"
said Paul.

"A blog," said Mitch. "Jesus."

"I'm going to look for him," said Paul.

In Legion's bathroom Paul read a text from Daniel that said
"come outside." Daniel, on the sidewalk, seeing Paul, began
crossing the street, toward White Castle, looking in different
directions while saying he knew the bouncers at Legion and

that Mitch shouldn't have panicked. Paul said Mitch had a high-paying job.

"Where is he?"

"White Castle," said Paul.

"Should I get some of this coke? I could've gotten in trouble."

"Yeah. If that's what you want."

"He's lucky it landed on this little ledge," said Daniel staring ahead as White Castle passed on their left. "I don't think any was lost."

"My groceries are in White Castle. Where are you going?"

"Let's go to your room to do some of this coke," said Daniel.

"It's too far," said Paul slowing his pace.

"We'll go there and come back, it won't take long."

"It's way too far," said Paul. "Just snort it off your hand."

They were on a dark street with no people, moving cars, or stores. Daniel's head seemed more elevated than normal—and his neck, swiveling and ostrich-like, more mechanical and controlled—as he looked in different directions while removing cocaine from the bag with what seemed to be his fingers, then somehow maneuvering his hand into a fist, which he put into his jeans pocket. Paul felt unsettled, imagining amounts of cocaine trickling between fingers and slipping off the sides of fingers and the curve of the palm and sticking as powder against Daniel's hand and pocket interior. Paul ripped a page from his Moleskine journal and said "here, use this." Daniel continued looking in different directions a few seconds before taking the page and putting it directly in his pants pocket.

"You should snort it off the Lincoln," said Paul.

"There isn't a Lincoln here," said Daniel.

"That looks like a Lincoln," said Paul pointing.

"That's a Pontiac," said Daniel looking elsewhere.

"You should hide between two cars," said Paul, and Daniel moved slowly toward the street. Paul used his phone to photograph Daniel kneeling between two cars and sent the photo to his own Gmail account and to Daniel's phone. He imagined them both sprinting in different directions the instant a spotlight appeared, gliding across the street, toward them, from a low-flying helicopter.

"Good job," said Paul walking toward White Castle.

"You know I don't usually do this to friends," said Daniel staring ahead.

"What do you mean?" said Paul grinning.

"I mean, do you think it's okay I did that?"

"Yeah. You were put in a dangerous situation."

"I was looking on the ground for it, but it was on this little shelf," said Daniel in White Castle.

"Jesus," said Mitch, who seemed distracted in a respiratory manner like, after Paul left, he'd become increasingly worried and hyperventilated a little and was still recovering. Daniel handed Mitch the bag and said "um, it was open, so I don't know how much fell out," with, it seemed, slightly averted eyes. Mitch put the bag in his pocket without responding and, with unfocused eyes, said he was going to the bathroom and went.

After snorting cocaine in Paul's room Daniel and Mitch moved into the kitchen, then into Caroline's room. Caroline's door, except when she was sleeping, was always partly open. Paul, whose door was almost always closed, listened from his mattress and when he heard someone say "chicken rings" stood without thinking and went to Caroline's room. Daniel and Mitch were aggressively looking at Caroline's shelves and walls, bending at their waists and craning their necks.

"Hi, Paul," said Caroline.

"Hi. I heard someone say 'chicken rings.'"

"Chicken rings?" said Caroline.

"I think I misheard," said Paul. "Never mind."

"Caroline was telling us she went to a Fuck Buttons concert tonight," said Mitch.

"Someone was talking about them before," said Paul vaguely. "I feel like . . . Daniel . . . you were telling me about them. Fuck Buttons."

"I don't think so," said Daniel.

"Last night, maybe," said Paul.

"Where were we last night?"

"Um," said Paul looking down with unfocused eyes, aware he looked like he was thinking but wasn't, an increasingly common deception for him. "I don't know," he said after a few seconds, then said "Shawn Olive" as a non sequitur and grinned and said "Daniel knows Shawn Olive" to Caroline, who had gone to school with Shawn Olive.

"Who's Shawn Olive?" said Mitch.

"I don't know," said Paul immediately while laughing a little. "I mean . . . seems hard to just answer that."

"We're good friends," said Caroline. "He's great."

"We saw *Robin Hood* last night," said Daniel.

Paul was alone, a few hours later, stomach-down on his bed, working on things on his MacBook—on 20mg Adderall— after eating most of his organic beef patty with an arugula salad containing flax seeds, alfalfa sprouts, cucumber, tamari, lemon juice, flax oil. He and Daniel, who'd left around 3:30 a.m. with Mitch, had been emailing steadily and were committed to meet at 9:30 a.m. to go to the Museum of Modern Art, where Marina Abramović was performing *The Artist Is Present,* for which she would be sitting in a chair for 736 hours over 77 days, staring at whoever was next in line to sit and stare back at her from an opposite chair. When Paul emailed Daniel at 9:22 a.m. that he was naked and hadn't showered Daniel responded that he was also naked and also hadn't showered. At 9:54 a.m. Paul texted "where the fuck are you." Daniel responded immediately that he was still naked and hadn't moved from his bed.

They met, an hour later, at an intersection near the Graham L train stop. One of them said the museum would be crowded on a Sunday and, within seconds, both had strongly committed to not going. They went to the bookstore adjacent Verb. "Shawn Olive," said Daniel holding the book with a black dot on its cover toward Paul and grinning. "Shawn Olive's book has the same cover. Almost the same cover."

"We already showed each other that," said Paul.

"What do you mean?"

"We showed each other this book. Are you joking?"

"No," said Daniel. "We talked about this book?"

"We talked about it where we're standing right now."

"Damn," said Daniel looking away. "I don't remember."

At Verb they each ingested 10mg Adderall. Daniel removed from his tote bag a glass jar with a peanut butter label and, with a neutral expression, not looking at Paul, poured around 4oz of whiskey into his iced coffee. Paul asked what Daniel was going to do about his financial situation. Daniel said Mitch, a week ago, had mentioned hiring him to write promotional copy for his band but hadn't mentioned it again. Paul suggested they shoplift things from Best Buy, or some other store, to sell on eBay.

Outside, walking steadily but aimlessly, they entered East River State Park and sat on grass, facing the river and Manhattan, which seemed to Paul like an enormous, unfinished cruise ship that had been disassembled and rearranged by thousands of disconnected organizations. They decided to sell books on the sidewalk, on Bedford Avenue, but continued sitting. Daniel began talking, a few minutes later, in a quiet, earnest voice about his lack of accomplishments in life, staring into the distance with a haunted, slightly puzzled expression, seeming at times like he might begin crying. Paul, grinning anxiously at Daniel's right profile, unsure what to say, or do, shrugged more than once, thinking that tears would have a restorative effect on the seared dryness of Daniel's eyes, which looked like they'd been baked at a low heat.

"What were we doing now?" said Paul leaving the park, around twenty minutes later.

Daniel looked distractedly in both directions after walking a few steps onto a street, then turned right on the sidewalk, staring ahead with a worried expression.

"We had a specific goal, I remember," said Paul. "What was it?"

"I don't know," said Daniel after a few seconds.

"We were just talking about it."

"I remember something," said Daniel absently.

"Oh yeah, selling books," said Paul.

"Let's do that," said Daniel.

"We just actually forgot our purpose, then regained it," said Paul grinning. "We still kept moving at the same speed, when we had no goal."

"Jesus," said Daniel quietly.

On the way to Paul's room, to get books to sell, they went in a pizza restaurant, because Daniel was hungry. Paul, rereading old texts, saw one he didn't recognize—"sorry, how was the party"—from Laura, more than a month ago, the morning after the Cinco de Mayo party. Between then and now, maybe two weeks ago, Paul had asked her in an email if she remembered referring to him as "my boyfriend," the night they attended two parties on Ambien. She'd said no, but was sorry if she did, but was sure she didn't, then later emailed to say her friends who'd been there confirmed she didn't. Paul was staring through glass at a pigeon eating specks off the sidewalk when he noticed the approach of what he briefly, with some sarcasm, began to perceive as another pigeon, inside the restaurant, but was Daniel. "Um, so, my debit card, either from cutting so much blow or being maxed out, isn't working," he said in a quiet, controlled voice with an earnest expression. "Could I borrow $2.75 for a slice of pizza?"

"Yeah," said Paul thinking he wasn't going to mention the pigeon illusion. "I'll add it to your tab."

Daniel stood near the center of Paul's room quietly saying that he felt "fucked" about his financial situation and generally, in terms of his life, then kneeled to a low table to organize two lines of cocaine with the last of what he had from Mitch's bag. Paul, stomach-down on his mattress, asked what music he should play and clicked "Heartbeats" by the Knife. They both laughed a little and Paul clicked "Last Nite" by the Strokes and said it sounded too depressing. He clicked "Such Great Heights" by The Postal Service and said "just kidding." He clicked "The Peter Criss Jazz" by Don Caballero. He clicked "pause."

Daniel said to put The Postal Service back on and snorted half his line. Paul moved a rolled-up page of Shawn Olive's poetry book in his right nostril toward the cocaine and exhaled a little after snorting half his line, causing the rest and some of Daniel's to spread in a poof on the table. Daniel lightly berated Paul, who sort of rolled toward his mattress's center, then—liking the feeling of unimpeded motion on a padded

surface—moved his MacBook to the floor and lay in a diagonal on his back with his limbs spread out a little, which felt
interesting because, he knew, it was probably the second or
third time he'd lain on this mattress, while awake and alert
and not impatient toward himself, without reading a book,
looking at his MacBook, or aware of his MacBook's screen.

At a certain age, he remembered, he had often lain motionless on carpet, or a sofa, feeling what he probably viewed, at
the time, as boredom and what now seemed like ignorance
of—or passive disbelief in—his forthcoming death, which
would occur regardless of his thoughts, feelings, or actions
in the unknown amount of remaining interim, upon a binary
absorption from some incomprehensible direction, taking
him elsewhere. Briefly, without much interest, Paul intuited
that if he were immortal, or believed he was, he might feel
what he'd felt as a child, which seemed less enjoyable than
obscurely unsatisfying, something he'd want to be distracted
from feeling. After a few minutes an out-of-view Daniel continued to say he felt depressed, but in a calmer voice that
Paul felt was "soothing," for him, to hear, from his bed.

They sat facing south at Bedford and North 1st with thirty
to forty books on a rollout carpet and, in a few hours, sold
around $25 of books and $60 of Paul's Adderall, which he
received monthly by mail at slightly-better-than-drug-dealer
price from a graduate student at Boston College. Four fash-
ionable black teenagers appeared and, Paul thought, "the
leader," who was much more interested than the others,
asked if he could "sample" Charles' book.

"I'll take it," he said after laughing loudly at something in
the book, which included poetry and prose about alienation,
boredom, science fiction, depression, confusion.

Daniel asked if the teenager liked Adderall.

"What is it?"

Daniel described it in a few sentences.

"So, it's like ecstasy?"

"Sort of," said Daniel. "But without the euphoria. It's good for doing work. It helps you focus."

The teenager asked if his friend was "in."

"No," said his friend. "But I'll watch you do it."

"Do you want your book signed? The author is here," said Paul pointing at Daniel, who had been pretending he was Charles, with Charles' approval gained by text.

Daniel wrote "best wishes, from Charles" in the book.

Charles' six weeks in Mexico and Guatemala, related in emails and Gmail chats, traveling hostel to hostel, spending much of his time in internet cafés feeling alienated from Americans doing what he was doing, but in groups, had taken on the tone and focus, after two weeks, of a comedic sitcom, which he'd named *Avoiding Jehan,* because his primary concern, most days, was to avoid or endure or try to permanently escape a person named Jehan, who had repeatedly—almost always inadvertently, obliviously—thwarted Charles' few romantic prospects and, in social situations, caused Charles to become "the third wheel" or "the fifth wheel." In one email Charles had wished Jehan would "become invisible." After getting stalled in Guatemala, on the way to South America, two weeks ago, Charles had returned cashless to his girlfriend and Seattle, where they now shared "a smaller, shittier apartment," he said, than when he left America, around two months ago.

The sky had begun to colorfully darken, a few hours later, with reds and purples and pinks that drifted away, like cotton candy, from an unseen horizon, as if something there was changing and releasing energy, when an Asian girl, who had slowed and passed a minute ago while talking into an iPhone, returned and said she recognized Paul from the internet and distractedly asked if Daniel was a cop.

"No," said Daniel, and the Asian girl said she was buying marijuana from someone with a business card, which she showed Daniel, at his request. She bought two books and three Adderall and kneeled and asked if Daniel or Paul had a driver's license, to move her friend's car from Crown Heights to the Graham L train station for money. They discussed the car for what seemed like fifteen minutes, without resolution, then the girl, whose name was Annie, which Paul heard initially as Addy, removed a Chinese magazine from her bag and asked if Paul was good at translating. Paul said he couldn't read Chinese or speak Mandarin fluently, and had an American accent sometimes, he'd been told. "I'm going to pee," he said, and went to Verb, two blocks away. In line, behind two people, he thought that, from a certain point onward— beginning with his book tour, maybe—he would only appear in public if he'd ingested sufficient drugs to not primarily be a source of anxiety, bleakness, awkwardness, etc. for himself and/or others.

When Paul returned to Daniel and Annie they were talking about Annie's boyfriend, who had attended the same college as Daniel, in Colorado. Annie's boyfriend had gone to India after college. When he returned to America, three years ago, he died for a reason that Paul, who was thinking of how spring was to summer like a morning was to an entire day, brief and lucid and transitional, didn't hear. Annie said her boyfriend's funeral, due to a request he'd made in India, had been organized and promoted like a party and was "weird," because it had been exactly like a party except everyone was wearing black.

• • •

In mid-July, a few weeks later, at a party that, instead of end-ing, had moved outside, through a window at the back of someone's bedroom, onto an eighth-floor roof, Paul and Dan-iel were on an additionally elevated platform—corner-set, wall-less, square, smooth—like a landing pad for tiny heli-copters.

Daniel was standing with limbs and neck uncoordinat-edly extended, slightly striding in place—the pre-predatory stance of a chained thing that had broken free and didn't yet know where to direct its vengeance, or what to do gen-erally. His vision was focused horizontally, as if across a flat expanse. Then, with his back to one of the two edges dropping to the street, he approached an already fearful Paul—sitting cross-legged at the platform's center, aware Daniel had been drinking steadily for hours and was probably on two or more drugs—who reacted preemptively, against what seemed like a purposeless entity unreasonably desiring his involvement, with defensive movements of his arms and hands, causing the situ-ation, in Paul's panicked state, to immediately seem like an unrestrained wrestling, though it probably looked more like an exaggeratedly confused handshaking. Paul tried to concentrate on flattening himself—on retaining a low, stable center—while repeatedly telling Daniel to "stop," because it was "dangerous," he heard himself say in a gravely serious, faintly humorous voice of uncertainly suppressed fear, but was distracted by how most of his thoughts were based on a reality in which he had fallen off the building. Should he close his eyes? What should he try to see? What would his mother do/feel? Could he grab things to disrupt his fall like in movies? Could one of these be his final thought? What would that mean? Why couldn't he comprehend this? Should he think other things?

3

Eight people were in Erin's five-seat car, which had gotten lost on its way from Paul's book-release reading in Brooklyn to DuMont Burger, also in Brooklyn, when it was stopped by a police car, in Manhattan, around two hundred feet from the Williamsburg Bridge. The officer shined a flashlight through the driver's window at the backseat without bending to see what was there, then asked Erin, 24, who had driven four hours that day from Baltimore to attend Paul's reading and visit friends, to step outside the car. Paul, in the front passenger seat, hadn't seen Fran, who was sitting partly on him, or Daniel, in the backseat, in five or six weeks, except once, briefly and separately, at a Bret Easton Ellis reading three weeks ago, when they'd avoided each other, and Fran, without context, had shown Paul a text from Daniel insulting her in a strangely formal, almost aristocratic tone. Paul had communicated regularly, the past month, only with Charles, by email or Gmail chat, mostly about what food they had eaten, or were thinking about eating, to "console" themselves. After being more social, April to July, than any other period of his life, Paul had returned to his default lifestyle, which varied, to some degree, but generally entailed (1) avoiding most social situations (2) not wanting to sleep most nights and not knowing why—he'd wanted since 2006 to title one of his books *I Don't Want to Sleep but I Don't Know What I'm Waiting For*—resulting usually in four to ten hours of looking at the internet, reading, masturbating, etc. until morning, when he would eat something and sleep until night.

Erin, back in her car, said the officer had looked at her two-months-expired, out-of-state driver's license an abnormally long time, like he'd forgotten what he was doing, before quietly saying "be careful" and allowing her to continue driving, in what seemed to be an egregious oversight, without a ticket or decreasing passengers.

Paul first learned of Erin twenty months ago, in January 2009, when she commented on his blog and he clicked her profile and read her pensive, melancholy, amusing accounts, on her blog, of her vague relationships and part-time bookstore job and nights drinking beer while looking at the internet and classes at the University of Baltimore, where she'd reenrolled after a two-year break. Paul found and read—and reread, with high levels of interest—three long stories, each focused on an unrequited or failed relationship, that she had published in online magazines. Erin, being an attractive and adventurous-seeming person, was probably almost always, Paul imagined, entering or leaving—or, in some way, maneuvering—one or more relationships, but probably, between relationships, as a person who seemed to enjoy being alone sometimes, would become more active on the internet, for weeks or months, which over months and years would overlap with Paul's nearly continuously high levels of internet activity. They would gradually communicate more and maybe begin emailing and—if neither died, entered long relationships, or left the internet—eventually meet in person. Paul viewed this process as self-fulfilling, not something he wanted to track or manipulate, so after one or two weeks had mostly internalized Erin's existence—as a busy person with a separate life, in a different city—and had stopped thinking about her by mid-February, when he met Michelle, with whom he was in a relationship both times, before tonight, that he met Erin in person.

The first time was in July, when Erin visited New York City for the release of Charles' poetry book. The day after the release Paul was amused and excited for them, at a BBQ, when Charles said he had kissed Erin.

The second time was in September, one year ago, when Erin attended Paul's reading in Baltimore. At a restaurant, with a large group of people, but talking only to each other, Paul asked about Charles, whom Erin had visited in August. Erin said she had changed her plane ticket and left earlier than planned because Charles had become gradually less affectionate, culminating with a night when, after sex, he said he didn't feel anything for her, then consoled her, as she cried, in his kitchen. Paul liked Erin's forthright, unhesitant, nonjudgmental answers and that she was able—already, despite what seemed like strong disappointment—to view and describe what had happened as at least partly amusing.

When Erin asked about Michelle, as they walked to her car, Paul automatically said Michelle was "good" while distinctly recalling a recent night when he complained he always offered her food or drink before himself, then after Michelle said she'd be happy to do that, now that she knew it mattered to him, said it didn't matter to him and she shouldn't change. Exiting Erin's car, at the hotel he was staying in for one night, because a mysterious Johns Hopkins professor, whose Facebook name was "Cloud Bat," had bought him a room, Paul thought that if he weren't in a relationship with Michelle he would ask Erin upstairs, where they would, he vaguely imagined, continue talking.

As Erin's car slowly accelerated away from the police car, onto the Williamsburg Bridge, one person, then another, said they were illegally carrying drugs. After a peculiarly awkward, car-wide silence that became comical when someone asked if every person in the car was illegally carrying drugs, eliciting three affirmations and a sort of confirmatory announcement that every person—Erin, Paul, Daniel, Fran, Mitch, Juan, Jeannie, Jeremy—was illegally carrying drugs, there was the immediately space-filling noise of a small crowd laughing, which continued for around five seconds, during which Paul (who, in sharing his seat with Fran, was partly turned toward the driver's window) watched the police car, or a police car, zoom past in the left lane, with emergency lights on and sirens off, quick and soundless as an apparition or the hologram of itself.

In DuMont Burger's bathroom Paul swallowed half of half a 30mg Oxycodone and .5mg Xanax, feebly amused to be already deviating, in moderate excess, from his plans to ingest specific amounts of drugs at certain times during his book tour, September 7 to November 4. To determine what amount of what drugs—MDMA, LSD, any benzodiazepine, amphetamine, opiate—he should ingest, on what days, to minimize anxiety and boredom for himself and others, he'd edited the seven-page itinerary from his publisher to fit on one page and, in an idle process he'd enjoyed, the past few weeks, studied each event in context, writing notes on the paper. He'd printed a final draft, currently in his pocket, that said he should ingest something—specified, in most instances, by type and amount—before twenty-two of his twenty-five events and some miscellaneous things such as the day a writer from *BlackBook* was writing an article about "hanging out" with him while doing that.

Paul splashed water on his face, which he dried, then returned to his seat, next to Juan, who was talking to Jeremy about whether a horse could win "best athlete of the year." Erin, the only person Paul felt like talking to, at the moment, was out of range, so when two acquaintances who didn't know anyone else arrived Paul sat with them at a four-person table, where he felt self-conscious about the tenuousness of his situation—he hadn't ordered food because he was nauseated from the Oxycodone and long car ride and he didn't have anything he wanted to say to anyone. When a friend of the acquaintances arrived, sitting at the table's fourth seat, Paul fixated on her—maybe partly to justify his increasingly pointless, idle presence—in an exaggerated manner (asking her questions continuously while sustaining a "concentrating expression" with such intensity, muddled by the onset of the drugs he'd used in the bathroom, that he sometimes felt able to sense the weight of the microscopic painting of the restaurant's interior, decreased by a dimension and scaled down to almost nothing, resting on the top curvature of his right eyeball) that felt conducive to abruptly stopping and leaving, which he did, after around fifteen minutes of increasingly forced conversation, walking six blocks to his room.

After blearily looking at the internet a little, then peeing and brushing his teeth and washing his face, he lay in darkness on his mattress, finally allowing the simple insistence of the opioid, like an unending chord progression with a consistently unexpected and pleasing manner of postponing resolution, to accumulate and expand, until his brain and heart and the rest of him were contained within the same song-like beating—of another, larger, protective heart—inside of which, temporarily safe from the outside world, he would shrink into the lunar city of himself and feel and remember strange and forgotten things, mostly from his childhood.

Paul's book tour's fourth reading—after another in Brooklyn and one at a Barnes & Noble in the financial district—was in Ohio, on September 11. Calvin, 18, and Maggie, 17, seniors in high school who'd been friends since middle school and were currently in a relationship, had invited Paul and Erin and other "internet friends" to read at a music festival and stay two nights in Calvin's parents' "mansion," as Paul called it.

The day after the reading Paul and Erin ingested a little LSD and shared a chocolate containing psilocybin mushrooms and sat in sunlight in Calvin's backyard, which had a hot tub and swimming pool and skateboard ramp and basketball hoop, "working on things" on their MacBooks. When Calvin returned from school they got in his SUV to go to Whole Foods, where Maggie was meeting them after work at American Apparel, and shared another chocolate. Calvin, who hadn't wanted any, meekly asked if maybe he'd feel good if he ate only a small piece, seeming like he wanted to be encouraged to try.

"We already ate it," said Paul, and laughed a little, in the backseat.

Erin, in the front passenger seat, was still holding a piece. Hearing Calvin she had seemed to slow its movement toward her mouth. She made a quiet, inquisitive noise and glanced slightly toward Paul, then resumed a normal speed and placed it inside her mouth. Paul lay on his back for most of the drive, sometimes sitting to noncommittally mumble something relevant, including that he liked Stereolab and Rainer Maria, to what he could hear of Calvin and Erin's conversation. Walking toward Whole Foods, across its parking lot, Paul said he was "beginning to feel the LSD, maybe."

"Really?" said Erin. "I feel . . ."

"I don't know," said Paul.

"I can't tell what I feel," said Erin, and automatic doors opened and they entered the produce section, where they held and examined different coconuts. Calvin stood looking back, seeming tired and a little afraid, like a reclusive uncle supervising his unruly niece and outgoing nephew.

"You should get one," said Paul. "It's refreshing."

"I'm . . . allergic," said Calvin a little nervously.

"Shit," said Paul grinning. "I forgot. Again. Sorry."

The next few minutes, while Paul and Erin went to three different sections—butcher, pizza, sushi—to get their coconuts opened, Calvin remained at a far distance, randomly and inattentively picking up and looking at things and sometimes glancing at Paul and Erin with a worried, socially anxious expression. Something about Calvin, maybe a corresponding distance or that they had similar body types, reminded Paul of Michelle, the night of the magazine-release party, waiting with slack posture at a red light, before she touched his arm and leaned on the metal fence. Paul, in line to pay, considered saying the word "Kafkaesque" to describe getting their coconuts opened, but was distracted by an eerily familiar actress's smiling face on a magazine cover and remained silent, then paid and maneuvered to a booth and sat by Erin, across from Calvin, who stared at them with wet eyes and a beseeching, insatiable, inhibited expression that alternated between Paul and Erin to keep both, Paul thought, locked into his meekly laser-like gaze. Paul held his left hand like a visor to his forehead and looked down and sometimes said "oh my god." Whenever he glanced at Erin, who seemed to be enjoyably displaying an unceasing grin, he laughed uncontrollably and, due to the contrast with Calvin's alienated demeanor, felt more uncomfortable. Unsure how to stop grinning, or what to do, he left the booth for straws. When he returned, after feeling mischievous and Gollum-like for two to three minutes while trying to secretly record Erin and Calvin with his iPhone, he lowered himself skillfully, he felt, in a 180-degree turn, like that of a screw, to a seated position, flinging a straw at Erin while connecting the awning of his left hand to his forehead. He moved his coconut to his lap and heard a partially metallic, imaginary-sounding noise. He stared without comprehension, but also without confusion, at Calvin's body, which was hunched close to the table with demonically jutting shoulder blades rising and falling in rhythm to what sounded like a computer-generated squawking. The cube of space containing Calvin seemed to be reconfiguring itself, against passive resistance from the preexisting configuration of Calvin, mutating him in a process of computerization. Paul thought he was witnessing a kind of special effect, then realized Calvin was imitating a pterodactyl.

"I feel so much better now," said Calvin. "Just doing what I want . . . what I want to do . . . yeah. Before, I was holding back, so I felt bad. I feel so much better now."

"You were making pterodactyl noises," said Paul in disbelief.

Maggie appeared as a desultory object, rapidly approaching the booth in a horizontal glide, seeming unnaturally small and eerily low to the ground. "LSDs, LSDs," she was saying in a high-pitched, taunting, witch-like voice. Paul, who was laughing and repeatedly saying "oh my god" and variations of "I can't believe this is happening," heard Calvin say "they're not on LSD." Maggie said "magic mushrooms" and seemed to be imitating an elf as she entered the booth behind Erin and Paul, who heard Erin say "we're on LSD and mushrooms," and briefly visualized the main character from *Willow*, the dwarf with magical powers. Things seemed defectively quiet, like before an explosion in a movie, the five to ten seconds before Maggie rose in the booth behind Paul, who turned and saw a faceless mound: Maggie, with her entire head inside a black beanie, saying "is this the front of me or back."

In the parking lot Maggie went alone to her car. Calvin was backing out of his parking space when Paul, leaning forward from the backseat, said he wanted to be in Maggie's car. Calvin braked and asked what to do, alternately looking at Paul and Erin with a helpless, besieged expression. Paul looked down a little, as if to suspend an intensity of visual input, to allow his brain to better focus on the question, but he wasn't thinking about the question, or anything, except maybe something about how he wasn't thinking anything, or was having problems thinking.

"I don't know what to do," said Calvin incredulously. "Should I call Maggie?"

"No," said Paul after a few seconds.

"Maggie already left, I think," said Calvin.

"Let's just go," said Paul.

"But . . . if you want to be in Maggie's car."

"I want to be here now."

"If you . . . are you sure?"

"I want to be in this car. Maggie's car is small."

"Are you sure?"

"Yes," said Paul leaning against the front passenger seat, aware of the distant municipality of the SUV's lighted dashboard. Things seemed darker to him than expected, a few minutes later, on the highway. The unlighted space, all around him—and, outside the SUV, the trees, sky—seemed more visible, by being blacker, or a higher resolution of blackness, almost silvery with detail, than normal, instead of what he'd sometimes and increasingly sensed, the past two months, mostly in his room, since one night when, supine on his yoga mat, his eyes, while open, had felt closed, or farther back in his head, and his room had seemed "literally darker," he'd thought, as if the bulb attached to his non-working ceiling fan had been secretly replaced, or like he was deeper inside the cave of himself than he'd been before and didn't know why. "My face . . . it feels like it's moving backward," Calvin was saying in a surprised, confused voice. "It keeps floating into me . . . itself . . . repeatedly."

"Jesus," said Paul. "Why?"

"Percocet. And a little Codeine."

"I didn't know you've been on those."

"I told you . . . at the house."

"Jesus," said Paul. "I remember now."

They began talking about a Lil Wayne documentary that focused on Lil Wayne's "drug problem," which Lil Wayne denied. Paul felt it was bleak and depressing that the filmmakers superimposed their views onto Lil Wayne. Calvin seemed to agree with the documentary. Paul tried, with Erin, who agreed with him, he felt, to convey (mostly by slowly saying variations of "no" and "I can't think right now") that there was no such thing as a "drug problem" or even "drugs"—

unless anything anyone ever did or thought or felt was considered both a drug and a problem—in that each thought or feeling or object, seen or touched or absorbed or remembered, at whatever coordinate of space-time, would have a unique effect, which each person, at each moment of their life, could view as a problem, or not.

In Calvin's room, supine on carpet, Paul felt circumstantially immobile, like a turtle on its back, and that Calvin and Maggie were pressuring him to decide on an activity. Then he was sitting on the edge of a bed, staring at an area of carpet near his black-socked feet, vaguely aware of his inability to move or think and of people waiting for him to answer a question. He grinned after hearing himself, in his memory of three or four seconds ago, say "I don't know what to do" very slowly, as if each word had been carefully selected, with attention to accuracy and concision. Erin silently exited Calvin's bathroom and left the room in a manner, Paul vaguely felt, like she was smuggling herself elsewhere. Paul heard Maggie say "all right, we're going to the hot tub" and remain in the top left corner of his vision a few seconds before vanishing. Paul walked lethargically into the bathroom, removed his clothes, stood naked in Calvin's room struggling to insert his left leg into his boxer shorts' left hole, which kept collapsing shut and distortedly reappearing as part of a slowly rippling infinity symbol, tottering on one leg sometimes and quietly falling once—mostly deliberately, anticipating a brief rolling sensation and a respite on the thick carpet—before succeeding and, after staring catatonically at nothing for a vague amount of time, aware of something simian about his posture and jaw, carefully going downstairs.

In the backyard, a few minutes later, Paul and Erin, holding each other's arms in an indiscernibly feigned kind of fear, hesitated before advancing, barefoot on the spiky and yielding grass, into the area of darkness Calvin and Maggie, after testing the swimming pool's water as too cold, had gone. Paul stopped moving when he saw the disturbing statue of a Greek god wearing a gorilla mask, which Calvin, that afternoon, had said someone put on last Halloween, then abandoned Erin by running ahead, on his toes a little. As he slightly leaped, followed closely by Erin, into the hot tub, he imagined his head shooting like a yanked thing toward concrete. He surfaced after exaggeratedly, unnecessarily allowing the water to absorb his impact, then stared in disbelief at a balled-up Maggie rolling forward and back like a notorious, performing snail. "Oh my god," he said, aware his and Erin's feet were deliberately touching. "Look at Maggie. What is she doing?"

"I was doing water sit-ups," said Maggie.

"I can't believe . . . that," said Paul. "Have you ever done that?"

"No," said Maggie. "What if we were all obese right now?"

"The water would be displaced," said Paul without thinking, and people laughed. Paul felt surprised he was able to cause authentic laughter at his handicapped level of functioning. The above-water parts of him were waiting patiently, he thought while staring at the soil beneath the bushes a few feet beyond the hot tub and remembering disliking the presence of soil while in swimming pools as a child in Florida, for the laughter to end and something else to begin. He became aware of himself saying "what would we be talking about right now if we were obese?" and, comprehending himself as the extemporaneous source of what seemed to be an immensely interesting question, felt a sensation of awe. He remained motionless, with eyeballs inattentively fixated on the obscure pattern of the bushes behind and to the left of Calvin and an anticipatory nervousness, as he imagined staring at each person, in turn, to confirm—or convey, depending on the person—that, despite his impaired functioning, he had, unforeseen to anyone, including himself, asked a question of nearly unbelievable insight.

"We would talk about if we were skinny," said Maggie.

"No, because it would be too depressing," said Paul, surprised again by the power of his mind but less than before, a little suspicious now of his own enthusiasm.

"You're right," said Calvin, and seemed to look at each person in disbelief—which confused Paul because he had imagined doing that himself.

"We would talk about food," said Maggie.

"I feel like people are staring at me," said Paul.

"Me too, a little," said Erin.

"I wish I could see how Erin and I are like on mushrooms now," said Paul.

"Me too," said Erin.

"I was going to bring my camera but didn't want to get it wet," said Maggie.

"People are staring at me weird, except Erin," said Paul. "I wish someone was recording us."

"Just ask me later and I'll tell you," said Maggie.

"Later," said Paul, confused. "When?"

Calvin said it was time for Maggie to go home and they left seemingly instantly. Paul was aware of having waved at them and of having meekly said "bye, Maggie," to himself, he realized, as he continued staring at where they had gone out of view—to postpone interacting with Erin, who'd been abnormally quiet most of the night, he uncertainly realized with increasing anxiety. Maggie should have stayed longer, because he and Erin were only visiting a few days, he thought earnestly for a few seconds before realizing, with only a little sheepishness, that Maggie had her own desires, separate from those of anyone else, which she expressed through her actions. Paul knew that, because he kept thinking about

101

Maggie, his demeanor and behavior, when he finally acknowledged Erin, would appear, if not obviously feigned, to convey
"I want to be elsewhere" or "I want to be doing things in service of being elsewhere," which Erin would easily discern, if
she hadn't already. Paul moved his mouth to where water was
bubbling and, partly facing away from Erin, said something
about it feeling "nice." Erin moved her mouth to a different
area of similar bubbling. After ten to fifteen minutes Calvin
appeared and said "you guys can come inside now, Maggie
went home," seeming to have assumed they had been waiting
for his approval to go inside. Paul had begun feeling comfortable and was confused why they couldn't—and weren't asked
if they wanted to—stay in the hot tub.

After showering in separate bathrooms Paul and Erin sat on
Calvin's carpeted floor. Calvin, covered by blankets up to his
underarms, with his upper body propped by pillows, seemed
like he was cautiously testing an unexpected feeling of health
and energy while on his "death bed." Maggie, he said in a
worried and slightly fascinated voice, had wanted to perform
oral sex on him, but he hadn't been aroused, which had upset
her maybe. Erin said it was normal for sexual desire to leave
sometimes. Calvin said he and Maggie hadn't had sex in four
months. Paul said that seemed normal because they'd been
together three years and that Calvin's drug use—Percocet,
Codeine, Klonopin, Adderall—the past few months, based
on their emails and texts, seemed high, which probably had
an effect. Then they discussed what to do now, for an activity,
but couldn't decide—each person seemed committed to not
deciding—and became locked into what felt like a three-way
staring contest, which they mutely sustained, each person
alternating between the other two, for thirty to forty seconds, until Paul bluntly said he wanted to "go for a walk with

only Erin, outside," and, after mumbling something incoherent about mushrooms—vaguely wanting to convey it was uncomfortable while on mushrooms to be around people not on mushrooms—quickly gained Erin's assent and repeatedly positioned himself to displace, or push, her toward where he was going, until both were outside the room, in a dark hallway, where they huddled together and maneuvered grinning to winding stairs, which they descended holding hands, toward the front door.

They walked down the driveway into the upper-middle-class neighborhood with their inside arms folded up and against each other. Most front yards had one or two fashionably sculpted trees and two or more colorful Boy Scouts–like patches of flowers and plants in independent organization. Paul saw, in a side yard, a pale fence with the colorless, palatially melancholy glow of unicorns and remembered how in Florida, in the second of his family's three houses of increasing size, both his neighbors had built fences—rows of vertical, triangular-topped slats of wood that had seemed huge, medieval—around their backyards. Paul said he felt like he was in *Edward Scissorhands* and they sat on a concrete embankment facing the street with their feet on a sidewalk. Paul slightly looked away as he said "there's so many stars here" without much interest.

Erin pointed and asked if one was moving.

"In place, maybe," said Paul uncertainly.

"It looks like it's vibrating," said Erin.

"It's, um, what thoughts do you have about UFOs?" said Paul looking away, as if not wanting Erin to hear him clearly. "I'm doing it . . . I'm saying stereotypical things that people say while on mushrooms."

"That's okay. UFOs are interesting."

"I know it's okay," said Paul, and asked if Erin had experienced "any UFO things." Erin said she wore purple and put glitter on her eyes every Friday in fourth grade because she thought, if she did, aliens would notice and take her away.

"That seems really good," said Paul feeling emotional. "All purple?"

"No. It just had to be one thing that was purple."

"Where did you think they would take you?"

"I don't think I thought about that," said Erin. "Just 'away.' Anywhere."

"What . . . did your classmates, or other people, think?"

"I've never told anyone."

"Really? But . . . it's been so long."

"I didn't have anyone to tell, really."

"You haven't told anyone except me?"

"No. Let me think. No, I haven't."

Paul had begun to vaguely feel that he already knew of a similar thing—something about purple glitter and fourth grade, maybe from a children's book—or was he remembering what he just heard? His voice sounded bored, he thought, as he told Erin about when, as a fourth or fifth grader, he really wanted to see a UFO and was on a plane and saw a brown dot and, without any excitement or sensation of discovery, repeatedly thought to himself that he'd seen a UFO. "I think I was aware at first that I was 'faking' it," said Paul uncertainly. "But . . . I think I convinced myself so hard that I made myself forget that part . . . when I was aware, and I think I really believed I saw a UFO."

"Whoa. Did you tell anyone you saw a UFO?"

"I don't think I've ever told anyone. I don't think I cared if anyone knew. I was just like, 'I saw a UFO.' I think I was extremely bored. I was like a bored robot."

The next night Erin and Paul met Cristine, 22—a mutual acquaintance from the internet—and Cristine's friend Sally,

22, in a public park that was closed for the night. Cristine sold Paul eight 36mg Ritalin and ten psilocybin chocolates, wrapped in tinfoil, like little hockey pucks. They each ate a chocolate and walked through the park, to the end of a beach, where they sat in the gently fluorescent light of a half moon that looked like a jellyfish photographed, from far below, in mid-propulsion, its short tentacles momentarily inside itself.

In the distance, Cleveland's three tallest buildings, each with a different shape and style of architecture and lighting, were spaced oddly far apart, like siblings in their thirties, in a zany sitcom. After spending their lives "hating" one another, in a small town, they moved to different cities and were happy, but then got coincidentally transferred by their employers to the same medium-size city. They were all named Frank. Paul felt reluctant to say anything weird because Cristine and Sally were behaving normally, with earnest expressions, as if pretending they weren't on mushrooms, except sometimes one would mention seeing beautiful colors, increasing Paul's apprehension because earlier he and Erin had bonded over feeling alienated by people who focused on visuals, instead of people, while on hallucinogens. Deciding, after around fifteen minutes, to drive somewhere in two cars, they walked on the beach toward the parking lot. The clear moonlight sometimes fleetingly appeared, on Lake Erie, to their left, as thin layers of snow, resting on the surface of the water, as if painted on, or briefly riding the shoreward, foamy fronts of tiny waves before vanishing. Sally's car, on the highway, got a flat tire. Paul and Erin couldn't stop grinning, due to the mushrooms, sitting on a sidewalk in downtown Cleveland, waiting for AAA, as a frowning Sally, whose car had a missing window covered by a garbage bag, persistently bemoaned her situation without looking at anyone. Cristine, grinning sometimes at Paul and Erin, drove everyone, in Erin's car, to Kent State University, where Paul and Erin walked far behind

Cristine and Sally, on a slightly uphill sidewalk. "When you said that thing about glitter and purple clothing I felt vaguely like I already knew about it," said Paul. "You really haven't told anyone?"

"The only person I've told is my friend Jennika."

"You said I was the only person you've told."

"I know," said Erin. "I shouldn't have said that."

"Did you forget? Yesterday?"

"No, I knew. I was nervous—I thought I was talking too much."

"But I was asking you about it."

"I thought I was boring you."

"You weren't," said Paul. "At all."

"I just wanted to, like, 'move on.'"

"Don't do that. If I ask something I really want to know."

"I know. I don't want to do that."

"You lied . . . to me," said Paul, and felt dramatic and self-conscious. "Wait, let me think. I'm thinking if I were you . . . if I would lie about that. I think . . . yeah, I would, if I didn't want to talk about it." He would if he didn't anticipate becoming close to the other person, or talking to them again. "I understand, I think." He imagined Erin's inattentive, half-hearted view of him as "vaguely, unsatisfactorily desirable," like how he viewed most people. "I would lie, like that, in that situation. Are you sure you haven't written it somewhere? Like on your blog maybe?"

"I'm really sure. I'm ninety percent sure."

"Only ninety percent? That's, like, 'unsure,' I feel."

"I'm really sure. I'm ninety-five percent sure."

"You can tell—"

"Paul," said Erin, and grasped his forearm. They stopped walking. More aware of Erin's perspective, looking at his face (and not knowing what expression she saw or what he wanted to express), than of his own, Paul didn't know what to do, so went "afk," he felt, and remained there—away from the keyboard of the screen of his face—as Erin, looking at the inanimate object of his head, said "if I did I would tell you" and, emphatically, "I'm not lying to you right now."

"Okay," said Paul, and they continued walking.

Sprinklers could be heard in the distance.

"I believe you," said Paul.

"Really?"

"Yeah. I haven't not believed you. I was just saying . . . maybe you got the idea or something similar to it from somewhere else, like a children's book we've both read, but we forgot about it, or something like that."

"I don't think I did," said Erin.

"I feel like I do that a lot."

"Maybe," said Erin quietly.

Around 1:30 a.m., after Cristine and Sally had left, Paul and Erin were walking in downtown Cleveland trying to find any open restaurant when they entered a hotel through an "employees only" door and ascended on an escalator and walked through dark corridors into an auditorium-like area, encountering no people. Paul imagined the building omnidirectionally expanding at a rate exceeding their maximum running speed, so that this goalless, enjoyably calm exploration of a temperature-controlled, tritely uncanny interior would replace his life, with its book tour and Gmail and, he thought after a few seconds, "food." Would he agree to that? "Yes," he thought "meaninglessly," he knew, because he'd still be inside himself, the only place he'd ever be, that he could imagine, though maybe he didn't know—not knowing seemed more likely.

At a Denny's near the airport Paul ordered a steak and minestrone soup. Erin ordered a grilled cheese sandwich and cheese sticks. They shared a 30mg Adderall and drove to the airport, listening to a '90s station, both immediately recognizing Natalie Imbruglia's "Torn," whose lyrics, to a degree that Paul couldn't stop grinning, seemed to be a near-unbroken series of borderline non sequitur clichés. Erin had a public-speaking class in Baltimore, eight hours away, in nine and a half hours. At the airport Paul left eight psilocybin chocolates with Erin, who said she would bring them to his reading in Manhattan in four weeks, if not earlier. They hugged tightly, and Paul, whose flight to Minnesota was in four hours, said he wished they had more time to listen to '90s songs together and that he "had a lot of fun," with Erin, the past few days.

The next three days they texted regularly and, Paul felt, with equal attentiveness. Paul texted a photo of a display in the Mall of America of books titled *I Can Make You Confident* and *I Can Make You Sleep* with the author grinning on each cover. Erin texted a blurry photo of what seemed to be a headless mannequin wearing a white dress and said she was in Las Vegas at a cousin's wedding. Then she texted less, and with less attention, and one night didn't respond to a photo Paul sent from a café in Chicago, where he was staying for four days, of a *Back to the Future* poster—

He was never in time
for his classes . . .

He wasn't in time
for his dinner . . .

Then one day . . .
he wasn't in his
time at all.

—until morning, when she texted "lol" and that she'd been asleep, but she didn't reciprocate a photo, or ask a question, so they stopped texting. Paul sensed she was busy with college and maybe one or more vague relationships, but allowed himself to become "obsessed," to some degree, with her, anyway, reading all four years of her Facebook wall and, in one of Chicago's Whole Foods, one night looking at probably fifteen hundred of her friends' photos to find any she might've untagged.

In a café in Ann Arbor around 10:30 p.m., two days later, Paul realized, when he remembered Erin's existence by seeing her name in Gmail, he'd forgotten about her that entire day (over the next three weeks, whenever more than two or three days passed since they last communicated, which they did by email, every five to ten days, in a thread Erin began the day she dropped him off at the airport, Paul would have a similar realization of having forgotten about her for an amount of time). Around midnight he drove his rental car to a row of fast-food restaurants near the airport and slept in a McDonald's parking lot. When he woke, around 2:45 a.m., he bought and ate a Filet-O-Fish from the McDonald's drive-thru. While trying to discern what, from which fast-food restaurant, to buy and eat next, he idly imagined himself for more than ten minutes as the botched clone of himself, parked outside the mansion of the scientist who the original Paul paid to clone himself and paid again to "destroy all information" regarding "[censored]." He drove across the street to a Checkers drive-thru and bought two apple pies, which he ate with little to no pleasure, almost unconsciously, while distractedly considering how once a bite of it was in his mouth, then chewed once or twice, there seemed to be no choice, at that point, but to swallow. He slept three hours, drove past McDonald's and Arby's, returned the rental car, rode a van as the only passenger to the airport, boarded the earliest flight to Boston.

Around two weeks later, in early October, he stayed for eight days in San Francisco in his own room, on the second floor of a house, which Daniel's ex-girlfriend and ex-girlfriend's sister shared. An employee at Twitter invited him to its headquarters, where he ate from two different buffets. Daniel's ex-girlfriend's sister's boyfriend sold him MDMA and mushrooms, which he ate a medium-large dose of before his reading at the Booksmith, which was livestreamed on the internet. His publisher left him a voice mail the next afternoon, asking him to call them to discuss "some problems." He emailed them late that night apologizing for missing their call and said he was available by email. He met someone from Facebook and ingested LSD, which she declined, before watching Dave Eggers interview Judd Apatow for almost two hours in an auditorium. On her full-size mattress, three hours after the interview, they watched a forty-minute DVD of a Rube Goldberg machine and kissed a few minutes, then Paul "fingered" her and, after seeming to orgasm, she rolled over and slept.

In Los Angeles, the night before a panel discussion at UCLA on the topic of hipsters, after privately ingesting a little LSD, half a capsule of MDMA, a Ritalin—the combination of which, at Paul's tolerance levels, had the effect of slightly distorting and energizing his base feeling of depression, so that he also felt many of its related emotions, such as despair and aggravation—he was designated, for some reason, to drive an NPR contributor's car to a house party on the steepest street he had ever seen in person. After the house party, in a bar staffed by Asians, with Chinese and Vietnamese food, Paul saw and approached Taryn, who seemed happy to see him, to his mild surprise (they'd only met once and vaguely, at the party where Paul put on "Today" by the Smashing Pumpkins). Taryn and a younger, sibling-like man, who at times seemed to be her boyfriend, but remained at a distance most of the night, went with Paul and the moderator of the next day's panel discussion and other people to an apartment whose only purpose, someone kept saying, was for partying in when bars had closed. Paul felt the same mysterious, vague attraction to Taryn he felt in Brooklyn but unlike then, when they'd spoken probably three sentences to each other, they talked continuously, energetically. Taryn said she moved here a month ago after securing a full-time job as a copywriter for a fashion website, where her coworkers did, or did not—Paul became confused which, at some point, after realizing he'd laughed at both—know she had an MFA in poetry. Paul gradually remembered Taryn was friends with Caroline, that she and Caroline—and many of Paul's acquaintances, including Shawn Olive, in Brooklyn—had been in the same one to three graduating classes for their MFAs in poetry at the New School and that most, or all, of them, as part of their curriculum, had read Paul's first poetry book that he wrote the summer after graduating, in 2005, with a BA in journalism. The moderator of the next day's panel discussion approached Paul and Taryn and said he had bought cocaine for them from a former Olympic soccer player whose father, before recently dying, had operated a major drug cartel. Paul and Taryn were led to a dresser, scattered on which were playing cards. The former Olympic soccer player indicated a six of spades, beneath which was twenty dollars' worth of cocaine.

On UCLA's campus the next night Paul photographed a piece of computer paper, taped crudely to a column, that said HIPSTER PANEL with an arrow pointing literally at the sky. In emails with the moderator of the panel discussion the past few weeks Paul had repeatedly half joked that he was going to "dominate the panel" and now, backstage peaking on one and a half capsules of MDMA and two Ritalin and an energy drink, he began openly conveying the same message to the other seven panelists, including a cofounder of *Vice*, the only person getting paid, everyone seemed to know, who was shirtless with 20oz beer and reacted to Paul's robot-like extroversion with what seemed like barely suppressed confusion, which Paul tried to resolve by overpowering any possible awkwardness with his temporary charisma, which resulted in what seemed to be intimidation but was maybe an intimidation-based attempt at a non-antagonistic guardianship, which caused Paul, who felt he solely wanted to interact with mutual sincerity, to hesitate a little, which maybe the cofounder of *Vice* sensed as anxiety because he slapped Paul's shoulder three times painfully. In his state of medium euphoria, with intensely dull eyes and an overall cyborg-like demeanor, Paul stared briefly at the cofounder of *Vice* before turning around and moving away with an earnest, uncertain feeling of disappointment. Paul arguably dominated the panel in a private way by multitasking (1) earnestly speaking on the topic of hipsters with uncharacteristic willingness to engage a matter of semantics (2) photographing other panelists and the audience and recording two videos with his iPhone (3) tweeting three times (4) interrupting people two or three times to defend audience members from the cofounder of *Vice*'s fashion criticisms (5) sustaining text conversations with Mia, who around a year ago had messaged Paul on Facebook, and Taryn, both of whom were alone in the audience of three to four hundred students and twenty to forty journalists (6) being asked the most questions during the Q&A, though almost all were negative and partially rhetorical, including why he kept writing after the "excrement" that was his previous book.

After the Q&A, during which Taryn had left due to a prior obligation, Paul talked a few minutes to Mia, vaguely remembering that she had lived, or something, in Crispin Glover's "castle," and wanted to spend more time with her, or Taryn, or the moderator, or the other panelists, at whatever post-panel party was probably beginning, but was driven in a sort of rush to the airport by two UCLA students, who in the front seats, talking to each other in voices Paul couldn't hear, for some reason, maybe because a window was open, seemed far away and illusory. At the airport Paul saw he had another voice mail from his publisher and felt dread, then realized he was accidentally listening to it and that it was over—a six-second message asking Paul to "please" call them. Paul rested his head on his dining tray, mostly facedown and awake, during the flight to Minnesota, where after six hours of a seven-hour layover, a few minutes after putting his things in his backpack and standing to wait to get on a plane, he got a long email from his mother, saying she knew she had promised she wouldn't anymore, but felt that she must, as a parent, continue telling Paul that she disapproved of his drug use. Paul could feel his intensely aggravated expression as he typed around three thousand words of stream-of-consciousness information about drugs and why the only way his mother could influence him to use less would be if she didn't view them as good or bad, but learned about them, as a friend instead of a parent, because he was 27, all of which he'd stated, he knew, clearer and more convincingly, in dozens of emails the past four months to seemingly no lasting effect. His mother replied in a manner like his email—the longest he'd sent from an iPhone—had no effect on her and he replied again, expressing futility, then flew to Philadelphia, where after a bleakly sober reading in a tiny bookstore, which sold only used and rare books, he slept on a mostly empty bus, dropping him off in Brooklyn's Chinatown, a place he'd forgotten existed.

In his room, around 2:30 a.m., he read a 2:12 a.m. email from Erin that said she'd "been using a lot of mental space to think about definitely ending a yearlong, 'on-and-off,' semi-vague relationship and actually did tonight"—in reference to someone named Beau—and that she was aware of the insufficiency of her email, half the length of Paul's email, from nine days ago, but wanted to say before sleeping that she was still coming, if it was "still okay," she said, to Paul's reading tomorrow and would bring the psilocybin chocolates Paul left with her one month ago as previously discussed.

Increasingly, as his memory occupied less of his consciousness, the past four to six months, whenever Paul sensed familiarity in the beginnings of a thought or feeling he would passively focus on intuiting it in entirety, predicting its elaboration and rhetoric in the presence of logic and world-view like a ball's trajectory and destination in the presence of gravity and weather. If he recognized the thought or feeling, and didn't want it repeated, he'd end its formation by focusing elsewhere, like how someone searching for a lost dog on a field at night wouldn't approach the silhouette of a tree. Paul, reading Erin's email, was vaguely aware of himself considering that, to some degree, Erin was "using him" to make Beau jealous, or to stay busy while Beau was doing other things maybe—that if things had worked with Beau she might not be coming tomorrow.

Without full awareness of what he'd begun to think Paul deliberately stopped thinking and texted: "Yes. Would like if you come, see you tomorrow hopefully." He called his publisher at 3:04 a.m., leaving a voice mail saying he understood what they probably wanted to say, that he was sorry and wouldn't do it again—vaguely he remembered that they had, at some point, told him they disapproved of him using mushrooms at a reading—and was available by email, then slept.

Paul was in Bobst Library around 3:30 p.m. and had just ingested a capsule of MDMA when Erin texted that she was around fifty minutes away. Paul walked ten blocks to the bookstore and sat on a tiny bench in the fiction section and tweeted and looked at his Gmail account. Erin texted she was in the store and had eaten a chocolate. Paul was surprised she was with a male friend, whom she introduced as a former coworker named Gary, who lived in Brooklyn.

"He's gay," said Erin, and gave Paul a chocolate, which he chewed into a gluey paste and swallowed with lemon water from the bookstore's café. After the reading Paul, Erin, and Gary walked to a bar for someone's 33rd birthday. Gary left after around ten minutes and Erin said he had whispered in her ear that he felt sad and wanted to talk. "I told him I couldn't now, I'm on mushrooms," said Erin. "Then he asked me for mushrooms. I said I didn't have any and he probably shouldn't have them now anyway and I'd call him tomorrow."

Around three hours later Paul and Erin were stomach-down on Paul's mattress watching YouTube videos of people answering the same questions sober and on hallucinogens. Paul, who kept clicking new videos, was amused by how he seemed to be comfortably and energetically, with only a little self-consciousness, "having fun," he kept thinking, in contrast to Erin, who seemed shy in a tired, depressed, distracted manner indicating to Paul that she was maybe thinking about someone else, probably Beau, whom she would probably rather be with, at the moment, instead of Paul, who felt intrigued—and further amused—why he was not affected by this information, which normally would make it impossible for him to enjoy anything. They slept without touching, woke in the afternoon, drove to Manhattan, where they separately "worked on things" (Paul in the library, Erin in a Starbucks) until 9:30 p.m., when they ate chocolates and watched a Woody Allen movie, which ended after midnight, on October 15, Erin's 25th birthday. Paul said he wanted to buy her an expensive dinner and they went in an Italian restaurant that seemed moderately expensive, sat in a corner booth, ordered medium-rare steaks and a shrimp appetizer. Erin asked if she should answer a call from Beau, who'd been calling and texting all night, she said.

"If you want, yeah," said Paul looking down a little.

Erin spoke to Beau in a jarringly, briefly absurdly different voice—one of impatient, dominating aggression—than Paul (who recognized the voice as similar to how he spoke, as a child, to his mother) had ever heard her use and which increased his interest in her, knowing she was capable of what to Paul was her opposite. After around fifty seconds, at a moment when she had the opportunity, Paul felt, based on hearing her side of what sounded like a mutual voicing of vague aggravation, to tactfully end the call and unambiguously convey she viewed their relationship as finished, Erin instead prolonged the call by speaking angrily, with sudden emotion indicating she wasn't indifferent. Paul felt dizzy with the realization, as Erin continued talking in a manner like she'd forgotten his presence, that his view of her was uncontrollably changing, that parts of him were earnestly, if dramatically, no longer viewing her as a romantic possibility. He intuited a hidden intimacy in Erin and Beau's hostility, a psychic collaboration—unconscious, or maybe conscious for one of them—assembling the structures, located days or weeks from now, where they would meet again to apologize and forgive and, while rescinding their insults, encouraged by the grammar and syntax and psychology of contrasts, near-automatically convey adoration, gratitude, compliments. Was this how people sustained relationships and sanity? By uninhibitedly expressing resentment to unconsciously contrast an amount of future indifference into affection? With quickly metabolized disappointment and a brief, vague, almost feigned restructuring of the mirage-like pile of miscellaneous items of his life Paul acclimated himself to this new reality, in which he would talk to Erin less and never with full attention, always distracted by, if not someone else, the ever-present silhouette of a possible someone else. Erin somewhat abruptly ended the call and asked if it had been entertaining, or interesting, or at least not too boring.

"I was really interested."

"It was okay? Not boring?"

"No. I felt high levels of interest."

"Oh," said Erin. "Good."

"I was surprised. You sounded angry."

"Yeah," said Erin. "I was angry."

"There was one part . . . when you started fighting more, instead of stopping, I felt, like, afraid," said Paul, and Erin said she knew what part he was referencing and that she had specifically considered if he would be entertained, or not, and had felt uncertain. As a waiter served their medium-rare steaks and, on multicolored rice, cooked into fetal positions, eight medium-large shrimp, Paul realized with some confusion that he might have overreacted. Staring at the herbed butter, flecked and large as a soap sample, on his steak, he was unsure what, if he had overreacted, had been the cause.

It occurred to him that, in the past, in college, he would have later analyzed this, in bed, with eyes closed, studying the chronology of images—memories, he'd realized at some point, were images, which one could crudely arrange into slideshows or, with effort, sort of GIFs, maybe—but now, unless he wrote about it, storing the information where his brain couldn't erase it, place it behind a toll, or inadvertently scramble its organization, or change it gradually, by increments smaller than he could discern, without his knowledge, so it became both lost and unrecognizable, he probably wouldn't remember most of this in a few days and, after weeks or months, he wouldn't know it had been forgotten, like a barn seen from inside a moving train that is later torn down, its wood carried elsewhere on trucks.

Erin was flying to the College of Coastal Georgia in the morning to read to writing students and stay five to ten days as a kind of vacation. They confirmed to meet in Baltimore in three weeks, at the last reading of Paul's book tour, to film themselves answering questions, on MDMA and while sober, to edit into videos like they'd seen on YouTube.

In Montreal, three days later, beneath a uniformly cloudy expanse, which glowed with the same intensity and asbestos-y texture everywhere, seeming less like a sky than the cloud-colored surface of a cold, hollowed-out sun, close enough to obstruct its own curvature, Paul walked slowly and aimlessly, sometimes standing in place, like an arctic explorer, noticing almost no other people and that something, on a general level, seemed familiar. He drank coffee and looked at the internet in a café, feeling gloomy and vertiginous when, after three hours, he went outside, where it had gotten significantly colder, to walk to a juice bar, twelve blocks away, near the café where the world's largest French-language radio station was interviewing him in an hour.

The sky darkened and was now almost cloudless, like it had been gently suctioned from an interplanetary pressure system. As a red truck, clean and bright as a toy, passed on the street, Paul realized Montreal, with its narrower streets and cute beverage sizes and smaller vehicles, reminded him of Berlin. He'd gone alone to Berlin early in his relationship with Michelle for the German edition of his first novel—a year and a half ago, in March 2009, he calculated after two to three minutes of focused effort containing two long pauses without thoughts, but it felt more than five years away, like part of himself, while in Berlin, had gotten lost on its way here, taking more than five years instead of one and a half, a feeling that confused Paul, who stopped thinking, then realized he hadn't thought about Erin, or maybe any person, today and that he had no romantic prospects. He visualized the black dot of the top of his head—from an aerial view of two blocks—slowing to a standstill and remaining motion-less on the sidewalk as other dots passed in either direction and the darkening city gradually brightened with artificial lights, the movie of his life finally ending, the credits scroll-ing down the screen.

Shivering, he walked with increasing speed toward the juice bar, wanting to stop moving in a way that he'd disap-pear, which didn't seem possible. He ingested two capsules of MDMA with a green smoothie, then walked four blocks to a café where he was interviewed by a small, balding, frequently laughing man of indiscernible age for around forty-five min-utes, during which Paul smiled uncontrollably, with almost continuously unfocused eyes, unable to discern stillness in the single image of everything, containing him in a sphere of blurrily passing scenery. He felt low in his seat, warming his hands on a cup of tea, and was sometimes aware that his face was arbitrarily pointing in strange directions, as if to consider his thoughts, or the interviewer's questions, from various perspectives, probably seeming genuinely eccentric or weirdly, insanely pretentious. His teeth chattered and his upper body sometimes "convulsed," he thought with brief interest, on the walk to the Drawn & Quarterly bookstore, where he sat absently in the audience in the back row with a slouched posture and, with a sensation of entering his body in medias res, at a moment when a decision, approved without his input, was about to actualize, said "is David Foster Wallace really big in America?" at a speaking volume to no one, it seemed.

Five or six people, ahead of him, facing the stage, which he also faced, shifted a little in their seats but didn't turn around. Paul realized he'd said "America" not "Canada" and, in his state of near immunity from shame and/or anxiety, acknowledged a theoretical embarrassment, which someone not on MDMA, in his situation, might experience. For one or two seconds, with tepid disappointment toward himself, before moving nearer to the stage, Paul dimly believed people had ignored him because they knew he was on drugs and were afraid he might say more things that would humiliate and further expose himself, in a completely non-funny way, as pathetic and troubling and drug-addled and sad. After the reading, then a Q&A—during which someone asked if Paul felt like his life had changed the past few years and he said no, which he qualified by saying it had, then after a pause said he honestly felt unable to answer accurately—the owner of Drawn & Quarterly approached and thanked Paul for coming to Montreal. Paul pitched a children's book, to be illustrated by a known graphic novelist who'd confirmed interest, based on one of his poems—

when i was five i went
fishing with my family

when i was five
i went fishing with my family
my dad caught a turtle
my mom caught a snapper
my brother caught a crab
i caught a whale

that night we ate crab
the next night we ate turtle
the next night we ate snapper
the next night we ate whale
the next night we ate whale
the next night we ate whale
the next night we ate whale
the next night we ate whale
the next night we ate whale

—with each line on its own page and the last line repeated as many times as needed. Maybe a different artist could illustrate each page to create a sort of anthology. As a children's book, due to the content, it would appeal to college students and teenagers and be a popular gift choice. It could become "one of those things," said Paul, who considered, at one point, while talking, if his behavior might be a little tact-less and easily concluded it might be to "normal people" but not the owner of Drawn & Quarterly, which had published many books, among Paul's favorites, sympathetic to socially dysfunctional characters.

When Paul finished talking, the owner, who'd sustained a polite, slightly tense smile and a tired and unblinking gaze, said "thank you" and walked away.

Paul's main feeling, an hour and a half later, in a café with six to eight strangers, staring at his hands wrapped tightly around his teacup, was an excruciating combination of social anxiety and, as the MDMA stopped working, disintegrating functioning, including tremulous fingers and what felt like an inability to control or predict the volume and pitch of his voice and a helpless sensation that his face—especially if he tried to mollify its severe appearance, which he would need to do if anyone asked him a question—might begin quiver-ing or flinching uncontrollably. His memory of what he now viewed as a "major, egregious faux pas," his interaction with Drawn & Quarterly's owner, was vague and nonlinear and dominated by a troubling suspicion that, with his pitch of a book in a genre Drawn & Quarterly didn't publish, he'd inter-rupted the owner's initial greeting.

Hiding in the bathroom, Paul remembered that, when he processed the identity of the owner, approaching from maybe six feet away, he'd felt a sensation not unlike click-ing "send" for a finished draft of a long email, setting off his children's book pitch. He probably had referenced his poem as if it were common knowledge because he didn't know how he could have conveyed its effect without reciting it in full. He remembered, or thought he remembered, seeing disap-pointment inside the owner's eyes—a faint off-coloring, like a woundless scar, a millimeter behind the cornea—which had seemed sad in a manner like his life (operating his publishing company, living in the same apartment for twenty years, accumulating obligations in the bleak world of graphic novels) was a pure, omnipresent, concrete reminder, Paul vaguely imagined while standing in a stall staring at his iPhone, that he was the only entity building and embellishing and imperialistically expanding his own unhappiness.

Around midnight, after everyone in the café had gone to a concert, Paul was alone in the Drawn & Quarterly bookstore's manager's apartment. He looked at Twitter for what felt like twenty minutes, alternating hands to hold his iPhone ten to fifteen inches above his face. He emailed Charles—

> I'm lying in bed on a sofa
>
> Feel strongly like I simply want to relate my feelings of bleakness in this email
>
> My legs feel cold

—with "Feeling bleak" as the subject. He was looking at Twitter again, a few minutes later, when for the fifth or sixth time since getting it in August he dropped his iPhone on his face, which did not register in its expression that anything had happened until after impact. He considered emailing Charles that his iPhone fell on his face. Then he tried to do what he couldn't specifically remember having done since college—he chose one of his favorite songs and, with a meekly earnest sympathy toward himself, listened to it on repeat at a high volume and tried to focus only on the drums, or bass guitar, until he was drowsy and decontextualized and memoryless, when he would half-unconsciously remove his earphones and turn off the music, careful not to be noticed and assimilated by the world, and disappear into the reachable mirage of sleep.

But he couldn't focus on the music. He couldn't ignore a feeling that he wasn't alone—that, in the brain of the universe, where everything that happened was concurrently recorded as public and indestructible data, he was already partially with everyone else that had died. The information of his existence, the etching of which into space-time was his experience of life, was being studied by millions of entities, billions of years from now, who knew him better than he would ever know himself. They knew everything about him, even his current thoughts, in their exact vagueness, as he moved distractedly toward sleep, studying him in their equivalent of middle school "maybe," thought some fleeting aspect of Paul's consciousness, unaware what it was referencing.

Paul arrived in Toronto the next night on a Megabus, then rode two city buses to the apartment of a Type Books employee and his girlfriend and slept on a sofa. In Whole Foods the next day, for around five hours, he ate watermelon and looked at the internet and typed answers to an email interview. He walked to a café near Type Books and asked on one of the two threads on 4chan about him that, for some reason, had appeared the last two days—and, with two to four hundred posts each, 90 to 95 percent derogatory, were the two longest threads on him that he'd ever seen—if anyone in Toronto could sell him MDMA or mushrooms within two hours. Someone named Rodrigo, who'd recently moved here from San Francisco, Paul discerned via Facebook, emailed that he could get mushrooms and maybe MDMA but not until after Paul's reading.

In Type Books people stood in an encroaching half

circle around a nervously grinning Paul, seated on a stool, "completely exposed," he felt, as an employee read a long, admiring, complicated introduction that seemed like it had incorporated sections of a dissertation. Paul, appearing sometimes openly frightened, honestly answered "I don't know" for almost every question during the Q&A, then in each ensuing silence, feeling pressure to elaborate, mumbled sentence fragments he knew were untrue or inaccurate before, in closing, reiterating "I don't know." Near the end, while saying "but I don't really know," he stuttered a little. After the reading he went to a restaurant with four Type Books employees and their friend Alethia, 22, who had published around six hundred articles since leaving college two years ago to write for Toronto's leading alt weekly. Paul asked if Alethia, whom he felt attracted to and curious about, wanted to interview him while, as a journalistic angle, he was "on MDMA."

In Rodrigo's apartment, a few hours later, Paul searched his name in Alethia's email account—signed in on Rodrigo's tiny, malformed-looking, non-MacBook laptop—while she was in the bathroom and saw she had pitched an article on him, two months ago, to the *Toronto Sun,* who had not responded, it seemed. Paul and Rodrigo each swallowed a capsule of MDMA. Paul said he felt "nothing" and swallowed another and, when it began taking effect, repeatedly encouraged Alethia to also ingest MDMA, "for the interview," but she declined, citing that when she tried LSD she rode a bus around Toronto for five hours. Rodrigo lay with his girlfriend on his bed as Paul and Alethia sat on beanbags on the floor and talked for two and a half hours, during which Paul sometimes wanted to hug or kiss Alethia, whose default expression, it seemed, was "worried," sometimes in an endearingly doe-like manner and sometimes like it was an effect of her job, as a full-time journalist, with its deadlines and copyediting, Paul thought half sarcastically more than once. Alethia said "you were saying you've been doing readings on drugs because it makes you feel more comfortable" and asked why.

"Um, actually, I just think it's more fun."

"More fun for you, or the people who are there?"

"In my view it's more fun for everyone," said Paul.

"So when you did that reading a few weeks ago on mushrooms . . . you stopped after two minutes?"

"Um," said Paul. "Two minutes?"

"Yeah. Is that what happened?"

"What reading?"

"Oh. I don't know . . . a few weeks ago."

"The Booksmith?"

"Yeah. In San Francisco."

"Oh. I was seeing 'tribal patterns' on the paper, because I was staring at it on mushrooms, and I felt like I was sweating, and I kept thinking 'Hunter S. Thompson.' Then I felt like I couldn't go on anymore. I was preparing to say something like 'I'm having a bad drug experience, I need to go home.' But I looked up, at the people, and regained control."

An hour later they were discussing a recent trend of Megabus accidents, described by Paul, who was riding a Megabus to Manhattan tomorrow, as "like, twenty people dying five times in the last few days," when Alethia asked if Paul was worried he'd be "the next to die."

"No. I don't care if I die."

"Um," said Alethia laughing.

"I feel like I honestly don't care if I die."

"Really? You're not worried about dying?"

"No, I think. I'm ready to die whenever."

"Because you've written enough books?"

"No, no," said Paul shaking his head a little. "I don't know. I'm just ready to die. Life just seems like . . . it's fine if I die.

Once I'm dead I'm dead." Rodrigo from his bed said "but in an interview you talk about eating healthy and not smoking because you'll be more productive." Paul said health and drugs and being productive were all in service of feeling good. Alethia said she took Ritalin almost every day, from ages 8 to 12, for "attention deficit disorder." Paul said "that seems horrible" and "that must've changed you."

"Yeah, I think it did," said Alethia. "I think it did."

"People who take the most drugs by far are the kids—"

"It's so true," said Alethia.

"—who get prescribed them," said Paul.

"Who's, like, your closest friend?"

"I just felt, like . . . really alone when you said that."

"Oh no! I'm sorry."

"Wait, there has to be someone," said Paul grinning. "I feel like I have close friends but we stop talking. Right now, I guess, what person do I feel closest to?"

"Yeah," said Alethia.

"Um, I can't remember right now. I feel close to different people over sets of days. Like if I've been texting someone, but then I'll forget about them."

"Do you sometimes feel like it sucks—to just, like, live in the world?"

"What do you mean?" said Paul slowly.

"Like, that the world can't provide us with enough to satisfy us."

"No," said Paul after around ten seconds, and covered his face with his hands. "I mean . . . the world is good enough, based on evidence, because I haven't killed myself. Like, if I killed myself . . . I could say the world is bad, on average."

"Like definitively," said Alethia.

"On average," said Paul through his hands. "Since the urge to kill myself isn't so strong that I actually kill myself, the world is worth living in."

• • •

Alethia left around 4:30 a.m., easily declining Paul's suggestions, bordering on "pleas," he felt, that she stay. Rodrigo and his girlfriend seemed asleep. Sitting on a sofa, in the common room, Paul texted Alethia: "This is Paul. Good night, glad we met." Alethia responded: "Me too. You are wonderful." Paul lay on the sofa, bristling with wakefulness, for around forty minutes, then put his MacBook in his backpack and wrote a two-sentence note to Rodrigo and walked outside into a silvery, wintry light.

On a Megabus to New York City—for around fifteen hours, due to a two-hour delay in Buffalo—he read all he could find by Alethia on the internet, becoming more "obsessed," he felt, after each article, lying on his back across two seats with knees bent, twice dropping his iPhone onto his face. His interest in Alethia naturally decreased, the next few days, then they texted a few times and he felt renewed obsession, but he didn't like her impersonal tone in their emails discussing their interview—which she'd spent eight hours transcribing—and, less than a week after they met, all he felt toward her, to his weak amusement, was an unexamined combination of indifference and vague resentment, which he described in an email to Charles, whose previous knowledge of Alethia was that Paul liked her "a lot," as "strong aversion," only half joking. Paul's next email to Charles said "I feel like I 'hate' her" and that it seemed, by the bureaucratic language and curtness of Alethia's emails, like she also "hated" him, that they "hated" each other.

On Halloween afternoon, in the library, Paul read an account of his Montreal reading, when he was on two capsules of

MDMA, describing him as "charismatic, articulate, and friendly."

He read an account of his Toronto reading, when he'd been sober, describing him as "monosyllabic," "awkward," "stilted and unfriendly" within a disapproval of his oeuvre, itself vaguely within a disapproval of contemporary culture and, by way of a link to someone else's essay, the internet.

After his book tour's last reading, on November 4, in Baltimore, Paul declined multiple dinner and bar invitations and went with Erin to her apartment—a bedroom, bathroom, tiny kitchen, TV room—where, using iMovie on Erin's MacBook, they recorded themselves on MDMA answering questions each had prepared for the other, then continued recording, sitting on Erin's bed, as they showed each other things on the internet, wanting to later be able to see how they behaved while on MDMA. Erin's iPhone made a noise, at one point, and Paul, who had wrapped himself in a thick blanket, asked if it was Calvin.

"No, Beau," said Erin.

"Nobo?" said Paul grinning.

"Beau. He said 'mons pubis.' Ew."

"What does that mean?"

"It's a part of the body," said Erin with a worried expression.

"You guys are seeing . . . you guys are together again?"

"No, we're not," said Erin shaking her head. "This is, like, unacceptable behavior."

"You're not together?"

"We were . . . but then I broke up with him . . . again."

"Again? After we ate steak on your birthday?"

"Yeah," said Erin.

"So . . . you got back together after that?"

"Well, no, but . . . he told me he was unemployed, and all this bad stuff was happening to him, and I felt bad."

Paul made a quiet, ambiguous noise.

"We've, like, hung out," said Erin.

"Oh," said Paul, unsure if he was confused.

"But we're not together," said Erin quietly, then drank a shot of tequila and most of a Four Loko (for a video she'd told someone she would post on her Tumblr) and an hour later, Paul saw after being in the bathroom a few minutes, was asleep with her mouth slightly open and her MacBook open on her stomach. After untangling a cord, then moving the MacBook to the floor, Paul lay beside Erin and meekly pawed her forearm three times, then briefly held some of her fingers, which were surprisingly warm. He lay stomach-down with his arm on her arm, thinking that if she woke, while he was asleep, this contact could be viewed as accidental. Maybe she would roll toward him, resting her arm across his back—they'd both be stomach-down, as if skydiving—in an unconscious or dream-integrated manner she wouldn't remember, in the morning, when they'd wake in a kind of embrace and begin kissing, neither knowing who initiated, therefore brought together naturally, like plants that join at their roots. After a few motionless minutes, unable to sleep in his increasingly tense position, he rolled over and gathered a blanket into a cushiony bunch, which he held like a stuffed animal of a brain, and slept facing a wall.

The next afternoon, at the University of Baltimore, in a lounge area, bright and warm from sunlight through glass panels, Paul and Erin sat on padded chairs and watched last night's footage, which they felt was "unseemly" and decided not to edit into a video to put on YouTube. At a soup-and-sandwich restaurant, two blocks away, they discussed what movies they wanted to make—

> *Heroin,* in which they inject heroin in each other and "work on things" on their MacBooks, recording six perspectives: their faces, their MacBook screens, their positions in the lounge area (from cameras on tripods in the distance) in sunlight on separate padded seats.

> *Cocaine,* in which a third person records them going to nightclubs and bars on a Friday night in Manhattan without a plan except that they must snort cocaine every ten minutes and will carry knapsacks filled with energy drinks and fried chicken.

> *Or Something,* in which "or something" is said hundreds of times, in a montage, sometimes with context, to convey a range of meanings: a grinning Erin "luxuriating" in her lack of specificity, a zombie-like Paul "tired" of his commitment in specifying uncertainty, Erin saying "or something, or something," earnestly to a Paul who has become "tolerant" to "or something."

—then returned to the lounge area and worked on things separately, until night, when they began texting people and asking on Facebook if anyone within fifty miles wanted to sell them drugs. Someone would walk to Erin's car to sell her cocaine and heroin, said Beau in a text, if she parked in a specific area of a shopping plaza.

"That's like . . . I don't know," said Paul quietly while trying to think about why Erin had texted Beau. Erin was quiet, then said she didn't want to try that option, then they walked four blocks to her apartment, where they used Xanax and Hydrocodone before driving to an apartment where someone had LSD, which they used with a little cough syrup. They drove to a movie theater and watched *Jackass 3D*, then couldn't find an open restaurant, so decided to drive to New York City. They arrived around 8:30 a.m., to an afternoon-like morning, not hungry or tired, due to Adderall.

They decided to film *MDMA* without a plan, except to use MDMA and go canoeing in Central Park. After showering in Paul's apartment, then riding the L train to Union Square and using MDMA in Whole Foods, then getting off an uptown 6 train four stops early by accident, they decided to go to Times Square instead of Central Park. They rode the Ferris wheel inside Toys "R" Us, then discovered that on MDMA they could easily speak in an unspecific, aggregate parody of (1) the stereotypical "intellectual" (2) most people in movies (3) most people on TV with a focus on newscasters and National Geographic–style voice-overs. They termed this manner of speaking (almost the opposite, especially for Paul, of the quiet and literal and inflectionless voice they normally used to speak to each other) "the voice," using it, in Barnes & Noble, with high levels of amusement and stimulation, to feign egregious ignorance, improvise seemingly expert commentary on specific objects, excessively employ academic terms and literary references.

That night, at Pure Food and Wine, an organic raw vegan restaurant near Union Square, seated outside the entrance in a kind of waiting area, they each ate a psilocybin chocolate with their salads. Their plan was to attend an Asian American Writers' Workshop fund-raiser in an art gallery, after eating, to record part one of *Mushrooms*. Exiting the restaurant, a woman looked down at Erin's MacBook with an affectedly bemused expression and asked with a French accent if it was recording.

"Yes," said Erin smiling.

"You are recording yourself?"

"Yeah," said Erin grinning.

"That is weird, no?" said the woman, and walked away.

"I feel like I hate everyone," said Paul a few minutes later, walking toward the art gallery.

"Huh?" said Erin. If she didn't hear something, Paul had noticed, she would sometimes appear confused in a frightened, child-like way, as if having assumed she'd been insulted.

"I feel like I hate everyone," said Paul.

"Yeah," said Erin, and smiled at him.

"Really?" said Paul, a little surprised.

"Yeah. Well, everyone on the street."

"I feel like I can't even look at anyone," said Paul.

They were on their sides facing each other on Paul's mattress, in his room, dark except for moonlight, around 3:30 a.m. After the fund-raiser, at which a saxophone player had ranted about identity politics until people, after maybe six minutes, actually began booing, they'd walked aimlessly into a gallery across the street, then had eaten dinner, four blocks from Paul's apartment, at Mesa Coyoacán. Paul scooted toward Erin, and they hugged five to ten seconds and began kissing and removing their clothes. Erin's eyes, whenever Paul looked, seemed to be tightly closed, which seemed like "not a good sign," as he'd read on her blog—or somewhere—that she liked sex with "a lot of eye contact." They were sweating, and their heads were on the opposite side of the mattress from before, when they finished, after around fifty minutes.

That night, in the library, Paul texted Erin, who'd left for Baltimore at 7:40 a.m. for a 12:30 p.m. public-speaking class, asking if she wanted to attend an event—*Caked Up!*—in two days in an art gallery, where cakes made by graphic designers, including Paul's brother, would be served buffet style. Paul texted it might not be worth the drive, since they would be driving eight hours the day after to Ohio, where Calvin had organized a reading and they would be staying three nights. When Erin promptly responded yes and that it wouldn't be inconvenient, because she liked driving, Paul was surprised how relieved he felt—how disappointed he would've been if she had declined—and realized, with excitement and a concurrent adjustment of his default mood to "eager and patient," that he was (or that he now, after Erin's response, viewed himself as being) in a stable situation of mutual, increasing attraction.

Their last night in Ohio, around midnight, when Calvin's parents and three brothers and Calvin were asleep, Paul and Erin decided to drink coffee and share a 30mg Adderall and each eat a psilocybin chocolate and, in the five hours before Erin would drive Paul to the airport—Calvin had bought Paul a plane ticket a month ago, as incentive to come—film part two of *Mushrooms* in the mansion's basement, which included a room with guitars and amps and a drum set, a game room with four arcade machines, a one-room gym, a billiards table, a home theater, a kitchen. They kissed for twenty minutes in the gym, then shut themselves in a room with two desktop computers and had sex for an hour in the dark, then showered together. They sat on a one-seat sofa in the living room with Erin's MacBook on their lap. Paul asked if Erin wanted to go with him next week to North Carolina and Louisiana, where he had readings at colleges.

"Yeah," said Erin.

"Are you sure?"

"Yeah," said Erin.

"You've said yes to other things you didn't want to do."

"Can you give me an example of one of those things?"

"Smoking weed with Calvin," said Paul about two nights ago, and extended a finger, then another finger. "Inviting Patrick to visit you," he said about someone Erin met at the College of Coastal Georgia and had spoken to twice on Skype and exchanged mix CDs and who, by Erin's invitation, had purchased plane tickets to visit her—for six days, in two weeks—but whose Facebook messages Erin had been ignoring. Paul closed his eyes and thought about how Erin seemed like she didn't want to talk to Beau anymore, but continued texting him and answering his calls.

"Just those two things," said Paul, and opened his eyes.

"I can explain those two things. Smoking weed with Calvin, I thought it could be a thing that I want to do, but in the moment I didn't feel like doing. And Patrick . . . I felt, like, bored for a long time . . . with romantic prospects. It seemed exciting that this person in Georgia was interested in me. I thought 'this could at least be something to do.' So . . . that's why. And I thought that maybe once he came it could be fun, or something."

"So, if it's just something to do, you'll still do it."

"Yeah," said Erin with the word extended. "But that's not what it would be like . . . with you. This," she said, and placed a hand on Paul's shoulder. "Interests me. A lot."

"But do I interest you enough for you to go through with it," mumbled Paul.

"With what?" said Erin after a few seconds.

"To go through with it," said Paul, unsure what he was referencing.

"What? What does?"

"I don't know," said Paul quickly. "Never mind. You want to come."

"I want to come."

"Okay," said Paul. "Good." They saw in Google Calendar

that Erin was scheduled to work two days next week. "So . . . you're not going with me?"

"I want to," said Erin.

"But you have work."

"I'd rather go with you than work," said Erin noncommittally.

"Then . . . what are you going to do?"

"I think I can get someone to cover my shifts. They don't really need me there those days."

"What . . . are you doing?" said Paul, and grinned. "What the hell are you doing?"

"I'm going with you," said Erin grinning, and patted his shoulder. "I'm going with you."

In North Carolina two Duke University students drove Paul and Erin from the airport, where they'd arrived on separate flights, to a hotel, returning at night to drive them to the reading. Paul and Erin talked calmly in the dark backseat, holding half-full cups of hot tea from the hotel lobby, as a college radio station played something fuzzy and instrumental and wistful. Erin said she emailed Patrick last night, while she was in Baltimore and Paul was in Brooklyn, that she started liking someone else and was sorry if he felt bad and would help pay for his plane ticket. Paul asked if Patrick might still visit Baltimore, as a kind of vacation.

"Probably not. He was going to stay in my apartment."

"What did Beau say last night?"

"He just really wanted to hang out," said Erin, who had mentioned in an email that she had "screamed" at Beau on the phone. "And I was like, 'I don't, really. I have other things to do and you shouldn't be here.'"

"He came over?"

"No, he was like 'fuck that, I'm coming over now.' Or like

'I'm walking there now.' I was like 'this is . . . scary,'" said Erin, and laughed.

"Jesus. What did you scream at him?"

"I screamed, like, 'this is done.' And I hung up on him."

"Did he call more after that?"

"No. He sent me . . . a mean text, insulting me. He was like, 'you're really great, but I've always thought your body sucked,' or something."

"Seems like a non sequitur."

"I know," said Erin, and laughed. "It was weird."

"Did you respond to that?"

"No," said Erin. "He's insane."

"Do you think you'll talk to him again?"

Erin said "probably not." The aquarium, sparsely forested darkness outside the car, on a street sometimes half-bracketed by shopping plazas, reminded Paul of traveling at night in Florida in his family's minivan. During longer drives he would lay alone, with a blanket and pillow, behind the third row of seats, beyond range of communication—not obligated to respond, he felt, even if he heard his name. In the dark and padded space, on his back, he'd see everything outside, reflected toward him, as one image—squiggling, watery, elemental, synthetic, holographic, layered—in fluid, representational reconfiguration of itself. Until 13 or 14, then sometimes habitually, he never sat in the front seat of cars, even if no one else was, except the five to ten times his brother, home a few weeks or months from college, would say "I'm not your chauffeur" and force Paul, who would feel immature and embarrassed, to sit in front. "I email with Michelle like once every three months," said Paul. "But in a manner like we're emailing every day. Like, if someone read our emails it would seem like we were emailing every day."

"That seems good," said Erin smiling.

• • •

In Louisiana, two days later, Paul and Erin were in a Best Buy, early in the afternoon, to buy an external hard drive, because their MacBooks from storing their movies were almost out of memory. Paul was walking aimlessly through the store with a bored expression, holding the Smashing Pumpkins' double CD below him, at waist level, where he scratched its plastic wrapping in an idle, distracted, privately frustrated manner. After finally tearing it off and lodging it, with difficulty, because it kept clinging to him by static electricity, behind some Beck CDs, he used "brute force," he thought instructionally, to pry open the locked case and get only the blue CD, which had "Tonight, Tonight" and "Zero" on it, to listen to in the rental car.

In Best Buy's security room, which was module-like and dimmer than the store, the sheriff of Baton Rouge shook his head in strong, earnest, remarkably unjaded disappointment when Paul, asked why he was here—he had a Florida driver's license, a New York address—said a college had invited him to speak to them, as an author.

"I felt ashamed," said Paul in the parking lot to Erin. "I feel like I was on shoplifting autopilot. I wasn't thinking anything. I was just already doing it." In Barnes & Noble, a few hours later, he stole Nirvana's second "greatest hits" collection. They ate watermelon and pineapple chunks in Whole Foods, then drove downtown and rode an elevator to the sixth floor of a darkly tinted building, where Paul read to LSU's graduate writing program for around twenty minutes ("from a memoir-in-progress that'll be more than a thousand pages," he said half earnestly) about a night he watched *Robin Hood* with Daniel at the Union Square theater, then went to a pizza restaurant, where Fran, who had whiskey in a Dr Pepper bottle, got drunker than Paul had ever seen her and the next day quit her job, after two days, as a waitress in a Polish restaurant. Paul felt self-conscious whenever mentioning a drug, in part because none of his previous books had drugs—except caffeine, alcohol, Tylenol Cold, St. John's wort—but the audience laughed almost every time a drug was mentioned, seeming delighted, like most of them were on drugs, which was probably true, Paul thought while reading off his MacBook screen. He imagined stopping what he was reading to instead say "Klonopin," wait three seconds, say "Xanax," wait three seconds, etc. He didn't notice until the word "concealment" that he was reading a sentence from something else he'd been working on that had been pasted apparently into the wrong file. He continued reading the sentence—

The transparency and total effort, with none spent on explanation or concealment or experimentation, of what the universe desired—to hug itself as carefully, as violently and patiently, as had been exactly decided upon, at some point, with gravity—was [something].

—until getting to "[something]," which he remembered using as a placeholder after trying combinations of synonyms for "affecting" and "confusing" and longer descriptions like "an actualized ideal, inside of which any combination of parts could never independently attain." He stared at "[something]" and thought about saying "Klonopin" or "Xanax." He thought about explaining the bracket usage. "The sentence I just read wasn't supposed to be there," he said. "I pasted it there by accident, I think. I'll stop here, thank you."

He sat next to Erin in the front row, then Mei-mei Berssenbrugge, a woman in her 60s, whose introduction included that she was married to Richard Tuttle—the artist Gabby said Daniel resembled—read poems for thirty minutes.

•••

At a flea market, the next afternoon, after drinking the equivalent of six to eight cups of coffee—in the form of 24x condensed coffee, which they bought from Whole Foods and had never seen before, in containers reminiscent of toilet-cleaning liquid—they pretended to be *Wall Street Journal* reporters and recorded themselves interviewing strangers about *Harry Potter and the Deathly Hallows: Part 1.* Erin meekly asked a large, young, thuggish-looking man and his smaller friend, both wearing backward caps, if they thought Darth Vader would "die in this one." After a long pause the large man laughed and said "man, I don't know," and looked at his friend, who appeared expressionless, like he hadn't heard anything that had been said.

"Darth Vader is *Star Trek,* not *Harry Potter,*" said Paul in a weak form of the "the voice," feigning he was remembering this aloud.

"No, no," said Erin grinning. "Really?"

"*Star Wars,*" said Paul laughing a little.

"Oh, I don't know, never mind, never mind, I need to check my notes," said Erin shaking her head and grinning as she and Paul walked away mumbling to each other, attempting to parody, Paul felt, a stereotypical comedy in which two high-level professionals are egregiously demoted into positions where they struggle to regain their jobs while nurturing between them an unlikely romance and mutually learning the true meaning in life. Erin said she felt "a strong need to be on more drugs." Without MDMA it was difficult to use "the voice," without which they felt uncomfortable talking to strangers, improvising, feigning behavior, trying to be witty.

•••

After ingesting their remaining Xanax, and more condensed coffee, they decided to drive to New Orleans, an hour away, because their flight to New York, from Baton Rouge, wasn't until the next morning. It became dark suddenly, it seemed, during the drive. Erin expressed concern about Paul's driving speed in residential-seeming areas. Paul encouraged her to nap (they'd both said they were sleepy, due to Xanax) and said he would be careful and, a vague amount of time later, became aware of a car that was parked, for some reason, on the street. After a few seconds of vague, unexamined confusion Paul realized the car, in the near distance, was stopped at a red light and abruptly braked hard, then harder, curling his toes with a sensation of clenching a fist. The screeching noise and forward thrust startled Erin awake, but she remained silent, seeming mostly confused. Paul drove sheepishly into a shopping plaza and parked near the middle of the mostly empty parking lot and turned off the car.

"I started feeling anxious before like where were we going and we were going fast and it was dark and you were running into things a little bit and I was scared and anxious and afraid," said Erin in one breath of wildly fluctuating volume and inflection and affect that seemed out of control and arbitrary, then in retrospect like she'd virtuosically sung a popular melody faster than anyone had ever considered trying.

"Sorry," said Paul with a worried expression.

"And I felt scared," said Erin with a slight tremble.

"Sorry," said Paul. "I'm really sorry." After he apologized more times they walked holding hands across the parking lot. Erin said she only felt slightly interrupted when she woke, that she had been like, "wait, I don't care, right now, about dying, but in the future I might not want to die." In a confused, intrigued voice Paul said "in . . . the future?"

"In the future I'll—" said Erin.

"But if you're dead you'll be dead," said Paul in a loud, murmured, strangely incredulous voice that he felt aversion toward and confused by.

"What?"

"But if you're dead you'll die," mumbled Paul in a quieter, slurred voice like a stroke victim.

"But I didn't really want to die right then," said Erin.

Around midnight, on the drive back to Baton Rouge, Erin said her father seemed to enjoy giving her Xanax and Adderall and that she used to get angry at him for smoking marijuana every night because it affected his memory and he would repeat himself—and, if stopped, would become defensive, argumentative—but now she didn't try to change him anymore. Paul said his father's default name for him, what he'd unconsciously say to get Paul's attention or to reference Paul in conversation, was "baby" until high school, or maybe college, when it became "old baby"—in Taiwanese, where both words were one syllable—which was what he now called almost all people and animals, including Dudu, the toy poodle, Paul remembered, that his parents had bought sometime in the past year, after he visited in December.

Paul talked about the panicked-seeming, alienating emails his mother had sent him the past five months, beginning in June—when he had published nonfiction on the internet mentioning cocaine and Adderall—and increasing during his book tour, when more information connecting him and drugs (tweets soliciting drugs, a "contest" on his blog to discern from the livestreamed video what drug he was on during his San Francisco reading, the interview with Alethia on MDMA) got on the internet. The emails had seemed complicatedly, strategically composed (referencing movies, news articles, celebrities who've "ruined their lives," etc.) to instill mostly fear and shame and a little guilt to reduce Paul's drug use, for the exclusive benefit, Paul believed his mother believed, of Paul's long-term happiness, which however Paul had repeatedly defined as "freedom" to do what he wanted and "trust," from his friends and family, that he was doing what, based on everything he knew, would result in the happiest results for everyone involved, which was what she also wanted, he'd told her many times. Paul had stated ultimatums like "if you mention drugs one more time I'm not responding to your emails for the rest of the month," which his mother had repeatedly agreed on and went against, saying she felt an obligation—that it was her duty—as a parent, to continue stating her disapproval. To an increasingly frustrated and, he sometimes suspected of himself, paranoid and distrustful Paul, the emails had begun, at some point, to tactically operate on, at the least, a base of reverse-reverse psychology, which was a cause of despair for Paul, who throughout had tried to stress—but seemed to have failed to convincingly convey—that their relationship would only worsen if they couldn't communicate directly, without strategy or hyperbole or deception, while aware of himself often not communicating directly.

The emails during the book tour culminated maybe with a series of emails sent after Paul and Erin posted their "event coverage" of *Caked Up!* They'd pretended to be from jezebel .com and an uninhibited Paul, on MDMA, had loudly shouted at strangers, at one point, at a volume and with an amount of belligerence that was normal for most people but, for him, was done, he'd felt, for comic effect. Paul's mother had emailed saying that the Paul in the video was not the Paul she knew and loved and that she was scared and, seeing what Paul "had turned into," had cried. Paul stopped responding to her emails, at that point, and, at the moment, in the car with Erin, couldn't remember offhand what he'd last said to her—either that he wasn't responding to her emails until

January, wasn't responding to any emails mentioning drugs, or wasn't responding until he believed she had internalized that their relationship would only deteriorate, causing them both to feel worse about everything and probably increase his drug use, if she continued mentioning drugs with intent to influence instead of learn or discuss, as friends, by asking questions. Paul vaguely remembered two or three emails asking when he was coming to Taiwan this year; he'd responded he didn't want to due to all the emails and broken promises. Paul believed he was doing what was best for them both and that his mother believed she was doing what was best for only Paul and not herself. Paul didn't want his mother to believe she had failed, as a parent, which he thought she must, on some level, if she was trying to change what she had created and raised, though maybe she was only focused on the task, not on her feelings.

Paul and Erin were walking near Bobst Library, a week and a half later, on a significantly colder night, in a sleet-like drizzle, when one of them said they wished it were warm and the other said they should fly somewhere warm. Las Vegas was the first suggestion. Paul said he wanted to lose all his money—around $1,200—while "peaking on MDMA" after eating at a buffet and relaxing in a hot tub.

In Think Coffee, an hour later, using Erin's MacBook, they bought a package deal for two round-trip flights and a rental car and four nights at the Tropicana, leaving on November 26, in five days.

4

"This is what the universe created, after whatever billion years," said Paul gesturing at MGM Grand and Excalibur and Luxor, around 9:30 p.m., on a walkway above the main street of casinos in Las Vegas, which was as cold or colder than New York City, they'd learned, with some amusement, upon arriving four hours ago.

"This is what we came into," said Erin.

"Look, beautiful," said Paul earnestly about the hundreds of red lights on the backs of cars, passing beneath the walkway, into the distance, like rubies in a mining operation.

"Whoa. Pretty."

"Life sometimes offers beautiful images," said Paul in a voice like he was in fifth grade reading a textbook aloud.

"But they're fleeting."

"Yeah," said Paul grinning.

"And you can't do anything with them—"

"Yeah," said Paul.

"—except look at them," said Erin.

"Maybe we should get drunk," said Paul, and they entered the casino at the end of the walkway, and Erin went to the bathroom. Paul sat at a slot machine and lost $20, then stared at two middle-aged men wearing backward caps, holding full glasses of golden beer, as they approached and passed with determined, unhappy expressions. When Erin returned, a few minutes later, she said "I think I feel depleted."

"What do you mean?"

"I feel kind of tired, depleted."

"But you shouldn't even have started feeling it yet."

"Huh?" said Erin.

"We had MDMA like twenty minutes ago."

Erin laughed. "I forgot."

"Jesus. You scared me."

"Sorry," said Erin grinning, and they sat on the floor of a carpeted hallway—darkly lit from an unseen source that cyclically pulsed from a near-ultraviolet purple to dark red— positioning Erin's MacBook to record themselves talking about their relationship.

"You go," said Paul smiling widely. "You go first."

"Okay, um, well I felt like I first wanted to kiss you when I dropped you off at the airport," said Erin quickly, with a stricken expression, as if confessing something intensely shameful.

"At the airport? After Denny's?"

"Yeah," said Erin. "I wanted to kiss you then."

"I thought you were hugging me really hard."

"Uh, I thought you were hugging me hard," said Erin seeming frightened, then for around five seconds didn't breathe. Paul laughed, in confusion. Erin said she felt a little nervous. Paul asked if she thought they were going to have sex, when they kissed, on his bed. Erin said no, that she just kept thinking things like "what's happening?" and "are we really going to do it?" Paul said he thought yes, because they wouldn't have been able to stop, except by finishing, because neither of them had said no to anything yet.

"We still haven't," said Paul. "Right?"

"Um," said Erin. "Yeah, I think."

"There was a period of like three days when I was really obsessed with you. But you weren't responding to my email and I kind of lost the obsessive nature."

"Whoa," said Erin. "When?"

"After one of the first times we hung out. We were sending picture messages, then you stopped and didn't email and I felt really depressed."

"Damn. Sorry. I didn't know."

"What was going on then?"

"I was kind of seeing Beau still then," said Erin, and as the MDMA took effect Paul began using "the voice" sometimes, including when Erin asked him which of his previous girlfriends he felt closest to and he said "I'm not really sure" in an extreme parody of a stereotypical romantic comedy, and they laughed for maybe ten seconds. Paul had stopped using "the voice," an hour later, when, during a silence, Erin asked what he was thinking and he said he was thinking why she hadn't read or mentioned the first-person account of his life from April to July he had emailed her a few weeks ago, at her request, which had, to some degree, been obligatory, he

147

knew. Erin said she felt strange reading about Paul's romantic interest in other people while she was beginning a relationship with him. "Like, I felt jealous," she said. "Of the Laura person, reading about her."

"That makes sense," said Paul earnestly.

"I also felt a little strange reading about your friendship with Daniel. I was like 'whoa, they could hang out a lot, then just not anymore; damn, what if that happens with me?'"

"Daniel was really interested in how Kyle and I just stopped talking," said Paul.

"Then you and Daniel stopped talking."

"You don't feel fine with that?"

"I do . . . I feel fine with that. I just think of all possible situations going into something . . . positive or negative. Does that make sense?"

"Yeah," said Paul nodding. "When I first met Michelle I was telling her that I've had a lot of friends who I've just stopped talking to, and she said she was afraid I would do that to her."

"That seems to be what happens with people."

"You don't have to read it at all," said Paul.

"Okay," said Erin.

"I trust whatever reasons you have . . . for doing anything," said Paul, and wondered if he had felt this before, or if he already no longer felt it.

The next night, after buying watermelon and salad ingredients from Whole Foods, they couldn't find a parking spot at the Tropicana, then found one in a different area and walked a different route toward their room. Paul noticed a MARRIAGE CHAPEL sign at the end of the hallway and, after a few seconds, as they approached it silently, said "we should get married."

"I was going to say that," said Erin.

"I would get married to you."

"Me too," said Erin. "To you."

"Let's get married."

"Let's do it tomorrow."

"Okay," said Paul. "I'm confirmed."

In Whole Foods, the next afternoon, Erin emailed her manager at the used bookstore that she was quitting her job, then scrolled through photos of Elvis standing between grinning, newlywed couples. Elvis appeared more energetic and alive than the couples in almost every photo, including one in which the couple was partially blocked from view by an over-eager Elvis who seemed to have lunged toward the camera, displaying the knuckles side of a peace sign.

"I don't get it, at all," said Paul.

"It's what people do. This is what people want."

"It really seems insane," said Paul.

"People are insane," said Erin.

"We should get an Elvis wedding."

"I'm fine with an Elvis wedding."

"Actually, I don't want an Elvis wedding," said Paul. "It seems extremely stressful." Erin made a next-day reservation for a "desk wedding." They discussed if they wanted to be on MDMA during their marriage ceremony. Erin said they should save it for the day after tomorrow, their last in Las Vegas.

"We might be dead by then," said Paul.

"They won't let us get married if we're on drugs," said Erin.

"They'll think we're on drugs if we're not on drugs. We're normal when we're on drugs."

Erin laughed weakly.

"We'll just—" said Paul. "We'll figure it out."

"We're going to be driving after the wedding, let's just do it after we drive," said Erin a few minutes later in a slightly pleading tone.

"Okay, okay," said Paul earnestly while nodding and patting her shoulder, then hugged her briefly.

Across the street from the marriage license office was a billboard that said MAKING THE RIGHT CHOICE about used cars and used car parts. In the office, which was bright and quiet and arranged like a post office, while filling out forms, Paul said getting married was like getting a tattoo, in that he just wanted to pay money and receive a service, not make appointments and go places and talk to strangers and be asked to confirm his choice. Erin said she was thinking that also and had been "having the same feeling" as before she got tattoos. Paul noticed a sign that said intoxicated applicants would be TURNED AWAY and focused, as they approached the window, on appearing normal, but realized he didn't know how.

"Look at the helpers," he said pointing at six to ten clips, each clasping an impressive seeming amount of paper, magnetized to the side of a cabinet. "I want one."

"Me too," said Erin grinning. "Which one do you want?"

"Any of them," said Paul after a few seconds.

"I want the curvy one," said Erin.

Paul stared at the identical, brown clips.

"The guy with the stripes," said Erin. "My own 'underling.'"

"I'm talking about the plastic paper holder things," said Paul.

• • •

Walking to their rental car they saw a shiny building and an abandoned building side by side, in the near distance. Paul expressed amazement at this second, also obvious, though maybe less egregious metaphor—the first being the used car billboard—and said their marriage would resemble the abandoned building in five years. After a pause, which functioned unintentionally for comic effect, he said "or, like, five days."

Erin laughed. "Five months, maybe," she said earnestly.

"Yeah," said Paul thinking that of the fives—hours, days, weeks, months, years, decades—months was, by far, most likely. "We'll be that tree," he said pointing at a tree that appeared healthy and, he thought, dignified.

"The apartments for rent," said Erin.

"The tree," said Paul.

"Yeah, the tree."

"The tree seems good."

"Nature. Natural."

"Jesus, look," said Paul pointing at an eerie building far in the distance, thin and black, like a cursor on the screen of a computer that had become unresponsive. He imagined building-size letters suddenly appearing, left to right, in a rush—*wpkjgijfhtetiukgcnlm*—across the desert.

The marriage chapel was less than a mile away in a building containing four to six businesses. Paul sat on a two-seat sofa, in a sort of hallway, while Erin used the bathroom. Around ten people, mostly children, surrounding what appeared to be a newlywed couple, passed through Paul's vision, on their way out of the building, then Erin sat by him, then the pastor (a large man with white hair and a serious but friendly demeanor) sat behind a tiny desk (six feet away, at the opposite wall) and read a prepared statement, completing the marriage, at which point—coincidentally, it seemed—a door opened and a smiling woman, with a tiny dog at her feet, congratulated Paul and Erin, after which, sort of huddled against each other, they moved toward the exit grinning.

"I immediately thought 'fuck you' to the stranger congratulating us," said Paul outside, on a sidewalk. Erin laughed and said she thought "pop-up ad," because "it went through the door," and they hugged and jumped repeatedly as one mass, spinning a little and sometimes saying "we did it" quietly. Paul ran suddenly away, onto the parking lot, in a wide arc that curved eventually toward the rental car in a centripetal force, accelerating to a speed that was, at this point in his life, unfamiliarly fast, but not near maximum, before slowing, as he neared the passenger door—and, knowing he would not collide with the car, briefly aware of the dream-like amount of control he had over his body—to a stop.

In Erin's car, two weeks later, on the way to Brooklyn—from Baltimore, where the past two nights he separately met Erin's parents, who were married but lived apart—Paul texted two drug dealers, Android and Peanut, to buy MDMA, ecstasy, LSD, cocaine to have in Taiwan, where they were going in the morning. Paul's parents had invited Paul and Erin to stay with them, as a kind of wedding present, all expenses paid including plane tickets, December 13 to January 2. The marriage, without which Paul likely would not be visiting Taiwan this year, seemed also to have drastically improved his relationship with his mother, who hadn't mentioned drugs, at all, the past three weeks, now that she had something positive to focus on and nurture.

It was dark out and neither drug dealer had responded, after two hours, when they arrived in Brooklyn and parked by Khim's. After buying lemons, celery, kale, apples, energy drinks, toilet paper they walked six blocks to Paul's apartment, then within ten minutes both drug dealers—and Paul's brother, to give Paul a Christmas present and presents to bring to their parents—texted that they were on their way. Android, named after the smartphone, Paul assumed, arrived first. Paul went outside, past the bronze gate, into Android's expensive-seeming car.

"How's it going? You all right?"

"Yeah, good. How are you?"

"I'm good," said Android.

"Here's $230," said Paul, and Android transferred a vial of cocaine and a tiny baggie of capsules into Paul's left hand. Paul asked if the MDMA was from the same batch as last time. Android said they were and, after a pause, in a voice subtly indicating auspiciousness due to rarity and increased quality, added that they were "double-dipped." Paul visualized a stock image, composite from movies he'd seen, of ethnic workers apportioning powder into capsules. "Oh, good," he said, and hesitated, then asked what "double-dipped" meant. Android, in response, seemed to shutdown, as a person, into a dormant state; when, after maybe two seconds, he returned to functioning, he seemed uncharacteristically bored and inattentive, like he wanted to be alone. "They do it twice . . . it goes through once, and they dip it again," he said unenthusiastically, with unfocused eyes and a subtle movement of his upper body that somehow effectively conveyed an additional, unrequired action within the process of an assembly line.

"Nice," said Paul. "Thank you for driving here."

"No problem," said Android in his normal voice. "Give me a call if you want some stuff over the holidays."

"We did it," said Paul in a monotone to Erin in his room, and they hugged. Peanut texted he was ten minutes away. Paul read a text from his brother and went outside and opened the bronze gate. Paul's brother followed Paul into the house, where Erin stood in the hallway outside Paul's apartment.

"Erin, right? Nice to finally meet you."

"Nice to meet you too," said Erin.

After a pause, during which they all grinned at one another, Paul's brother gave Paul a duffel bag and a check and, due to pressure from their mother, Paul assumed, a winter coat, and said "this is for Mom and Dad, you have to remember to give it to them," indicating a department store bag inside the duffel bag.

"Okay," said Paul looking in the duffel bag.

"You have to remember."

"I will," said Paul.

"You can't forget. Okay?"

"I won't," said Paul.

"Okay," said Paul's brother in a slightly child-like voice, then looked at a vacantly grinning Erin and hastily said "we'll have a formal dinner later on together, all of us," with a scrunched expression conveying he knew that she obviously already knew this information, which he was saying aloud as a kind of indulgence to himself. Peanut texted five minutes later when Paul was sitting on his yoga mat, absently organizing his drugs in his six-compartment plastic container.

Paul got in the backseat of a car that, relative to Android's, did not seem expensive. The same middle-aged woman as the previous four or five times Paul bought from Peanut, the past few months, was driving. Paul distractedly imagined himself asking if the woman was Peanut's mother as he bought two strips of LSD and thirty ecstasy—half blue, half red—from Peanut, who was in the front passenger seat.

Paul and Erin, sitting on Paul's mattress, were wearing earphones and doing things on their MacBooks, an hour later, after each ingesting "double-dipped" capsules of MDMA and 10mg Adderall and sharing a zero-calorie energy drink. They'd decided to use drugs throughout the night and sleep on the plane. Paul, worried because he didn't feel like talking even after the MDMA and Adderall should've taken effect, inspected the capsules and asked Erin on Gmail chat if they seemed less full than in the past; they didn't, to her, but she also wasn't feeling a strong effect. They concluded the problem was their tolerance levels and each ingested a blue ecstasy and continued doing things separately. "I feel something now, but I'm not sure if I feel like talking," thought Paul looking at his Gmail account. "But I think I'll be okay."

The next four hours they had sex (and showered) three times, shared 50oz kale-celery-apple-lemon juice and 30mg Adderall, typed accounts of a cold and sunny afternoon one week ago when they walked around SoHo on MDMA shouting and screaming iterations of Charles' name (initials, first, first and last, full) at each other while holding hands. Paul packaged a strip of LSD, four MDMA, twelve ecstasy inside the CD case for Nirvana's second "greatest hits" album, which he wrapped in transparent tape, then in four issues of Seattle's leading alt weekly with his face on the cover, which his mother had requested he bring, then in a shirt, which he fit snugly inside a shoebox.

Around 4:30 a.m., after deciding to use all their cocaine before leaving for the airport, they recorded Erin licking cocaine off Paul's testicles and serving cocaine off an iPhone to Paul reading a purple-covered *Siddhartha* while seated on a high chair he found on a sidewalk in August and until now had used only as a clothing rack; Erin snorting cocaine off her MacBook screen; Paul snorting cocaine off Erin's face; both snorting cocaine off vacuum-wrapped Omaha Steaks, which Calvin's father had ordered for Paul for Thanksgiving. They discussed, relative to Adderall, not liking cocaine, which was inferior in price, effect, length of effect, aftereffect, convenience, availability but fun to have in group situations, in terms of thinking of funny places to snort it from. Paul said he wanted to shower before finishing the cocaine and walking to Variety, a café four blocks away, to relax, drink iced coffee, wait for their airport taxi.

After showering Paul dried himself and put on clothes and, while Erin was showering, stood in a corner and stared at his room without thinking anything or, he realized after a vague amount of time, moving his eyeballs. He sat on his yoga mat and stared at his Gmail account, remembering after a few minutes that he'd wanted to stand in a corner and look at his room to double-check he'd packed everything. When Erin, looking at herself in the wall mirror, finished blow-drying her hair, around fifteen minutes later, Paul looked up from where he'd remained on his yoga mat—absently scrolling through bohemianism's Wikipedia page after clicking "bohemian" on Kurt Cobain's page, which he'd looked at, while rereading emails from his mother, to see if he died at 26 or 27—and asked if Erin was "ready," with what felt like a self-consciously neutral expression, vaguely sensing his question to be antagonistic, because he didn't know exactly what it referenced.

"Yeah," said Erin with a blank expression.

"No," said Paul pointing at her MacBook and small pile of miscellany by her red backpack, which he felt aversion toward, in a manner that would become a problem, for him, in the future, he realized, with aversion toward himself, because it always seemed dirty.

"What," said Erin.

"You're not finished packing."

"I thought we were doing that first?" said Erin pointing at the cocaine.

Paul felt himself blinking. "Oh," he said. "Yeah. I forgot. Sorry." He stood and stepped carefully over his yoga mat and kneeled by the low table and asked with unfocused eyes and a controlled voice if Erin wanted to use the remaining cocaine at Variety—to extend their usage and, he vaguely thought, soften their forthcoming "depletion," or "depleted serotonin levels," as they had, with a kind of feigned affection, been referencing their periods, after feeling good on drugs, of feeling bad.

"Okay," said Erin after a pause. "But we should cut it first."

"We can do it there," said Paul after a long pause.

"It'll be easier to do it here," said Erin.

Paul stared at her tired, confident expression.

"I don't want to do it there," she said.

"Okay. But we'll have to put it back in, after taking it out, if we do it here. We have to take it out and put it all back in again."

"That's fine. We aren't in a hurry . . . are we?"

"No," said Paul after a few seconds, and heard himself thinking, in a voice like he was practicing a speech, that an amount, even if only a trace, of cocaine would remain outside the vial—and it would all just clump together again, when back inside. There was also the risk of sneezing or otherwise uncontrollably disrupting the cocaine. "But we'll lose some, when you take it out," he said slowly. "It just . . . seems inconvenient." Erin said she could "cut it really fast" and that she'd done it many times, arguably referencing, for the second or third time, a somewhat mysterious period of her life, when she did cocaine with Beau and other people every night or something. Paul felt aversion toward himself for feeling bothered by how Erin, or the situation itself, seemed to be indicating that, by not defaulting to Erin's greater experience in cutting cocaine, Paul was behaving irrationally. "It just seems inconvenient," he was saying. "It's just inconvenient."

"We can cut it there," said Erin with a bored expression. "It doesn't really matter."

"We'll just cut it here," said Paul, and slowly swiveled his head toward the cocaine. He grasped the cute, orange-capped vial with the thumb and middle finger of his right hand, whose full weight rested on the table. "I don't care about cutting it. When we put it back in, won't it, just, like, turn into a clump again?"

"We don't have to," said Erin. "I don't really care."

"Why cut it, though? Doesn't it all just go in you?"

"It doesn't hurt as much," said Erin, and gestured at the top half of her face and said things about sinuses, that it was "healthier" and that "more of it gets absorbed, instead of going in your stomach," as Paul thought about referencing *Cocaine: A Drug and Its Social Evolution,* a book he knew Erin knew he'd been reading. "It all gets absorbed," he said. "It's the same if you eat it or snort it."

"Then why does everyone snort it," said Erin seeming neither curious nor rhetorical.

"People do a lot of things. I don't know why, probably a lot of reasons. It's the same as long as it's inside of you. I read the book. The cocaine book."

"That's true," said Erin.

"So, you should listen to me," said Paul grinning slightly.

"The book said it's the same if you eat it?"

"Yeah, or something," mumbled Paul looking away. "I don't remember what it said."

"What else did the book say?"

"A lot of things. I don't know. I haven't finished it yet. I'm going to pee." Paul stood grinning and went in the bathroom and peed a little. He splashed water onto his face. He dried his face with a hand towel and entered his room. "That was our first 'drug fight,'" he said still grinning a little.

"I was going to say that," said Erin.

"I feel like we handled it well."

"It was good," said Erin absently.

"I tried using the book," said Paul grinning. "The cocaine book."

"I noticed," said Erin with a neutral expression.

At Variety, after snorting the remaining cocaine in Paul's room, they decided to type accounts of their "drug fight." Paul finished and left for Union Square to mail drugs to Taiwan. The shoebox, on his lap, felt "like a cat," he kept thinking on the L train. He walked in a distended circle, like a comet's orbit, on the wide sidewalk outside FedEx, which at 7:54 a.m. was locked and dark, listening to music through earphones, until an employee, seeming to slightly feign, Paul felt, being rushed, unlocked the door and entered and turned on the lights. Paul's package would cost $89 to mail, said the employee, then walked out of view, toward the back of the store. Paul slowly filled out a form, then carried the form toward the exit, stood uncertainly in place a few seconds, returned to the counter, walked distractedly toward the exit, put the form in the trash, left FedEx. He rode the L train five stops. He bought two containers of pineapple chunks from a deli. "It would've cost $89 to mail," he said at Variety. "I'm just going to put it in my bag. If I go to jail I'll just write *Infinite Witz*," he said referencing two very long novels, *Infinite Jest* and *Witz*.

"What?" said Erin with an inattentive expression.

"If I go to jail I'll just focus on writing *Infinite Witz*," said Paul, and in the time and location of waiting, for himself to repeat what he'd said, he imagined the scenario and was a little surprised at the ease and speed with which he felt he would accept it—and that he would be relieved, to be removed from the confusing, omnidirectional hierarchy of his life. Erin smiled and said "good" and patted his shoulder, and he felt surprised again, as he hugged her, realizing that he wouldn't be removed from his life—only dying would remove him—so would feel the same probably. He would still be—and be inside—the invulnerable dot of himself, irreducible and unique as a prime number, on or off, there or not, always following itself perfectly. Paul pushed the shoebox toward the bottom of his duffel bag, wedging it between layers of clothing, and they read each other's "drug fight" accounts while eating pineapple chunks.

"We both wrote it in a Raymond Carver–esque manner."

"I was thinking that," said Erin. "The story with the baby."

In the taxi, at one side of the backseat, Paul felt surreally distant from Erin, at the other side, like he would need to turn his head more than 90 degrees to see her. Through the window, against his face, the early-morning light had the vertical glare and the accumulated, citrus heat of a late-afternoon sun. "I feel really depleted, I'm closing my eyes until we get there," said Paul in a voice that was agitatedly boring for himself to speak and hear and that seemed to echo inside his mouth, staying where it began.

At the airport, when they got out of the taxi, Erin asked how Paul felt and he murmured "zombie-like" without moving his head. They held hands while standing in line for luggage check-in, but Paul avoided looking at Erin, facing away from her as much as possible, to try to convey, without speaking, that he did not want to be asked any more questions, be looked at, or otherwise feel pressured to do or think anything. Unsure if Erin, at whatever moment, was receiving his communication, or not, or to what degree she was, or was not, Paul felt a constant dread of what might happen next, mostly that Erin might ask him another question. He wanted to hide by shrinking past zero, through the dot at the end of himself, to a negative size, into an otherworld, where he would find a place—in an enormous city, too large to know itself, or some slowly developing suburb—to be alone and carefully build a life in which he might be able to begin, at some point, to think about what to do about himself.

They lay on their backs on a padded seat continuously lining one side of a cafeteria with no restaurants open yet. When Paul woke, drooling a little, he moved into a sitting position with his elbows on a table, and saw that Erin was gone. Before forming any thoughts, or discerning any feelings, he saw her, in the distance, outside the cafeteria, walking parallel to a moving walkway with her iPhone to her ear, becoming out of view. Paul noticed a scrap of paper on his lap, from Erin, saying she was going to the bathroom and calling her friend and would be back by 9:15 a.m. Paul saw her at 9:08 a.m. hurriedly enter a store outside the cafeteria. She approached with pineapple chunks and bottled water, smiling at Paul's neutral expression. "I got you this," she said, and Paul mutely held the container of pineapple chunks a few seconds before placing it distractedly on the table.

"Where did you go?" said Paul self-consciously.

"I went to the bathroom and called my friend Jennika. Did you see my note?"

"I didn't until like five minutes after I woke," said Paul with aversion toward himself, aware he saw the note within a minute maybe. He asked why Erin didn't stay within view to talk on the phone. Erin said she hadn't thought of that and Paul said it was okay and—finally, self-conscious at the delay—thanked her for the pineapple chunks and opened the container and moved a chunk, with a fork, toward Erin's mouth. Erin shook her head. Paul moved the chunk into his mouth and, after his mouth stopped moving, asked what Erin talked to Jennika about on the phone.

"I told her I got married and was going to Taiwan, and she got angry and just started sobbing and yelling at me," said

Erin, and without noticeable change in her slack posture, facing the empty cafeteria, began crying a little. Paul carefully held her—weakly, tiredly "hating himself," he felt—and, after she stopped crying, asked why Jennika had been angry. "She was angry I didn't tell her sooner. She kept saying she would never do that to me and that I was a bad friend."

Paul continued asking questions and was slightly affected by Erin's extrasensitivity, it seemed, in not relating unsolicited information. Erin said Jennika had previously always been okay with periods without contact—with respecting the other person's availability—and that after Jennika she had called her mother to say she felt scared that Paul didn't want her to go to Taiwan with him.

"Why do you think that?"

"I started feeling paranoid. I felt like you didn't want me around and I'm bothering you just by being around."

"No," said Paul shaking his head.

"You've been so quiet," said Erin.

"I'm quiet from being depleted. I said I felt zombie-like."

"I know, but I still felt paranoid. I thought 'what if he's just tolerating me. I'm going to be around him for the next three weeks.' And things like that."

"We're depleted big-time. Don't trust what you feel now."

"I felt all this even after factoring in depletion," said Erin, and Paul eased her into a lying position, on her side with her head on his lap, and alternated feeding her and himself pineapple chunks.

On the fully booked, thirteen-hour twenty-nine-minute flight to Narita, where they would transfer to a three-hour fifteen-minute flight to Taiwan, they had middle seats in consecutive, three-seat rows. Before takeoff, standing in view of the four relevant passengers, Erin asked if "anyone" wanted to trade seats for $40 so she could sit with her husband and was egregiously ignored except by the middle-aged woman, to Paul's left, who said "no thanks" cheerfully, as if she'd misconstrued the situation to believe she was doing a favor by declining. Paul sometimes stood to lean forward and hug Erin's head, massage her shoulders, or grin at her after certain lines of dialogue during *Eat, Pray, Love,* which they excitedly agreed to watch together and both felt nearly continuously amused by.

After the movie they stood hugging by the "lavatories." Erin said she felt better than when she'd been paranoid, but seemed reluctant to reciprocate Paul's enthusiasm when, with a child-like sensation of wanting to be encouraged to believe a fantasy, or that an aberration was the norm, he said, for the third time since getting on the plane, as if stressing the unexpected discovery of something worth living for, in an existence in which most things were endured, not enjoyed, that it seemed good they used "all those drugs and energy drinks" and hadn't slept and still felt "okay." Paul was surprised and confused when it occurred to him that if they felt almost anything other than happy, or at least content, *Eat, Pray, Love* (with its montages and fortune cookie–like monks and unacknowledged but knowing, it had seemed, usage of clichés) would've been incredibly depressing. He felt self-consciously, annoyingly optimistic when Erin reacted to this information, which had felt to him like an epiphany, with little interest and no enthusiasm, seeming less glad or curious than troubled, as if the message was to retroactively not enjoy the movie.

Before Paul visited his parents twelve months ago (which had been his first time in Taiwan in almost five years, during which most of the Taipei Metro, or Mass Rapid Transit, had been completed) he had no concept of Taipei's size or shape or layout, only an unreliable memory of how many minutes by car separated certain relatives' apartments and department stores. After using the MRT and idly studying its maps on station walls and Wikipedia, then walking between stations—to and from different routes, one night to six continuous stops, some days while far from his parents' apartment to illuminate a distant area, placing a candle there for perspective, or as a reminder that there was more—he had, with increasing interest, begun to view and internalize Taipei less like a city than its own world, which he could leisurely explore, he imagined, for years, or maybe indefinitely, as it reconfigured and continued to expand, opening new MRT stations until 2018, according to Wikipedia.

To Paul, who'd stayed mostly in his uncle's sixteenth-floor apartment on previous visits, the vaguely tropical, consummating murmur of Taipei, from his parent's fourteenth-floor apartment, had sounded immediately and distinctively familiar. The muffled roar of traffic, hazily embellished with beeps and honks and motorcycle engines and the occasional, looping, Doppler-effected jingle from a commercial or political vehicle—had been mnemonic enough (reminding Paul of the 10 to 15 percent of his life on the opposite side of Earth, with a recurring cast of characters and no school and a different language, almost fantastically unlike the other 85 to 90 percent, in suburban Florida) for him to believe, on some level, that if a place existed where he could go to scramble some initial momentum, to disable a setting implemented before birth, or disrupt the out-of-control formation of some incomprehensible worldview, and allow a kind of settling, over time, to occur—like a spaceship that has exhausted its fuel and begun falling toward the nearest star, approaching what it wants at the rate it's wanted, then easing into the prolonged, perfectly requited appreciation of an orbit—it would be here.

5

Paul's father looked the same as last year, Paul thought at the airport, except maybe, as part of a long-term change, a little more child-like, in his mindfully cheerful manner, seeming always slightly distracted by some earnest, interior activity, which Paul sometimes imagined to be the low-level focus required to retain the mysterious, untransferable, necessarily private wisdom that powered his contentment. Paul thought of how, as one aged, more people became comparatively younger, so that, among an increasingly child-like population, one might unconsciously behave more like a child. While buying bus tickets, then waiting for the bus, Paul's father said he had found Paul's Taiwanese publisher on the internet and called them—learning it was one person, in his apartment— and arranged for Paul to give a reading for the Taiwanese edition of his first novel on Christmas, its release date.

On the bus Erin slept with her head on Paul's lap. Paul's father slept one row behind. It was around 10:30 p.m. Paul stared at the lighted signs, some of which were animated and repeating like GIF files, attached to almost every building to face oncoming traffic—from two-square rectangles like tiny wings to long strips like impressive Scrabble words but with each square a word, maybe too much information to convey to drivers—and sleepily thought of how technology was no longer the source of wonderment and possibility it had been when, for example, he learned as a child at Epcot Center, Disney's future-themed "amusement park," that families of three, with one or two robot dogs and one robot maid, would live in self-sustaining, underwater, glass spheres by something like 2004 or 2008. At some point, Paul vaguely realized, technology had begun for him to mostly only indicate the inevitability and vicinity of nothingness. Instead of postponing death by releasing nanobots into the bloodstream to fix things faster than they deteriorated, implanting little computers into people's brains, or other methods Paul had probably read about on Wikipedia, until it became the distant, shrinking, nearly nonexistent somethingness that was currently life—and life, for immortal humans, became the predominate distraction that was currently death—technology seemed more likely to permanently eliminate life by uncontrollably fulfilling its only function: to indiscriminately convert matter, animate or inanimate, into computerized matter, for the sole purpose, it seemed, of increased functioning, until the universe was one computer. Technology, an abstraction, undetectable in concrete reality, was accomplishing its concrete task, Paul dimly intuited while idly petting Erin's hair, by way of an increasingly committed and multiplying workforce of humans, who receive, over hundreds of generations, a certain kind of advancement (from feet to bicycles to cars, faces to bulletin boards to the internet) in exchange for converting a sufficient amount of matter into computerized matter for computers to be able to build themselves.

As the bus moved into denser parts of Taipei, nearing Paul's parents' apartment building, Paul felt like he could almost sense the computerization that was happening in this area of the universe, on Earth—could imagine the three- or four-minute simulation, in a documentary that probably existed, of occurrence and eventual, omnidirectional expansion, converting asteroids and rays and stars, then galaxies and clusters of galaxies, as they became elapsed in space, into more of itself. Paul had read about this in high school, lying on the carpet in his room, in *The End of Science*, with excitement, intuiting that, from the perspective of the computer at the end of everything, which he would be a part of and which would synthetically resemble an undifferentiated oneness, it didn't matter if he had never kissed a girl, was too anxious to communicate with his peers, had no friends, etc. When Erin woke, seeming depressed and confused, avoiding looking at anything as she sat up, Paul patted his lap and she lay there again. Paul asked if she could think of a newer word for "computer" than "computer," which seemed outdated and, in still being used, suspicious in some way, like maybe the word itself was intelligent and had manipulated culture in its favor, perpetuating its usage.

"I'm still thinking," she said after a few minutes.

"I don't think my question made sense," said Paul. "There can't be a newer word . . . for the same word."

• • •

More framed pictures of Paul were on display in his room, it seemed, than last year. Seeing them (two as a baby, four as a small child, one as an adolescent, two as a teenager in his marching band uniform) arranged on shelves, in two corners, Paul imagined his mother placing them strategically to affect him to use less drugs. He gathered all but one (in which he was nine or ten and grinning and holding, for some reason, a Three Musketeers–style sword, with his parents and brother, in a professional studio in Taipei, with an outer-space-themed background, unfurled like a scroll, he vaguely remembered, on the wall, pre–green screen) and stacked them—so many the room had felt like a memorial—facedown on a dresser, saying they made him uncomfortable. Erin asked why and said he looked cute and happy in them. Paul said he would feel uncomfortable seeing that many of anyone's face.

The next afternoon, walking to a street market, Paul and Erin stopped to look at a two-story McDonald's with five employees outside speaking into megaphones, sometimes in unison, waving banners and flags. Paul said there were fewer McDonald's in Taiwan than fifteen years ago, that this was probably a "last-ditch effort," which seemed to be working (the first floor—they could see through the glass front—was entirely filled with customers). Erin said they should improvise a documentary titled *Taiwan's Last McDonald's* or *Taiwan's First McDonald's*. They walked to the end of the street market and back, on the same route, buying and eating things, then bought and ate egg tarts from two different bakeries, then with nervous grins earnestly discussed eating however many egg tarts it would take for them to not want more, but resisted and returned to the apartment building, where they lay for an hour in the building's sauna and dog-paddled, in a heated pool, to six different massage stations, including one—partly simulating a waterfall, maybe—where water fell eight to ten feet in pummeling, faucet-like columns onto the tops of their heads.

• • •

"My face won't stop being red from the thing," said Erin, an hour later, in Paul's room, in a voice like she was mostly thinking about something else. Paul was trying to open the taped CD case for Nirvana's second "greatest hits" collection. He looked at Erin briefly. "It looks good," he mumbled looking at the CD case. His mother, in the hallway outside the room, whose door was open a few inches, said something in Mandarin.

"What?" said Paul in Mandarin.

"Bring your phone," said Paul's mother in Mandarin.

"Okay."

"What?"

"Okay," said Paul in Mandarin. "Don't worry," he said in Mandarin in a louder, agitated-sounding voice.

"Okay. Your father and I are going to eat."

"Okay," said Paul in Mandarin.

"Do you . . . want to come eat together?"

"No," said Paul in Mandarin.

"They're leaving," said Paul after a few seconds.

"Oh," said Erin in a staccato with a worried expression.

"We'll wait till they leave."

"Oh," said Erin.

"Before we—" said Paul.

Erin nodded attentively.

"They're going to eat," said Paul, and walked to a bookshelf and stared at two hardbound Animal Life volumes with the same image of a cheetah climbing a tree on their spines. He opened and closed a drawer, aware he wasn't thinking anything, then put on black socks and hugged Erin from behind. They looked at themselves, being recorded, on the screen—uniquely neither reflection nor movie, but viewable perspective—of Paul's MacBook, smiling sarcastically. Their plan for tonight was to ingest MDMA, after Paul's parents left, and go to a shopping district where the streets, closed off to cars, were used as giant sidewalks. Paul showed Erin its Wikipedia page ("Ximending is the source of Taiwan's fashion, subculture, and Japanese culture) and typed "ximending" in Google Images.

"Whoa," said Erin. "Looks like Times Square."

"We're leaving," shouted Paul's mother a few minutes later, when Paul and Erin were looking at the Wikipedia page for *28 Days Later,* which Erin had said was one of her favorite movies. Paul was rereading a sentence ("As he gets hit by a car in his flashback, he simultaneously dies on the operating table") for the fourth time, in idle confusion, when the apartment's metal door closed in a loud and distinct but, Paul thought, non-ominous click.

Ten minutes later Paul was at the dining table staring at an email from Calvin ("hi bro. did you get the steaks my dad sent you? lol . . .") while waiting for Erin, who was in the bathroom. Paul typed "hi" and his eyes unfocused. He typed "," and saved "hi," as a draft. He minimized Safari and saw his face, which seemed bored and depressed, his default expression. He maximized Safari and imagined millions of windows, positioned to appear like one window. He closed his eyes and thought of the backs of his eyelids as computer screens; both could display anything imaginable, so had infinite depth, but as physical surfaces were nearly depthless. Paul typed "ppl are powerful computers w 2 computer screens & free/fast/reliable access to their own internet" in Twitter, copied it, closed Twitter, pasted it in his Gmail draft of tweet drafts. He was thinking about the fast-food restaurant Arby's, which he'd always felt a little confused by, when Erin appeared behind him and patted his shoulders with both hands moving up and down.

"Let's hug as hard as we can," said Paul, and stood and they did. "I think being squished really hard is what people who cut themselves get . . . to feel."

"Have you cut yourself?"

"No. Have you?"

"No," said Erin carrying the MacBook toward the front door.

"Why would being squished feel good?" said Paul absently.

"Hm," said Erin. "Do you have m—"

"Raarrr!" screamed Paul with his mouth open.

"Jesus," said Erin grinning.

"Does it smell?" said Paul about his breath.

"Maybe like coffee a little bit. But it's okay."

Paul jogged to the bathroom, brushed his teeth and tongue, rinsed his mouth, jogged to the front door. Erin asked if he had her "ID thing"—he did—then touched his arm and quickly said "do you feel okay?" in a high-pitched voice. Paul, who'd begun to feel the MDMA, looked at Erin's hand and imagined feeling utter disbelief, increasing to uncontrollable rage, that she would touch his arm, at a time like this. "Yeah," he said with a neutral expression. "Do you?"

"Yeah," said Erin. "Wait, is my—"

"Smells vaguely of barbecue, but it's good," said Paul, and patted her shoulder.

"Vaguely of barbecue," said Erin grinning.

In the mirror-walled elevator they stared at themselves on the screen of Paul's MacBook, which Erin held waist level. Paul moved in a parody of a robot and lightly slapped Erin twice. Erin slapped Paul once and, after exiting the elevator, yawned audibly, as they approached an atrium of spiral staircases and a gigantic Christmas tree.

"Look," said Paul with a fish-like expression.

Erin laughed loudly. "Jesus," she said.

"You made a Jack Nicholson facial expression."

"Really?" said Erin, and laughed.

"Your eyebrows went," said Paul demonstrating.

"Whoa," said Erin loudly. "I made a soundboard laugh."

"Oh," said Paul. "Oh," he said quietly, and moved toward a potted plant and, before reaching it, jumped in place, slightly confused by his own behavior. Erin said she thought Paul was going to "jump on." There was a suctioned, whooshing noise as they exited automatically opening doors onto a wide sidewalk. Paul turned left—into Erin, who almost dropped the MacBook—and sustained an uninhibited, yelping noise for three or four seconds, imagining himself as a butler in a Disney movie in comically prolonged recovery from almost dropping an elaborately layered tray of desserts and drinks. Paul had an urge to practice the noise repeatedly, with increasing frustration, trying to perfect it—cutscene to him in a straitjacket.

"Jesus," said Erin grinning. "Should I get dramatic shots of the street?"

"Whatever you want."

"Dramatic ass shots," said Erin.

"It's your night," said Paul in vague reference to the Cinderella archetype of a beautiful, oppressed, sympathetic character that experiences a hectic reversal of fortune. "I keep thinking 'this is our night' for some reason," he said a few minutes later, and his eyes felt shiny, and he thought of shyness, acceptance. "I wonder what it's going to be like for us, for our twenty days here," he said as they crossed a street. "What are we going to . . . do?"

"What if we get divorced by then?"

"It seems possible," said Paul. "Twenty-eight days."

"Twenty-eight days," said Erin grinning. "Twenty-day immersion technique."

"Have you ever spent twenty straight days—"

"Yeah," said Erin.

"You have?"

"With Jennika. This summer, in Seattle."

"I mean with a boyfriend," said Paul, and imagined himself becoming physically faceted by rapidly facing different directions, in 15-degree movements, advancing blurrily ahead as a barely visible, wave-like curvature.

"Oh. Yeah. Probably."

"Who?"

"First boyfriend. Kent."

"Sleeping together?" said Paul suppressing an urge to scream it in mock disbelief. Erin said they were together "like every day" in the beginning and that "it seemed okay." Paul asked what she meant by "okay" and visualized "it seemed" darkening and "okay" brightening colorfully. He mock studied "okay," which suddenly enlarged and disappeared by "flying" through him, it seemed. Paul felt vaguely, uncertainly amused. Erin was explaining that she and Kent didn't fight until she used his computer to write a paper and saw a folder of naked girlfriend pictures, which Kent said were from so long ago he couldn't remember and that the girl lived in Poland and he didn't talk to her anymore, all of which were lies.

"How do you feel about our fights so far?"

"I feel . . . they seem to be okay," said Erin descending stairs into a powerfully air-conditioned MRT station, marbled and quiet and clean, with the austere plainness of an established museum. "I still feel the same amount of interest toward you. But I think I worry more. I worry like 'he might actually have a reaction toward this so I'll think about it more.' Or something. How do you think about them?"

"They seem fine," said Paul.

"Is . . . this how it usually goes?"

"Yeah," said Paul with the word extended.

"Like the fights are similar?"

"Um, yeah . . . I don't have the kind of fight where it's, like, 'fighting,'" said Paul as they passed a bakery where he photographed and ate a crispy, red-bean-paste-filled croissant last year. "Like, yelling at each other and trying to 'win,' or something. Or, like, forgetting about it."

"Or like what?"

"Like 'winning.' I don't have that kind of fight."

"Oh," said Erin.

"Ever," said Paul quietly.

Erin said with Kent she had the kind of fight where it turned into "proving a point," then escalated into yelling. Paul asked if she fought with Harris, her second boyfriend.

"No," said Erin.

"You have a curling effect," said Paul touching her hair. "I like it. Is that what you're going for?"

"Yeah," said Erin smiling endearingly.

"You didn't fight with the second one at all?"

"We had fights like you and I, like discussion-style things," said Erin. "I don't think we ever yelled at each other. Except, did we ever, no—no, we never yelled."

"How do you feel about me compared to your other boy-friends?"

"I like you more," said Erin.

"Than all of them?"

"Yeah," said Erin.

"I like you—"

"You—" said Erin.

"—more also," said Paul.

"Really?"

"Yeah," said Paul.

"Sweet," said Erin. "You seem to encompass major things of what I want, in ways I feel like only segments of other people . . . have." She patted Paul's chest and said "I like you" as they approached an intersection of corridors, wide as four-lane streets, where last year, leaning against a pillar in the left corridor, Paul read the last few pages of Kōbō Abe's *The Face of Another,* which ended with the narrator, hiding behind a pillar, about to attack his "imposter." Paul realized they were walking the wrong direction, and they turned around.

"What do you think your parents think about me?"

"They . . . like you," said Paul, and laughed quietly.

"Do they usually act like . . . the way they did?"

"Yeah," said Paul uncertainly. "I think they're always focused on me, not the other person. But, yeah."

"I wondered about that."

"My mom's probably thinking about drugs a lot," said Paul, and Erin laughed and hiccupped, it seemed, at the same time. Paul said "I mean worried about drugs."

"Is she addicted? Do you think?"

"Yeah," said Paul grinning.

Erin said she'd noticed that Paul sometimes sounded "really angry" when talking to his mother in Mandarin. Paul said he didn't feel angry, that he had gotten into a habit, from being a spoiled child, of talking to her like that and that it used to be "way worse." Until he was 7 or 8 his voice, incomprehensible to anyone outside his family, had been a harmonica-like, almost electronic, squealing-bleating noise, which wholly outsourced the task of articulation, in the form of deciphering, to the listener. Paul's brother would tell him to "stop screaming" or "stop whining." Paul's mother, the listener probably 95 percent of the time, a shy and anxious person herself, probably had strongly encouraged and liked how unrestrained and unself-conscious Paul had been.

"I was surprised," said Erin. "I've never heard you talk like that."

"I really don't like it," said Paul.

"It's interesting," said Erin stepping onto a down escalator.

"I'm embarrassed about it."

"I do it with my parents," said Erin smiling.

"What have you read by Kōbō Abe?"

"Just *The Woman in the Dunes*."

"What else do you think about me?" said Paul, and laughed sarcastically, which Erin also did, then both abruptly stopped and hugged and, stepping off the escalator, approached one of eight automated turnstiles. Paul said "just hold it to the thing" about Erin's MRT card, then in a deeper voice than normal "wait, wait" and, after a pause, that he was "going to poop."

Paul could see himself, after exiting the bathroom, shakily enlarging on the screen of his MacBook, which Erin pointed at him, as he maneuvered toward it in a flighty zigzag, perpendicularly against people walking to and from turnstiles, escalators. "I just vomited, like, water," he said.

"Oh my god. Really? Are you sick?"

"No, I'm just getting the feeling of a lot of emptiness."

"Oh. I was going to go poop but the—"

"Go, go," said Paul.

"—like the thing, or, okay," said Erin.

"Wikipedia? What?"

"The thing in the floor? I wasn't sure how to use it."

"You went in there?" said Paul.

"It's just, like, a hole in the floor, interesting."

"What if I couldn't find you?"

"Huh?" said Erin with a confused expression.

"What if I couldn't find you? You went in the bathroom?"

"I just went in for a second, with the intention of—"

"Go, go," said Paul patting Erin's shoulder, and she went. Paul set his MacBook on the floor. His legs moved in and out of view for a few minutes. "Hello?" he said in Mandarin into his iPhone. "Okay, okay, we're leaving now, okay, bye." Erin was skipping toward him and, it seemed, flapping her arms. Paul said his mother called to remind them they can't eat or drink on the train. Erin smiled and said "oh, helpful" sincerely and they passed turnstiles, descended two floors, waited two minutes, sat in a train. Paul asked what Erin hadn't liked about her other boyfriends.

"Like, things that have just bothered me?"

"Let's just talk about . . . Harris," said Paul.

"Okay. Um, bothered me that he, like, had a lot of friends and a big social life. And didn't seem to be okay with how I just had him and one other friend. He'd be like 'you need to focus on me less and get more friends.' I felt bothered that that was constant. And I didn't like it that sometimes he seemed to make insensitive comments. There was one incident where I had to get a . . . surgery-type thing on my, like, cervix . . . thing."

"What was it?"

"To remove precancerous cells, or something."

"Whoa," said Paul.

"They had to, like, burn—"

"Is that normal?"

"Yeah, relatively, but I couldn't do anything for three weeks, then finally when we did . . . this weird-looking thing came out? And, I don't know, I felt really self-conscious, and the first thing he was just like 'ew' and, like, backed away from me and I was like 'I can't help it.' I don't know. It bothered me at the time but now . . . I don't know."

"Are you on birth control right now?"

"No. I haven't had my period but I've also taken three pregnancy tests, I'm not pregnant."

"When did you take three pregnancy tests?"

"Periodically. One time I didn't have my period for a year and a half. I feel like I should get on birth control. Because I have my period when I'm on it."

"Isn't it healthier to not be on it?"

"Yeah. That's why I'm not on it."

"It seems fine," said Paul vaguely.

"Really?"

"Yeah," said Paul trying to remember something he wanted to say on the topic of friends. "It . . . doesn't matter to me if I come in you or somewhere else."

"Okay," said Erin.

"Um," said Paul distractedly.

"This is probably the most that a guy has come in me without being on it. But I figure if anything happens we're probably similarly . . . minded." Erin looked at Paul with an ironic expression and placed a hand on his shoulder. "Because you want to have kids," she said in a mock-serious voice. "Soon. Right?"

Paul nodded, aware he probably appeared confused.

"That was our goal in getting married," said Erin.

Paul patted her thigh twice and grinned a little.

"We're not in sin anymore," said Erin completing the joke, mostly to herself, it seemed.

"I've always, um, felt like . . ." said Paul quietly.

"Huh?" said Erin staring at his blank expression.

"Weird about friends," murmured Paul. "I never hang out with other people if I'm in a relationship."

Erin nodded rapidly, seeming a little anxious.

"We're here," said Paul, and they exited the train as it said XIMEN STATION (and something about Chiang Kai-shek) in Mandarin, Cantonese, Taiwanese, English in a female, robot voice. Paul sneezed and looked at his hands rubbing the front of his shirt, aware of Erin also looking, both with neutral expressions. "Um," said Paul on an up escalator to another train platform. "How did you deal with Harris having that many friends?"

"I would hang out with them. Harris and I were similar in the way we would joke about things, and I liked that his friends seemed to like me . . . or, like, they laughed at me, and him, when we were together. But it was weird because it was obvious that I never became friends with any of them. What problems . . . do you have?"

"With friends?"

"Girlfriends. The same question you asked me."

"With . . . who?"

"Uh, with Michelle," said Erin.

"Just . . . her friends," said Paul on an up escalator to the station's main floor. "She would want to hang out with friends. And I wouldn't want to . . ."

"Is there anything about her? Like, as a person."

"I feel like we weren't perfectly—we weren't, um, optimally excited by each other."

"How? How?"

"Just, like, she didn't like the same things that I liked . . . as much."

"Oh," said Erin. "Like *On the Road* things?"

"Yeah," Paul said, who hadn't liked *On the Road* as much as Michelle, who had rated one of his favorite books, *Chilly Scenes of Winter*, which she'd said she "liked," two out of five stars on Goodreads, after their relationship had ended. "And then, uh, I felt like maybe she . . . had a slightly neurotic aversion toward blow jobs, I feel," said Paul.

"Seriously? I wouldn't expect that."

"She would do it, but not as much as I would to her, I think," said Paul as they reached street level, at an intersection, where two corner buildings seemed armored with layers of billboards and lighted signs and, near the top of one, like a face, a giant screen, showing a movie preview. On a plaza was a donation bucket decorated like a Christmas tree and a grand piano without a player. "Sometimes she would joke about how it was 'degrading,' but I feel like she wasn't completely joking."

They entered the area blocked off to cars.

"So maybe I wasn't satisfied with that," said Paul.

"What other things sexually?"

"Sexually?"

"About her, or about anybody."

"Uh, I don't have that many sexual complaints. What about you?"

"With Kent it got really boring and routine."

"How?"

"It was just the same thing. He would go down on me, then we would have missionary style, and that's it . . . that's, like, it. Harris, similarly, we never really gave each other oral sex, toward the middle and end. But I really like that, both ways. And it also became sort of the same thing with him, where we would do missionary. Then I would . . ."

"Then you would . . ."

" . . . like, finger myself," said Erin at a lower pitch with a complicated expression that Paul saw peripherally.

"You would finger yourself? While he was doing it?"

"Yeah," said Erin.

"Did you like that?"

"It was okay. Seemed business-oriented. So we could both . . ."

Paul made a noise indicating he understood.

"How do you feel about . . ."

"What?" said Paul, dimly aware and liking that they'd

remained focused on their conversation instead of acknowledging their new, intense environment, which was bright and chaotic and crowded but, without vehicles, relatively quiet, more calming than stressful. Paul felt like he and Erin—and their conversation—were in the backseat of a soundproofed, window-tinted limousine.

"How we have sex?"

"Seems fine," said Paul.

"Do you have any critiques? Any."

"Critiques," said Paul. "Um, no."

"Really? You can say."

"Critiques," said Paul.

"Or anything. Any thoughts."

"Um, no. I don't think it's that big of a thing for me: sex."

"Yeah," said Erin vaguely.

"What do you have about that—with me?"

"I have none for you," said Erin.

"Are you sure? You can say it."

"No, you're good at everything—"

"Really?"

"—and you keep it interesting," said Erin.

"Really?"

"And I have orgasms . . . regularly."

Paul made a quiet noise of acknowledgment.

"Everything's good," said Erin.

Paul repeated the noise.

"But I also don't feel like it's a big thing. Do you feel thirsty?"

"We'll get something," said Paul nodding distractedly. "What else?"

"Hm. For sex?"

"Anything," said Paul.

"Anything," said Erin in a child-like voice.

"Um," said Paul, and from somewhere behind them someone began playing piano. Paul instantly felt a sheen of wetness to his now "horizontally seeking," it seemed, eyeballs. In the movie of his life, he knew, now would be the moment—like when a character quotes Coleridge in *Eternal Sunshine of the Spotless Mind* as the screen shows blurry, colorful, festive images of people outside at night—to feel that the world was "beautiful and sad," which he felt self-consciously and briefly, exerting effort to focus instead on the conversation, which was producing its own, unmediated emotions. "Um," he said shifting his MacBook.

"I can hold," said Erin taking the MacBook.

"What else for you?"

"Nothing," said Erin.

"What other questions do you have?"

"I was mainly wondering about the sexual stuff. I like asking questions like this, though."

"Ask me," said Paul mock pleading.

"Do you usually ask questions like this?"

"Um, no. I think it's—some of it's—because we're on drugs."

"Oh yeah," said Erin.

"But we also ask questions at other times."

"Yeah," said Erin. "What do you feel about the drugs thing? In terms of your life, long term."

"Um. I think it's sustainable, as long as I'm healthy. Or I think if I'm really healthy I'll be better off than someone who isn't healthy and doesn't do drugs. And doing drugs encourages me to be healthy, which increases productivity, which seems good. What do you think?"

"I feel like this is the most drugs I've ever done in a period in life," said Erin. "But it's also the healthiest I've been, in life. I think similarly about it."

"In some relationships I would use food to console myself."

"Me too," said Erin. "Big-time."

"There's not that, with us, so that's good."

"Yeah," said Erin. "I've done that a lot."

"Me too. Eating a ton of shitty food. Being excited with the other person about food . . . seems depressing. We also don't drink alcohol, which seems good."

"Yeah," said Erin. "I did the food thing with Harris. And Beau. When you and I had started hanging out, but not romantically or something, I was eating sushi and Beau got something fried and was like 'don't you just want to eat unhealthy things together and bond over that?'"

"None of your boyfriends cared about you eating a lot?"

"Kent wanted me to, like, gain some weight. Harris . . . quietly resented my body, I think, or something. He was really skinny. And I gained like five or ten pounds in the course of dating him. And—"

"What did he resent?"

"Just that—"

"Was he skinnier than me?"

"Maybe . . . yeah. Or, like, less muscular. He was maybe a little bit taller but really small."

"What did he resent?"

"I think 'resent' isn't the right word. I think . . . no, he did resent it because I weighed more than him and I think he didn't like that he had to put up with it, instead of being with a naturally smaller body."

"Then wouldn't he care if you ate a lot?"

"Yeah, but we never stopped eating a lot."

"Oh," said Paul.

"Or maybe he would care, but not that much. I don't know. What is my body . . . do you have problems with my body?"

"No . . . what problems?"

"Or, do you like it?"

"Yeah," said Paul at a higher pitch than normal.

"If you don't you can . . . something," said Erin lightly.

"No, yeah, I do," said Paul. "What would your ideal body be?"

"For me?"

"For a boyfriend," said Paul.

"I don't think I've thought that. Just, like, skinny and healthy looking. Like, I've never minded if . . . hm."

"Not 'minded.' 'Ideal.'"

"Oh. Then yeah."

"What," said Paul.

"I guess weigh a little more than me. Enough to not be self-conscious about it. Or just not care. I don't know. What about—"

"I think my ideal is, like, the same, I think, or—"

"Really?" said Erin.

"Yeah," said Paul, who was an inch taller than Erin and weighed a little less.

"Oh," said Erin anxiously.

"Or, like—" said Paul.

"The same," said Erin.

"But I think overall it doesn't matter that much."

"Yeah," said Erin.

"Because Michelle . . ."

"She seemed really skinny," said Erin.

"I think what matters to me most, in terms of that, is just that things aren't getting worse."

"Yeah," said Erin. "Me too."

"I think I can get fixated on that neurotically."

"I do with myself definitely," said Erin. "You mean for yourself?"

"No," said Paul. "Other people."

"How do you mean?"

"I can become fixated on it."

"On, like, in what way?"

"On what the other person weighs."

"Oh," said Erin.

"I feel like it's neurotic to some degree," said Paul.

"I don't care that much," said Erin ambiguously.

"If they weighed the ideal I would find some other neurotic thing to focus on."

"You would find something else to focus on?"

"Yeah," said Paul.

"Like body-wise, or something else–wise?"

"Something else–wise."

"Oh," said Erin.

"It's not a solution, or something, to find someone with the ideal . . . but focusing on not getting worse seems fine to me."

"Yeah," said Erin.

"Yeah," said Paul slowly.

"Yeah," said Erin. "That seems like . . ."

"You have to focus on something, and—"

"7-Eleven," said Erin pointing.

"Huh?" said Paul, distracted from the conversation for the first time since he heard the piano, and couldn't remember what he'd wanted to say. He followed Erin into 7-Eleven, feeling imponderable to himself, like his brain was of him, external as a color, shooting away from its source.

"I feel irritated by all the stuff going on," said Erin on a wide sidewalk parallel to a four-lane street, outside the area of closed-off streets, around twenty minutes later. "Or like I can't concentrate on talking." Paul had become quiet after 7-Eleven and had talked slowly and incoherently, he felt, on topics that didn't interest him, with increasing calmness, and now felt peacefully catatonic, like a person in a photograph, except for a pressure to speak and a vague awareness that he couldn't remember what Erin had last said.

"Do you feel anything from the MDMA?"

"Yeah," said Paul in a bored voice.

"How do you feel?"

"About what?" said Paul.

"Do you feel happy? Or do you feel what?"

"Right now?" said Paul, as if stalling.

"Yeah," said Erin.

"Yeah, happy," said Paul looking down a little, aware his face hadn't moved in a long time. "Physically uncomfortable a little. I want to poop."

"You what? What was the last thing?"

"I want to poop," mumbled Paul.

"I feel like I want to hit people, a little," said Erin grinning.

"Let's go in one of those places," said Paul slowly, with a sensation of not being prepared to speak and not yet knowing what he was saying. He listened to what he'd said and pointed at a building that said PARTY WORLD and, seeing his arm, in his vision, sensed he hadn't carried his MacBook in a long time and should offer to carry it soon.

"Yeah," said Erin distractedly.

They walked silently for around forty seconds.

"What are you thinking about?"

"I don't know," said Paul honestly. "What are you?"

"I thought 'I wonder what we're going to do.' Then I thought 'we aren't talking anymore—oh no, why aren't we talking anymore.' You're not upset about anything?"

Paul shook his head repeatedly.

"Okay, okay," said Erin.

"No," thought Paul emotionlessly.

"People seem to be looking a lot, at the computer."

"I haven't . . . noticed anyone," said Paul.

"Oh," said Erin uncertainly. "I haven't—"

"I haven't been looking at anyone."

"I haven't either, really, except sometimes if I look out somebody will be looking. I forgot we're not in America."

"I like how quiet it is," said Paul.

"Me too," said Erin.

"In New York it would be so loud."

"Yeah. There would be, like, layers upon layers of noises."

"I don't like places . . . where everyone working is a minority . . . because I feel like there's too many different . . . I don't know," said Paul with a feeling like he unequivocally did not want to be talking about what he was talking about, but had accidentally focused on it, like a telescope a child had turned, away from a constellation, toward a wall.

"Like, visually?"

"Um, no," said Paul. "Just that . . . they know they're minorities . . ."

"That they, like, band together?"

"Um, no," said Paul on a down escalator into the MRT station they exited around an hour ago.

"What are we doing?" said Erin in a quiet, confused voice.

Paul felt his diagonal movement as a humorless, surreal activity—a deepening, forward and down.

"Minorities," said Erin at a normal volume. "What were you saying?"

"Just that . . . here, when you see someone, you don't know . . . that . . . they live like two hours away and are um . . . poor, or whatever," said Paul very slowly, like he was improvising an erasure poem from a mental image of a page of text.

"Is this the mall? Thing?"

"No, bathroom," mumbled Paul.

"Huh?" said Erin.

"Bathroom," said Paul after a few seconds.

•••

In the MRT station Paul said he tried masturbating and couldn't and that he was worried he vomited some of his MDMA earlier, because he didn't feel much. Erin said she felt like she was "feeling it a lot more" than Paul and laughed a little and said Paul should "go back and take more."

"Really?" said Paul quietly.

"Yeah. Because I feel like if you were also feeling it . . ."

"What," said Paul.

"Now I feel myself being chill, or something. Or I don't know. I didn't know what was going on. I thought it seemed like you weren't feeling anything."

"Really?" said Paul with earnest wonderment.

"Yeah. Let's just go back and do more, then come back."

"All right," said Paul in a voice as if reluctantly acquiescing.

"Do you want that?"

"Yeah. I'll take two, you take one."

"Okay," said Erin.

"But . . . now I'm going to have it stronger than you."

"I'll take one and a half," said Erin.

After both ingesting two ecstasy and, almost idly, as sort of afterthoughts, because it had been very weak the past few times, a little LSD, they exited Paul's room, and Erin went to the bathroom. Paul's mother asked Paul what clothes he bought. Paul said he didn't yet and his mother said he should buy thicker clothing and they discussed where, at this time, around 10:30 p.m., to find open stores. When Erin exited the bathroom Paul's mother asked if she bought any clothes.

"No," said Erin smiling. "Not yet."

"Okay," said Paul in Mandarin. "We're going now."

"Cell phone," said Paul's mother in Mandarin.

"I've got it," said Paul in Mandarin.

"Bring a cell phone," said Paul's father in Mandarin from out of view, watching TV.

"Why are you bringing your computer?" said Paul's mother in Mandarin.

"We, just," said Paul in Mandarin.

"Oh, you're going to record again," said Paul's mother in Mandarin in a slightly scolding voice, but without worry, it seemed, maybe because she could see that Paul was the same as last year. "The 'video thing,' isn't it better?"

"What video thing?"

"I sent it to you. I bought it for you. For your birthday. Did you already sell it?"

"No. I have it in my room."

"What's it called?"

"Flip cam," said Paul.

"Dad went to many different places asking which was the best. Why don't you use it?"

"What are you all talking about?" said Paul's father idly in Mandarin from out of view.

"My mom probably knows we're on drugs, or something," said Paul after they'd walked around two minutes without talking. "She sounded suspicious when she saw us recording. But she seemed okay with it. I searched my emails with her earlier and . . . she said something like 'it's okay to experience new things but don't overdo it,' or like 'it's probably good for a writer to experiment,' and she was talking about cocaine, I think."

"I thought your mom was completely against drugs."

"Me too," said Paul. "I forgot an entire period of emails where she seemed okay with it. My brother, I think, told her, at one point, that I had too much self-control to become addicted to anything. My brother told her not to worry, I think. I don't know."

"I haven't swallowed the LSD yet," said Erin at a red light a few minutes later. "My throat won't push it down to my stomach, it's weird." Paul distractedly pointed at a billboard of disabled people, then looked at Erin's tattoo of an asterisk behind her earlobe as she looked at the billboard. "In Taiwan only disabled people, I think, can sell lottery tickets," said Paul slowly while imagining being heard by thousands of readers of a future book, or book-like experience, in which Erin's name had an asterisk by it, indicating the option of stopping the narrative to learn about Erin, in the form of a living footnote, currently pointing the MacBook at the three-lane street, on which hundreds of scooters and motorcycles passing, in layers, with more than one per lane, at different speeds, appeared like a stationary, patternless shuffling.

"Swarming," Erin was saying. "Swarm. Swarm."

"My mom warned against getting hit by a car," said Paul.

"Does it happen a lot?"

"I don't know," said Paul as a car honked. "I don't know."

"I kind of have to pee again," said Erin crossing the street.

"You have to pee? We'll find somewhere."

"In my public-speaking class, on the last day, this guy spoke about how he has kidney failure and can't pee. At all. He poops his pee."

"He doesn't even have a tube?"

"No," said Erin.

"How old is he?"

"Twenty-four," said Erin.

"Whoa," said Paul.

"Yeah. And he has a big thing in his arm—his dialysis machine."

"From drinking alcohol?"

"He didn't say why," said Erin, and a man wearing a motorcycle helmet in the near distance walked briskly across the sidewalk, seeming "too comfortable in his motorcycle helmet," thought Paul with mock disapproval, into a 7-Eleven.

"What if we just moved here," said Paul.

"Let's move here," said Erin with enthusiasm.

"Since we don't have friends. What would we do all the time?"

"Work on writing," said Erin. "We'd have to go back, to do promotion things."

"We can pay people to pretend to be us."

"Interns," said Erin.

"Backpacks," said Paul a few minutes later about a vat-like container of generic-looking backpacks, outside a footwear store. "What do you think of these?"

"They seem good. Simple."

"Your red backpack . . . is really dirty," said Paul, and laughed nervously.

"It only looks dirty. I clean it a lot."

"Backpack," said Paul touching a black backpack.

"I would buy one but my mom said she's buying me one for Christmas," said Erin.

After peeing in an MRT station they decided to find a McDonald's and improvise *Taiwan's First McDonald's*. Paul's MacBook had seventy-two minutes of battery power remaining. They couldn't find a McDonald's, after around five minutes, but two Burger Kings were in view, so they decided to do *Taiwan's First Burger King*, then crossed a street and saw a McDonald's, six to ten blocks away. "Let's not talk until we get there," said Paul. "But start thinking."

"Let's not think of what to say, let's just do it," said Erin.

"Just as an experiment, let's not talk until we get there."

"Oh," said Erin. "Okay, okay."

Paul stared at her with an exaggeratedly disgusted expression, which she reciprocated. They ran diagonally across three lanes to a median and held their open palms out to motorcyclists advancing in the spaces between slow-moving and stopped cars, as if by vacuum suction. Two people on one motorcycle shouted "hey, hey, go, yeah!" and slapped Erin's palm. Paul and Erin, both smiling widely, crossed to a sidewalk and turned toward McDonald's. Paul took the MacBook and stared in earnest fascination—feeling almost appalled, but without aversion—as Erin ran and leaped stomach-first onto the front of a parked car, then speed-walked away with arms tight against her sides, crossing Paul's vision, supernatural and comical as a mysterious creature on YouTube, before calmly taking the MacBook. Paul stared angrily at the sidewalk with his body bent forward, imagining a powerful magnet dragging him by a strip of metal at the top of his forehead. He began hitting his head with balled fists. Erin hit his head, and he instantly stared at her in mock disbelief. Erin grasped the floor of an invisible opening midair with both arms extended, not fully, above her. Paul, staring with earnest astonishment, imagined a ventilation-system-like tunnel and pulled her arms down while trying to feign an expression of "feigned disgust unsuccessfully concealing immense excitement," as if Erin had unknowingly discovered the entrance to a place Paul had recently stopped trying (after a decade of research, massive debt, the inadvertent nurturing of an antisocial personality) to locate. He laughed and continued ahead and—two blocks later, nearing McDonald's, which had a suburban-seeming front yard of quadrilaterals of grass, a sidewalk, gigantic Christmas tree, lighted menu, driveway for the drive-thru—he accelerated and entered McDonald's saying "let's get a shot with a lot of background activity to lure them back with the rewatches," and after a few seconds, because the first floor had only an ordering counter, was ascending stairs, to the second floor, where eight to twelve people were in forty to sixty seats.

"Try to find a celebrity face to stand in front of," said Erin.

"I'm going to wash my face, I can't appear like this," said Paul grinning, and went to the bathroom. When he returned Erin was picking at her hair, with elbows locked above her head, hands moving inward in a kind of puppetry, or to cast spells on her head. She left for the bathroom. Christmas music played on a loop, repeating every forty or fifty seconds. Paul looked at what seemed to be a group of mute people in a separate, attached, somewhat private room and thought of a documentary about a woman who became deaf and mute as a teenager and remained on her bed feeling depressed, she said, for fifteen years before devoting her life to traveling across Germany teaching the deaf-mute language and "bringing out" those, born deaf-mute, with whom communication had never been attempted. Paul was absently drumming the table with his hands when Erin returned. He stood and said they should start the documentary outside, pointed at the attached room, said "look, those people are mute, I think."

Erin seemed confused and slightly frightened.

"Mute," said Paul. "It's a group of mute people."

"Oh, mute. Jesus, I thought I was having a drug thing."

"Jesus," said Paul.

"They're like how we were," said Erin.

"Oh yeah," said Paul.

"When we couldn't talk, I felt like I had to talk," said Erin descending stairs. "But I had nothing to say. I just felt encompassed by the limits."

They sat on a grassy area of the median—after deciding to begin *Taiwan's First McDonald's* "in the middle of traffic"— and criticized their own, while complimenting each other's, hair and faces for three minutes until Paul abruptly stood and said "let's go inside" with a sensation of "surveying" the premises, though his eyes were unfocused.

"I started feeling things big-time," said Erin.

"Me too," said Paul.

"Big-time style," said Erin, and they ran across the street into McDonald's, to the second floor. "We're back . . . here . . . again," said Paul, and laughed a little while feeling the situation was hilarious.

"Yeah," said Erin laughing, and they returned outside.

"You be the host," said Paul pointing the MacBook at Erin, who stood in front of the lighted menu the size of a blackboard.

"For Bravo," said Erin.

"Use 'the voice.' Just don't grin."

"Okay, okay," said Erin.

"Just don't grin," said Paul.

"Well, here's the flagship, uh, Taipei's fir—"

"Let me try," said Paul giving Erin the MacBook.

Erin made noises indicating failure, self-disgust.

"So this is the first McDonald's to open, in, um, well, Taiwan," said Paul. "It opened on . . . Tuesday. They had the grand opening special of three patties." He moved his ear to an image of a Double Filet-O-Fish on the menu and said "it doesn't want to be filmed" to Erin, who said "the camera is not on" with exaggerated enunciation to the Double Filet-O-Fish. "Here is . . . this is Hillary Clinton's hairstyle," said Paul pointing at lettuce protruding from a chicken sandwich.

"Tactical, um," said Erin.

"Explosions," said Paul after a few seconds.

"Well, yeah," said Erin.

"Jesus," said Paul, and they both grinned a little. "All right. Now we'll go inside for a closer look . . . at the conflict, the controversy." Through the glass front a deliveryman, wearing a motorcycle helmet, peeked around a corner at the ordering counter. "It's been said that he's actually the founder of McDonald's," said Paul. "They stole his idea, now he just looks. I actually just heard someone talking about it over there. That guy!"

Erin pointed the MacBook at a man scurrying away from McDonald's.

"He won't go 'on the record,'" said Paul. "He's too afraid."

"Let's move inside," said Erin, and pointed at a PUSH sticker. "Oh, this is actually—"

"They had to add that. Because people actually were trying to, um—"

"Pull," said Erin.

"Yeah, pull," said Paul grinning, and didn't move for two seconds, unsure if there was more to say about the PUSH sticker, then took the MacBook and entered McDonald's. "Now, this," he said about a tall structure obscured by colorful balloons.

"It's been said that this is actually a performance art piece. It's meant to represent . . . just universal peace," said Erin, and an employee walked between the structure and the MacBook with an expression like everything but his mouth was grinning.

"I noticed this employee is running a little," said Paul following him to the second floor. "Does that mean something?"

"Well, it's sort of characteristic of our times," said Erin.

"Who are these people?" said Paul pointing at one of four preadolescent Caucasian girls in a blown-up photo on a wall.

"These are all Cameron Diaz's children," said Erin.

"Why are there spaces between this one's teeth?"

"Well, the meat fills in, then they put it into one burger."

"And the rest is just hair and stuff?"

"That's—actually, we shouldn't reveal that," said Erin.

"And this is for . . . ten thousand chicken nuggets?" said

Paul pointing at the space of a missing tooth. "The gelatin required from the teeth."

"Yeah," said Erin. "And actually for some . . . if you pay extra you can get a little bit of a tooth, from an actual child, and you can also get it memorialized, in a locket."

"If a country pays extra, their nuggets get more gelatin?"

"Yes," said Erin. "The quality is just slightly raised."

"I heard that Canada did that," said Paul.

"Um, just the Saskatchewan. They're the prime testing markets. Because they eat . . . they primarily eat teeth there. That's their diet, I didn't know if you knew that."

"The Weakerthans wrote an album about that, right?"

"Yeah, they—" said Erin.

"*Fallow*?" said Paul.

"*Fallow*," said Erin confidently.

"That was about the teeth—" said Paul.

"The Saskatchewan teeth crisis," said Erin.

"This is where the district managers have their weekly meetings," said Erin a few minutes later in a circular room—wallpapered with blown-up photos of children on bikes, and pogo sticks, in the foreground of a playground, at dusk—with a padded floor and, at its center, a playground of two slides, monkey bars, a pole, a tiny bridge. Paul said a girl had different eye sizes because she was on a "McFlurry-only diet" and asked Erin about a Hispanic girl wearing giant, padded headphones. "She's actually producing right now," said Erin. "She's a producer."

"What's her favorite McDonald's meal?"

"She just gets a side salad," said Erin.

"Are you serious?"

"Yeah, that's her thing," said Erin pointing at what seemed

like an Ash Wednesday marking on her forehead. "See? She's Zen."

"Let's go to the opposite side of the spectrum: this girl."

"She gets six Big Macs," said Erin about a pale, red-haired girl sitting in a sandbox. "She puts it all in the McFlurry machine. And the Oreos come down."

"Jesus. She puts it in the machine? This girl?"

"She extracts the sauce from the Big Macs, and she puts that in a cup," said Erin.

"So she brings it home?"

"It's 'on the go.' She'll just bring it anywhere."

"Then what?"

"Then her interns are instructed to massage her, because she's actually a candidate for the next McChicken sandwich."

"You could be eating her tomorrow," said Paul to an imagined, future viewer of *Taiwan's First McDonald's*, and turned the MacBook to the girl with giant headphones. "You ate her. Now you might be eating the other one." He panned the MacBook across half the room. "Or one of these, anyway."

"Can you talk about him?" said Erin about a chubby, closed-mouth smiling boy on a bike with training wheels, and took the MacBook. "You shouldn't leave him out."

"Sure. This is one of the great failures of the Chicken McNugget raising program. This photo is actually . . . they told him he was supplying Thailand's artificial flavoring from 2010 to 2020. He was really happy, which was his mistake."

"They're actually going to tell her," said Erin pointing at a girl, half obscured by a bored-looking dog, midair on a pogo stick. "She's supplying Thailand until 2020, with a nonexclusive option at extending her contract."

"Nice," said Paul.

"She's Miss Thailand," said Erin.

"This one doesn't know he's also going to be one," said

Paul about a boy on swings at the apex of his backward movement. "They're all going to be one."

"Well, yeah. Someday."

"Even you," said Paul.

"I'm . . . uniquely . . ."

"You know you're going to be a Chicken McNugget."

"I've accepted it," said Erin.

They approached stairs—blocked by a dry mophead and
what seemed to be a traffic cone—to a third floor, a few minutes later, ascending to a small dark room of additional seat-
ing, kaleidoscopically lit from outside sources through two
windows.

"It took them five years to Photoshop this," said Paul
pointing at the letter *M* inside a circle on a wall. "They had to
wait for Adobe to answer a question they had, on a message
board."

"The mother brain," said Erin.

"Shh," whispered Paul tracing the circle with a forefinger.

"Sorry," whispered Erin. "The brainstorming process is in
action."

"Jesus," whispered Paul taking the MacBook carefully.

"This is—" said Erin pointing at a pile of plastic-wrapped
plastic utensils.

"Leftovers," said Paul.

"—just the scraps of ideas that get sold to Burger King
and Arby's on eBay."

"Arby's needs to update its credit card information."

"It will, it always does," said Erin, and approached the
darkest part of the room. "And here we have the brainchild,
really, of this whole operation," she said pointing at where
the wall, due to lack of light, was indiscernible in color and
texture.

• • •

"So, we've shown you what it's about, and what it does, for the country," said Paul in front of the Christmas tree. "Now let's go over the main points again: one."

"Cameron Diaz's foundation," said Erin.

"Two?"

"One-A," said Erin.

"One-A?"

"One-A," said Erin. "And then one-B."

"Um," said Paul grinning, and pointed at the third-floor windows. "We were there."

"The brainstorm. The conspiracy."

"And—remember this?" said Paul pointing at the Double Filet-O-Fish.

"Yeah, whoa. Seems like so long ago."

"And then," said Paul moving toward the entrance.

"The performance art for world peace. Highly suggested."

"The, um," said Paul noticing a headset-wearing employee inside McDonald's, looking at him suspiciously, it seemed. "The arts sector."

"We didn't do the drive-thru."

"Um," said Paul distractedly.

"One of the first, and worst, in Asia," said Erin, and someone behind them said something that Paul didn't comprehend. The person repeated himself. Paul turned around and the headset-wearing employee—a manager, it seemed—repeated himself again, in a sort of pleading voice.

"We aren't," said Paul in Mandarin. "We're only doing video. We finished."

The employee said "you can't" in Mandarin and a word Paul didn't comprehend.

"We won't," said Paul in Mandarin. "There's just us two only."

"Skype," said Erin quietly.

"Vacation," said Paul, and the employee looked at Erin, then Paul. They were standing where cars, after ordering, would pass to get to the pickup window.

"Oh, okay," said the employee, and smiled a little and, after a pause, moved backward a few steps before turning around, walking away.

"Vacation," said Paul grinning.

"Skype," said Erin.

"We're on vacation," said Paul.

"Skype," said Erin grinning, and they entered a dark, quiet, residential area of tall buildings behind McDonald's, then briefly explored "one of the more glamorous alleyways in Taipei," said Paul, before returning to McDonald's "front yard," where a young man wearing a scratched, black, melon-like helmet and thick-lensed glasses, standing at a bike rack, with two McDonald's bags in his bike's basket, stared carelessly into the distance as his hands, below him, fumbled idly with his bike lock, it seemed.

"The binge in action," said Erin. "Yet another successful binge operation."

"This is the best part of the binge. He's imagining the nuggets. He's already imagining his next trip. So much so that this is it . . . this is the next trip."

"The infinite loop of binge eating," said Erin.

"We're looking at his mental projection of himself."

"We're inside his brain right now."

"We're looking at our creator," said Paul grinning wildly.

"Shit," said Erin, and laughed. "That's why he can't move." She noticed a few minutes later that the MacBook was "depleted," a word they'd begun using to sympathetically reference anything that had temporarily exhausted a replenishable means.

• • •

On the way back to the apartment, to get a charger, they decided instead of a documentary to make a science-fiction movie, on the conceit that they existed because a young man in Taipei, while eating a bag of Chicken McNuggets, allowed himself (despite knowing this would definitely increase his unhappiness) to realistically imagine his next binge, when he would have two bags. Paul and Erin were constructed by the young man's unconscious, for verisimilitude, as passersby in the peripheral vision of his imaginary next trip to McDonald's. Their memories were not based on a concrete reality but on the meager imaginative powers—enough for only a very short-term, working memory—allotted for the "artificial intelligence" of peripheral passersby.

Paul and Erin discussed their movie in a dialogue that sometimes overlapped with their inner monologues, which they sometimes introduced to the dialogue, or abandoned to focus on the dialogue, or both externalized, like pets into a shared space, to observe. That the universe was how it was, and that certain things seemed incomprehensible, that Paul couldn't, without increasingly unexertable amounts of effort, remember what he didn't store outside himself, as words, in books, that remembering seemed to require as much, or much more, energy as imagining, all seemed, while on LSD, in a context of science fiction, explainable in excitingly interconnected and true-seeming ways.

At the apartment, around 1:30 a.m., they got a charger and Paul wrote a note to his mother that he and Erin were at McDonald's or downstairs. They somehow didn't remember they were on LSD, so didn't discern and attribute the effects of LSD until, on their way to a different McDonald's, crossing a street, Paul realized he was repeatedly becoming conscious of things in medias res, like the information he received from sensory perception wasn't being processed immediately, but at a delay sometimes, resulting in microseconds to seconds of partial—but functioning—unconsciousness.

At the McDonald's where five employees had stood outside with megaphones and banners they sat in a corner on the second floor—the only two customers on the floor—and recorded more footage, using their iPhones, for their science-fiction movie. They regularly reminded each other that the LSD would soon start weakening, as it continued intensifying, to a degree that Paul could sense the presence of a metaphysical distance, from where, if crossed, he would not be able to return, therefore needed to focus, with deliberate effort, against a default drifting in that direction. Around 4:30 a.m. they walked twelve blocks to the apartment, holding hands and concentrating on and reminding each other of the task—to walk to the apartment without getting lost or hit by a car.

They looked at the internet in a downstairs area until Paul's parents woke, then showered and went outside to a sunny, warm morning. They lay on a suburban area of grass in front of a stadium by the apartment building, no longer excited or interested in their science-fiction movie, having forgotten or become tolerant toward its most exciting, beginning elaborations—discussed most intensely after Paul's MacBook stopped recording. If they existed only in abstraction, as an unconscious aside in someone's brain, this forgetting, indicative of decreasing interest, would be exactly what he would predict to happen, he weakly thought with predictably less interest and clarity, on his back, with eyes closed.

• • •

The next two times they ingested ecstasy they both felt what they termed "overdrive," which for Paul was a whirring, metallic, noise-like presence that induced catatonia and rendered experience toneless—nullifying humor, irony, sarcasm, intimacy, meaning—so that he became like a robot that could discern (but not process, consider, or interrelate) concrete reality. Both times, after forty talkative minutes, Paul became silent and thoughtless and expressionless and suddenly disinterested in Erin and intensely—only sexually—interested in strangers and he tried masturbating in public bathrooms and couldn't orgasm or feel pleasure, to any degree, as if lacking the concept, but felt continuously aroused "somewhere," including sometimes, it seemed, outside his body, a few feet in front of him, or far in the distance, in a certain store or area of sky, or in an overlap, shifting in and out of his chest or head or the front of his face.

Their brand of ecstasy, Erin learned from the internet, contained MDA, which they attributed—unconvincingly, because they'd previously enjoyed the same brand—as the cause of "overdrive."

One night, while sober, they were at a red light at a busy, quiet—unnaturally muffled, it seemed—intersection of a four-lane street and an eight-lane street, into the X of which a two-lane street asymmetrically stopped, as if the intersection had been built to memorialize where a traveler, by choice or not, had stopped going somewhere.

Paul felt an oppressive sensation of being confined by the most distant things he could see in any direction, like after Michelle had walked away and he'd stood motionless in the rain, except then there'd also been a feeling of possibility, a glimmer of eagerness as he walked over the shiny, wet street, to return to the party. In an effort to distract from this feeling he asked, somewhat unexpectedly, what Erin was thinking—they'd stopped asking because it was always something depressing—and, with a slight grin, he saw peripherally, she said she'd been thinking that Paul needed to return her, like a broken appliance to a store, because she needed to be replaced with a newer, upgraded model. Paul stared ahead, wishing she hadn't said that. "No," he said grinning vaguely, unsure exactly how—but suspecting strongly that—their relationship due to what she'd said had changed in some notable, irreversible manner.

The next night in a bookstore near Taipei 101, the third-tallest building in the world, an hour after ingesting MDMA, walking aimlessly with held hands, Paul "grimly," he earnestly felt, asked what Erin was thinking about, and she said she was having paranoid thoughts again, "like maybe it's not the drugs, maybe we just don't have anything to talk about anymore." Paul thought she was right, but argued against her by saying they had been spending too much time together—that, in his other relationships, one or both people would have work or school. They sat holding each other on the floor in the fiction section and decided to not ingest their remaining two ecstasy and to be apart from each other four hours a day. Paul was wearing a striped sweater he and Erin bought, a few days ago, solely because it was comically not his normal style.

Manually descending a down escalator, about an hour later—holding Erin's hand, leading them past people standing in place—Paul realized he was (and, for an unknown amount of time, had been) rushing ahead in an unconscious, misguided effort to get away from where he was: inside himself. Concurrent with this realization was an awareness of himself from a perspective thousands of feet above, plainly showing he was doing what he logically knew he did not want to do (that he dreaded doing, in the same way he dreaded the remaining seconds on the down escalator, the minutes walking to the MRT station and waiting for the train, the six-minute walk from the station to the apartment, waiting for the elevator and lying in bed until an instantaneous transport to the next day's minutes—was there no reprieve even in sleep?—he'd always felt comforted by sleep and now felt confused by it) and yet, even now, discerning this, kept doing what caused this realization.

On Christmas Eve, when Erin returned from the bathroom and lay on the bed, ready to sleep, it seemed, Paul asked if she'd had any thoughts, since arriving in Taiwan, about showering.

"Not really," she said after a few seconds.

"I noticed you don't shower at night anymore. Or haven't the last two nights."

"I don't shower every night."

"You did . . . before Taiwan."

"I only shower at night if I noticeably smell," said Erin. "There've been nights I haven't, with you."

The next few minutes, sensing something combative and offendable in her—that he hadn't before—Paul felt increasingly careful of his word choice and tone of voice. Erin stood, at some point, and was moving around the room. Paul said something about an area of the bed smelling bad, and Erin said "I'm stinky, all right, you're right, I'll go shower, I have stinky feet" loudly, and left the room, closing the door with force. When she returned, maybe ten minutes later, Paul's heart was still beating considerably harder than normal and he immediately left the room. In the nearly pitch-black hallway Dudu's wet nose softly touched the back of Paul's leg, when they apparently moved in the same direction, toward the bathroom. In the shower Paul earnestly thought about how to extricate himself from the marriage—what to do about their film company, how to behave the next ten days, what he and Erin would separately do each day, what to say to his parents—but when he returned to his room Erin apologized, which he hadn't expected, and he reiterated that they'd happily agreed, a month ago, that if either person wanted the other to shower or brush their teeth, or anything like that, they'd state it immediately and directly and impersonally, instead of accumulating resentment.

"There are things I'm still sensitive about," said Erin.

Paul said he had felt most upset by her sarcasm when she said she was stinky and how she left suddenly and sort of slammed the door. Erin said she had been joking, in an effort to downplay the situation, and hadn't meant to slam the door. Paul said he hadn't felt—or suspected, at all—that she was joking. Erin slept on her side facing away.

In the morning Paul read an email from his mother, whose bedroom shared a wall with his, asking him to please try to be nicer to Erin, who remained on her side facing away, though she seemed awake. Paul showered for around forty-five minutes, continuing to mentally prepare to be single, and was unaware of the time until, after putting on clothes, his father said the taxi he'd called to drive them to the café hosting Paul's reading—his mother was already there—was downstairs. Paul expected no response—or a begrudging one, maybe—as he explained to Erin, who was still facing away, in a voice he controlled to sound neutral that a taxi was waiting and that she didn't have to go to his reading but it would be awkward if she didn't because reservations had been made for dinner immediately after, in a nice restaurant, with many relatives, to celebrate their marriage. Paul felt emotional and surprised when, after a few seconds, during which her body visibly relaxed, easing a tension Paul hadn't discerned, Erin stood and softly said she didn't know the reading was today and, prioritizing the situation, over her feelings, became accommodating and goal oriented, quickly and gracefully getting dressed and preparing to leave.

In the taxi's backseat, between Erin and his father, Paul pointed at a bright red, metal, pointy roof outside his father's side's window. "Look at that roof," he said in Mandarin, and pushed a blue ecstasy into Erin's mouth—against teeth, then inside, touching her tongue a little—while his father talked about slanted versus flat roofs. Paul, grinning convolutedly, pointed again and asked how to say "corrugated" in Mandarin and put their last ecstasy in his own mouth.

Dinner, after the reading—with Paul's parents, uncle, uncle's girlfriend, uncle-in-law, great-uncle, two aunts, five cousins—was in a restaurant whose interior lighting, circuited into pillars and walls and the ceiling and bathrooms, though probably not in the kitchen, had been coordinated to undulate fluidly and cyclically, as one, yellow to red to purple to blue to green, seeming egregiously LSD themed.

Paul's father talked the most, by far, usually to no one specific, during the hour-long dinner. When he spoke people became attentive to him, but passively, at their leisure, with neutral expressions, as if watching an infomercial, neither annoyed nor entertained, feeling no obligation to respond or engage. Whenever he finished with a topic, sometimes to the accompaniment of his own laughter, people seemed to uniformly and inhumanly return, like foam mattresses, to how they were before, profoundly unfazed. At one point, in what seemed like a major faux pas, in part because Paul's cousin's father, Paul's uncle, was present and seemed depressed, Paul's father tried—for maybe five minutes, with no external feedback except two or three grunting noises from his target—to recruit Paul's cousin, a few years older than Paul, to work for him selling lasers on commission. He'd tried the same, at previous dinners, with both Paul and Erin—and, at dinners last year, just Paul, who suspected his father felt as amused by his behavior, in this regard, as Paul and Erin, who'd said "your dad tried to recruit me to work for him" four or five times the past week.

Paul's relatives, though somewhat withdrawn and/or alienated from one another, seemed peaceful as a group, maybe because there didn't appear to be any pressure for anyone to do anything they didn't want to do, such as talk or smile. Paul's mother and her older sister, best friends for decades, now seemed like polite, recent acquaintances who secretly disliked each other for admittedly irrational and/or superficial reasons.

After dinner Paul and Erin followed Paul's uncle and Paul's uncle's girlfriend to their car, to be driven, at Paul's mother's suggestion, to where young people went to buy clothes. Failing to operate a refrigerator-size parking meter, which Paul had never seen before, Paul's uncle grinned and said something in Mandarin conveying idle bemusement regarding his decreasing ability to comprehend and maneuver himself through an increasingly surreal environment. In the BMW's backseat Paul remembered, with embarrassment, when as a child, on the way to Ponderosa, in this car, his uncle suggested to Paul's mother, his little sister, a restaurant that was the same as Ponderosa but used "fresher ingredients." Paul's mother had asked Paul, who had responded with a noise, causing six to ten relatives to eat at Ponderosa.

Paul didn't notice his uncle had turned around in his seat, and was grinning slightly, until he heard him say "you're getting out here also" in Mandarin. The car was parked on the side of a street and Paul's uncle's girlfriend had gotten out.

Paul's uncle, who spoke English fluently, congratulated Erin then carefully said two sentences to her and maybe Paul, who was remembering how he'd been surprised—and complicatedly moved—once when his uncle talked about buying and liking Michael Jackson's music, in this car, after asking if Paul, who doesn't remember what he answered, or how old he'd been, maybe 10 or 11, liked Michael Jackson.

At the airport, after a silent taxi ride, around 7:30 a.m., Paul's mother stood with Paul and Erin in line to check in luggage. Paul peripherally noticed his mother facing away, a little, with only her neck slightly turned. He looked at her and she turned her neck farther, so that he was looking at her looking elsewhere, then she turned, openly crying, toward him and said in a child-like but controlled voice that she was leaving before she started crying harder. She reflexively opened her mouth in a similar manner as when Paul had "caught" her, last year, putting sugar in her coffee, but the effect now was of further embarrassment, past helplessness, to disengagement, then withdrawal.

Paul, whose eyes had become instantly watery, hadn't seen her like this before. He thought of her mother, who had died before Paul was born—and was aware, with momentary clarity, which did not elucidate or console, but seemed to pointlessly reiterate, of how, in the entrance-less caves of themselves, everyone was already, always orphaned—and they briefly hugged and she hugged Erin and uncharacteristically left.

6

Paul was in Bobst Library's first basement floor, seated at a computer, becoming increasingly, "neurotically," he knew, fixated on his aversion toward Erin's red backpack, on the possibility that she would have it with her when he went upstairs, in fifteen minutes, to meet her and that, in its presence, he would feel upset. He hadn't seen her in three weeks, since a few days after returning from Taiwan, when she returned to Baltimore, where a drunk driver had repeatedly rammed her mother's car, breaking her mother's hip and badly injuring Erin's face, which the hospital had said would heal, without scarring, in four months. Erin was wearing large, black-rimmed glasses—to block her face, she said, and they hugged.

"Sorry," said Erin with a blank expression.

"About what?" said Paul, aware he'd felt only self-conscious when he noticed the red backpack, in his vision like a dot on a screen during an optometrist's exam.

"Face," said Erin. "My face."

"You look good, don't worry."

They walked holding hands toward Union Square, ten blocks north. Paul sometimes looked away, so Erin wouldn't see his depressed expression. He'd begun to worry, some days, for hours at a time, that he was permanently losing interest in Erin, despite earnestly wanting, he felt, the opposite, if that were possible. "You have the red backpack," he said grinning slightly, with some confusion.

"I do," said Erin in a tired voice.

Paul sustained his grin tensely.

"What do you feel about that?"

"I don't know," said Paul looking away.

"I know you don't like it."

"It's . . . just," said Paul.

"I'll buy a new one tomorrow."

"No," said Paul quietly.

"I have a gift card."

"I thought your mom was buying you one for Christmas."

"So did I," said Erin.

On his mattress, on their sides, holding Erin from behind, Paul thought he wouldn't end the relationship now, or at any time while Erin's face, which after two and a half weeks looked like it had been recently stung by eight to twelve bees, was still healing, even if he knew he wanted to, which he didn't.

But he wouldn't not end the relationship now, if he knew he wanted to, because it would be pitying and misleading, which Erin wouldn't want, based on what he knew, but maybe she wouldn't care, if she didn't know, which she wouldn't. Paul thought that he would stop thinking about himself and focus on Erin, but instead, almost reflexively, as a method of therapy, began thinking about suicide, then became aware of himself, a few minutes later, earnestly considering—or maybe only imagining—trying to convince Erin that they should commit suicide together. After an initial, default "open-mindedness" they could easily become fixated, then would want to do it quickly, while it made sense. They would find information on the internet and hurry to a subway station, or wherever, collaborating intimately again, looking out at the world from a new and shared perspective. Paul began to feel, in a way he hadn't before, like he comprehended double suicide—the free and mysterious activity of it, like a roller coaster descending only into darkness, but accessible from anywhere, on the theme park of Earth, always open.

He sensed his vicinity to a worldview—or a temporary configuration of preferences, two or three ideas introduced to a mood—in which double suicide would be as difficult, as illogical, to resist as a new sushi restaurant to a couple that likes sushi and trying new restaurants. He felt scared, and to distance himself from what he might accidentally engage in, or be absorbed by, in a moment of inattention or daydreaming, he opened his eyes and leveraged himself and looked over Erin's shoulder with an extremely troubled expression. To his surprise—and self-consciously private confusion, relocated immediately away from the front of the face, to study later—she looked serene and was smiling a little, it seemed.

•••

Three weeks later they were seated in Sunshine Cinema—at a showing of *Somewhere* that would begin in five minutes—and had ingested Xanax, which hadn't taken effect, when Paul, staring at the screen, said in a monotone that he wanted to talk about their relationship. Immediately, in a sort of rush, which indicated to Paul that she wished she had said it first, an otherwise unfazed Erin said she also wanted to talk about their relationship. Paul said he felt bad about it, but didn't know what to do, or what else to say. Erin said she felt the same. They talked, staring at the screen, during previews—mostly reiterating that they felt bad, didn't know what to do, didn't know what else to say—and stopped, when the movie began, without resolution.

At some point, the past two or three weeks, Paul had begun to imaginarily hear Erin quietly sobbing—whenever she was in a bathroom with the sink on, and sometimes when in bed, beside him—in a manner as if earnestly trying to suppress uncontrollable crying, not like she was crying for attention, or allowing herself to cry. He would concentrate on discerning if the crying was real, and would become convinced, to a large degree, every time, that it was, despite learning, every time—seeing, to his consistent surprise, a friendly expression mostly—that it was not.

Paul became aware of himself staring, "transfixed," at the center of the screen, with increasing intensity and no thoughts. He focused on resisting whatever force was preventing him from moving his head or neck or eyeballs until finally—suddenly, it seemed—he calmly turned his head a little and asked if Erin was bored.

"I don't know. Are you?"

"I can't tell," said Paul. "Are you?"

"Maybe a little. Do you want to go?"

"Yeah," said Paul, and slowly stood.

• • •

On the L train Paul held Erin in a way that her head and upper body were on his lap, but her legs remained as if she were sitting upright, aware he was doing this—was holding her head to his lap—to mitigate pressures to talk to, or look at, each other. Erin sat up, at some point, and Paul began to speak, in vague continuation of their conversation before the movie, slowly and mostly incomprehensibly, unsure what he was trying to say. Gradually, by focusing on what he'd already said, in the past ten to twenty seconds, he learned that he seemed to be trying to convey that both he and Erin were depressed, which he realized they both already knew. He only felt motivated to say anything at all because he was on Xanax, he knew, and remembered he had Ambien in his pocket and shared one, then another, with Erin, who had sat up, then became aware of himself trying to passive-aggressively convey something by directly saying he wanted to feel pressured to concurrently be a depressed writer and fashion model.

"I don't know what you're talking about," said Erin.

"I just feel . . . depressed," said Paul, and weakly grinned.

"Is there anything I can do to make you feel less depressed?"

"I don't think so," said Paul. "You're depressed."

"What can I do, at this point, to help our relationship?"

"I don't know," said Paul feeling that he was more expressing himself than answering a question, and they got off the train.

"Anything at all," said Erin in a hollow voice.

"I don't want to tell anyone what to do," said Paul staring ahead.

"You wouldn't be. You'd just be answering my question."

•••

In Sel De Mer, a seafood restaurant four blocks from Paul's apartment, seated at the bar, Erin asked if Paul wanted more Xanax and he said "shouldn't we not 'go overboard'?"

"What do you mean?"

"We had Ambien and Xanax."

Erin appeared unresponsive.

"Never mind," said Paul. "Yes. I want more." After sharing 2mg Xanax, then ordering, he absently ate all the free bread and butter, and they sat staring ahead, not speaking or moving, until Erin said she felt weird.

"Me too. I don't know what to say."

"Let's just stop fighting," said Erin.

"Okay," said Paul.

"Okay," said Erin after a few seconds.

"Do you want more Xanax? I don't feel that much."

"Yeah," said Erin, and they shared 2mg Xanax.

When Paul's salad and clam chowder arrived he moved something fried from the salad, with a feeling of efficacy, into the soup, then ate it with a spoon. His steamed lobster with fries and Erin's broiled monkfish with mesclun salad arrived. He ate his fries using all his butter and ketchup and, at her offer, most of Erin's butter. "I feel better," he murmured.

"What?"

"I feel better, due to Xanax, I think. How do you feel?"

"I don't know," said Erin. "Okay, I guess."

At Paul's apartment they drank green juice and showered, then performed oral sex on each other, showered again, turned off the light to sleep. Paul said they should be on Xanax all the time. Erin said "we're probably ideal candidates for Xanax prescriptions."

"I'm sure that we are," said Paul, and went to the bathroom with his MacBook and, seated on the toilet, looked at lobsters' Wikipedia page. He typed "immortal animals" in Google and clicked "The Only Immortal Animal on Earth" and saw a jellyfish on a website that looked like it was made in the late '90s. He copied a sentence, a few minutes later, from Taipei Metro's Wikipedia page—"The growing traffic problems of the time, compounded by road closures due to TRTS construction led to what became popularly known as the 'Dark Age of Taipei Traffic'"—and emailed it to Erin.

Paul entered his room carrying his open MacBook. "This is what you ate," he said showing Erin a photo, captioned "a monkfish in a market," of a glistening, black, mound-shaped mass—grotesque in a melancholy, head-dominated, almost whimsical manner—and she laughed a little.

Ten days later they were on Erin's bed in Baltimore, around 3:45 a.m., watching a Japanese movie about a woman who tortures and murders men. The past two nights they'd ingested large doses of MDMA and low-to-medium doses of Percocet, Adderall, Xanax and today they'd only used a little Adderall. Paul began to sometimes leverage himself above Erin, who would roll onto her back, or remain on her side, loosely enclosed by Paul's arms to either side, as he stared vertically down at her with fixed, impractical, "scary" expressions.

Erin laughed and, the first two times, complimented his effort, then told him to stop, after which he did it again, and thought he wouldn't anymore, then did again, five minutes later, on an impulse, almost uncontrollably—hovering low, with bent elbows, feeling both insane and, in the private room behind the one-way mirror of his exaggeratedly happy expression, like an experimental psychologist—and she began crying in a helpless and cowering manner, which Paul, to some degree, thought was feigned, so remained motionless, for two seconds, during which Erin's face appeared unrecognizable, like the irreducible somethingness of her, in the form of a coded overlay, or invisible mask, had abruptly left, revealing the frightening activity—the arbitrarily reconfiguring, look-less chaos—of a personless face. Paul hugged her so she couldn't see his face and repeatedly said he was sorry and variations of "it's me" and "it's okay." Erin's eyes appeared strangely collapsed beyond closure, like rubber bands overlapping themselves, for a few seconds, after she stopped crying. "It's just that my car is broken," she said earnestly. "I can't get away."

"I would have stopped if I knew you were this scared," said Paul, confused by what she'd been thinking to have imagined escaping in a car.

"You should have stopped when I said stop."

"But people always say to stop. And you were laughing."

"I told you to stop," said Erin.

"You did other times and I kept going and you liked it."

"I know," said Erin, and described how she'd lately felt depressed in a new and scary way, which Paul also had felt lately and described as a sadness-based fear, immune to tone and interpretation, as if not meant for humans—more visceral than sadness, but unlike fear because it decreased heart rate and impaired the senses, causing everything to seem "darker." Sometimes it was less of a feeling than a realization that maybe, after you died, in the absence of time, without a mechanism for tolerance, or means of communication, you could privately experience a nightmare state for an eternity. More than once, the past few weeks, Paul had wondered—idly, without thinking past hypothesis—if books and movies he viewed as melodramatic might be accurately depicting what, since before his book tour, he now sometimes felt. They diagnosed themselves with "severely depleted serotonin levels," caused by forty to eighty doses of MDMA the past three to five months. As Erin's apartment brightened from the morning sun, through sixth-floor windows, they prepared to sleep. Erin stood at a window eating pink tablets that seemed huge—"disk-like," thought Paul with a blanket covering all but his head.

They looked at each other neutrally.

"I feel like those aren't good for you," said Paul.

Erin said a doctor had recommended them and Paul said something implying it was healthier to never listen to doctors.

"How do you know it's not good for me?"

"You'll become dependent, to some degree."

"No, I won't, I rarely take it," said Erin.

"You'll become dependent to a little degree, I'm just saying."

"Did you read about that somewhere?"

"Not specifically," said Paul.

"How do you know, then?"

"Based on what I know, from things I've read and experienced, about tolerance, I think your body will be less able to produce something each time you use those."

"That's not how everything works," said Erin.

"I'm not trying to argue with you, based on what I know," said Paul, aware it was funny to qualify "I'm not trying to argue with you" with "based on what I know," but not feeling humored. He was standing, around twenty minutes later—and had bought a ticket with his iPhone for a bus leaving in an hour—looking at Erin, sitting on her bed facing away. They were both crying a little. It was below freezing and gusty outside, but Paul declined Erin's offer of a jacket and multiple offers to drive him to the bus stop—on an unsheltered bridge—and said bye and self-consciously left.

• • •

In early May, more than two months later, Paul was outside Bobst Library waiting for Peanut—to buy drugs for the next three days, when he and Erin would be in Pittsburgh, for a reading, then in Calvin's mansion for two nights—when he saw Juan walking past and asked what he was doing. Juan said he was buying a Clif Bar and going to the gym and asked what Paul was doing.

"I'm meeting someone to buy drugs."

"What drugs are you buying?"

Peanut was approaching on the sidewalk.

"I'll tell you after, he's there, he probably won't want to see you," said Paul remembering once when he and Erin got in Peanut's car and Peanut became very still a few seconds before quietly saying "yo," and that he'd expected one person.

"I didn't know you was a writer," said Peanut.

"Yeah," said Paul.

"What books you've written?"

"Like five books," said Paul.

"A book's a book," said Peanut, and Paul got in his car. The middle-aged woman in the driver's seat was wearing a baseball cap. Paul wasn't sure if she'd worn it every other time or no other time. Paul asked if Peanut had mushrooms. "No," said Peanut. "But I'm working on that for you."

"What else do you have on you?"

"On me? I've got a bundle of dope."

Paul, walking toward Think Coffee, where Erin was working on writing, told Juan he bought Ketamine, MDMA, Xanax. Juan said when he tried Ketamine he felt like he could feel the solar system flying through space and that he had been on his bed and had pointed the top of his head in the same direction. Paul said he also bought heroin and Juan said he knew people when he was in high school (in Kansas, where he had been arrested for selling marijuana, Paul uncertainly knew) who used heroin and one had died.

"What do you mean?" said Paul vaguely.

"I think he died," said Juan, and they slowed to a kind of loitering, as a policeman, behind them, walked past. They stood in place, then continued walking.

"When did they die?"

"I'm not really sure," said Juan.

"He died," said Paul grinning. "How?"

"I don't know."

"Why did he die?"

"I don't know. I just know he died."

In the morning, while driving, Paul listened to music through earphones and photographed Erin—asleep with her head, against the passenger window, cushioned by the fluffy, patch-work, faded blanket loosely wrapping all but her face, like an oversize astronaut suit with no visor—around ten times with his iPhone. In Baltimore a few days ago she had been drinking tequila alone while cleaning her apartment—she was moving into her father's small house, in which a middle-aged couple rented a room—and later while driving had been stopped by the police. Her mother had screamed at her in an out-of-control manner—for the first time in six years—and her father, somewhat unexpectedly, had gone into "nice mode." Paul remembered a night, eating dinner with Michelle in her mother's house, when he had said he felt depressed. Michelle had gone upstairs silently—the house had thick, soft carpeting everywhere, even on the stairs, so that people sometimes appeared or disappeared without warning—and cried on her bed. Paul was surprised he'd forgotten that night, and emailed himself with his iPhone—

> Remembered being depressed at dinner w Michelle in empty house
>
> While driving to Pittsburgh w Erin asleep
>
> Typed on iPhone in Gmail w right hand
>
> Listening to P. S. Eliot
>
> Left hand on steering wheel

—then vaguely remembered another time when he had remembered the same dinner and had also felt surprised that he'd forgotten.

Paul and Erin were both upset—their default, while sober, at this point—when they arrived in Pittsburgh and each ingested 2mg Xanax. Paul, on a sidewalk outside Erin's car, watched Calvin and Maggie, both grinning, as they approached and hid behind a dumpster, then walked to Paul, who had a depressed expression, which he didn't attempt to hide or mollify.

"Hi," said Calvin after a few seconds.

"We should go to Whole Foods," said Paul.

"Is there a Whole Foods here?" said Maggie.

"Yes, I've been there like ten times," said Paul peripherally aware of Erin exiting her car. "This is where my ex-girlfriend lived. Michelle." He looked at Calvin and Maggie, unsure if they knew of Michelle. In Whole Foods he walked aimlessly at a quick, undeviating pace, with a sensation of haunting the location. He ladled clam chowder into the largest size soup container, chose a baguette, stood in line.

• • •

After the reading, which was on the second floor of a bar, Paul stood in a shadowy room, at a billiards table, eating his baguette and soup. He said "we should have an orgy tonight" to Calvin, who seemed hesitant but curious. Maggie entered the room and stood with them and Paul said "we should have an orgy tonight."

"Yeah, seems good," said Maggie in an uncharacteristic monotone.

"But we should film it," said Paul.

"No, I don't know," said Maggie with unfocused eyes.

"Once we're on MDMA we won't care," said Paul. "About anything."

"Maggie's seventeen," said Calvin grinning weakly.

"That's not underage. We can black out her face."

"I'm not doing that," said Maggie.

"It's not worth doing at all if it's not filmed," said Paul.

"I don't want to be filmed," said Maggie.

"She doesn't want to be filmed," said Calvin.

Erin entered the room and began playing catch with Maggie with a billiards ball. Paul sat on a stack of ten to fifteen chairs and continued eating his baguette and soup, feeling distantly like he was avoiding something that would eventually end his life, except it wasn't avoidable and when it did end his life he wouldn't know, because he wouldn't know anything.

"Should we switch cars, on the drive back?" said Calvin. "Like, Paul and Maggie in Maggie's car, me and Erin in Erin's car?"

"I don't know," said Paul.

"Someone else decide, I'm going to my car to get my sandwich," said Maggie, and went downstairs. Erin was cleaning a stain on the billiards table, it seemed, at the edge of Paul's peripheral vision. Paul went downstairs, where he sat alone in a booth and texted Maggie, asking what kind of sandwich she was eating.

At a red light, around half an hour later, Paul threw a clementine at Erin's car, which was ahead. The light turned green and the clementine missed Erin's moving car. Paul got back in Maggie's car, said he wondered what Calvin and Erin were talking about. "I feel sleepy from the food and Percocet," he said around ten minutes later.

"I like sleeping when I'm cold rather than when I'm warm."

"Me too," said Paul. "Are you going to be hungry tonight?"

"Yeah," said Maggie after a pause.

"I kind of want to eat spaghetti," said Paul, and laughed a little. "Or something."

"I'll make spaghetti," said Maggie.

"No, I don't want to eat spaghetti," said Paul.

"Oh, I thought you wanted to eat spaghetti."

"I don't know," said Paul quickly, and a few minutes later Maggie said her brother turned 4 recently and would say things like "my three-year-old self hates cucumbers" but wouldn't talk about his two-year-old or one-year-old self, which Maggie thought was interesting and wanted to ask why, but kept forgetting.

At Calvin's house everyone ingested more Percocet and Xanax and went in the basement, where Maggie and Calvin each ate a bowl of cereal and Paul, ignoring everyone, to a large degree, talked to Charles on Gmail chat, eventually eating three bowls of cereal. In bed, around 1:30 a.m., Erin asked what Paul and Charles had talked about.

"Nothing," said Paul automatically. "We just talked about feeling depressed."

"What else did you talk about?"

"I don't remember," said Paul.

"Try to," said Erin.

"You can just read it tomorrow."

"Can I read it now?"

"Just read it tomorrow," said Paul.

"Why can't I read it now?"

"Okay," said Paul, and opened his MacBook.

He woke, on his back, to Calvin looking at him from the doorway. He asked if Calvin had used any drugs today. Calvin said he hadn't, and they looked at each other.

"You haven't?" said Paul. "Today?"

"Well, a Percocet, when I woke up."

"When you woke up," said Paul in a monotone.

"Oh yeah—your alarm is going off," said Calvin to Erin. "That's what I came here, to tell you."

"Oh, damn," said Erin, and left the room.

"Are . . . you and Erin . . . having problems?"

"No," said Paul, and laughed a little.

Calvin appeared tired, slightly anxious.

"I mean . . . no," said Paul looking at the ceiling. "No."

"I'm going to my room," said Calvin after a few seconds.

When Erin returned, five minutes later, Paul asked where she'd been.

"In the bathroom," she said. "Where were you?"

"What do you mean? I've been right here."

"I was in the bathroom. Sorry I didn't tell you."

"What do you mean 'where were you?' I was here when you left."

"I know. I'm sorry. I was trying to make a joke. It was . . . 'in bad taste,' I guess."

"Don't apologize about that," said Paul.

After a few seconds Erin rolled over. "I misinterpreted what you said," she said facing away. "I don't want to do that in the future."

"Stop apologizing," said Paul.

"I'm not apologizing," said Erin.

"Okay. Just stop talking about it."

Erin went in the bathroom attached to the guest room, and when the shower turned on Paul immediately heard a quiet, soporific crying like something from nature. He saw Calvin and Maggie jogging into the room and covered himself with a blanket and they jumped on the bed, then repeatedly in place.

In Calvin's SUV, that night, on the way to Target to buy hair dye, because Calvin wanted to dye and cut his hair "really weird," and Maggie had earnestly said "I think I want to color my face too," Erin asked if anyone wanted Xanax; everyone did, in different amounts, which she apportioned. To her right, gently isolated in a one-person seat, holding half a Xanax bar, which was guaranteed to have an effect on him within forty minutes, Paul felt a quaintly affecting comfort and a self-conscious, fleeting urge to ask someone a question or say something nice to someone.

He thought of how, from elementary through high school, if a girl had been nice to him at school or if he got a valuable baseball or Magic: The Gathering card or if he accomplished something in a video or computer game—if for whatever reason he felt significantly, temporarily happier—he would get an urge to talk to his mother and sometimes would go find her, at her makeup station in her bathroom, or outside watering plants, then reveal something about his life or ask her a question about her life, knowing he was making her happy, for a few minutes, before running back to the TV, Nintendo, or computer. Sometimes, half mock scolding, mostly as an amused observation of human nature (she'd also say she recognized the behavior in herself, that she was the same way, with certain people), Paul's mother would tell Paul, who almost always answered her questions, her attempts at conversation, with "I don't know" in a kind of vocal cursive, without disconnected syllables, that he shouldn't only talk to her—to his "poor mother," she'd say—when he felt like talking.

Gradually, after being the target a few times of a similar capriciousness, which he discerned as default behavior for most people, and not liking it, Paul learned to not be more generous or enthusiastic or attentive than he could sustain regardless of his mood and to not talk to people if his only reason to was because he felt lonely or bored.

In college, junior and senior year, when he'd deliberately remained friendless—after his first relationship ended—to focus on writing what became his first book, he would force himself to email his mother (his only regular communication, those two years, once every two to four days) even when he felt depressed and unmotivated. He would always feel better after emailing, knowing his mother would be happy and that, by mastering some part of himself, he'd successfully felt less depressed without bothering, impeding—or otherwise being a distraction in—anyone's life.

Target was closed for an unknown reason. Paul was quiet during the ten-minute drive back to Calvin's mansion, dimly remembering once sitting close with Erin in another backseat, also at night, holding cups of hot tea for warmth. His memories had increasingly occurred to him without context, outside of linear time, like single poems on sheets of computer paper, instead of pages from a book with the page number and book title on top.

They used all their MDMA in Calvin's basement while eating cake, ham, salad, cookies—the first time Paul had eaten food for comfort while on MDMA—then went upstairs to Calvin's room, where Calvin and Maggie drank beer, which Paul and Erin, who had eaten only a little food, declined. Paul began recording, at some point, with his MacBook. "Isn't it a thing?" he said after ingesting Codeine and Flexeril. "That people warn against? Combining drugs."

"Yeah," said Calvin, and laughed.

"I don't think that's true," said Erin shyly.

"I'm on like eight things now," said Paul.

Calvin asked if Erin wanted to smoke marijuana and she asked if Paul would be okay with that and Paul said yes, thinking he didn't like that she had asked. While Erin and Calvin smoked in the bathroom, with the door closed so Calvin's parents wouldn't smell it, Paul and Maggie created a GIF of a baseball cap moving around on their heads. Maggie, when Paul said he wanted to smoke marijuana, said he shouldn't because of his lung collapse history. Paul began coughing nonstop after smoking and repeatedly said his chest burned and fell, half deliberately, to the floor, grinning in a stereotypically marijuana-induced manner, he could feel, as he tried, with his MacBook, to find information on the internet about his situation.

"I feel like I'm unsarcastically viewing this as a major ordeal," said Calvin.

"I'm just trying to Google 'burned lung,' I'm not doing anything to indicate what you said," said Paul in an agitated voice while grinning. "I'm just idly looking up 'burned lung' variations on the internet."

"I was also viewing this as major until Paul just said that," said Erin.

Paul lay facedown, at some point, on one of the two beds in the room and heard Calvin say "what if he's dead?" and imagined Erin shrugging. When he woke, four hours later, on his side, Erin was holding him from behind.

They spoke once—at a rest stop, when Paul said it was his turn to drive and Erin said she was okay with continuing—during the eight-hour drive to Brooklyn, arriving around midnight and sleeping until late in the afternoon, when Erin said she was buying groceries from LifeThyme and driving back to Baltimore. Paul asked if she wanted to "stay and eat dinner on Xanax" before leaving.

At Sel De Mer, that night, Erin said Paul had been ignoring her all weekend and that she felt depressed. Paul said he'd focused on doing what he wanted, on talking to Charles, instead of complaining that he was unhappy. Erin said Paul did complain, to Charles.

"I don't remembering complaining to him," said Paul.

"You said you don't feel happy around me," said Erin.

"I said I don't feel happy no matter what. I also said I don't feel interested in anyone except you."

"You said you felt interested in other girls sexually."

"That isn't complaining," said Paul. "We talked about a lot of things." Charles had seemed to be having the same "relationship problems" with his girlfriend as before Mexico and had said he was planning a similar, solitary trip to Asia. Paul had suggested Charles write a novel called *Mexico,* plotted around his problems with Jehan, who was still in Mexico but had been active on the internet, regularly writing on Charles' Facebook wall and, unless it had been a different Jehan, adding Paul on Goodreads.

• • •

After dinner, in Paul's room, Erin asked if she was "going home now." Paul lay unresponsive on his mattress facing away. Erin said she "wanted to buy groceries from LifeThyme before leaving." Paul rolled onto his back and, with only the top half of his head visible, said "I think it would be better if you didn't stay tonight" through the muzzle-y screen of his blanket. He felt "completely motionless," he thought, on his mattress, with his eyes closed, as Erin gathered her belongings. He heard her say "I agree with what you said about how if it doesn't work out then it doesn't work out, but I wanted to say that I like knowing you and I hope it works out."

Without knowing exactly why, but sensing, on some level, that his feeling was mostly vicarious—that he was experiencing what he suspected Erin would experience, in a few seconds, once she discerned his sincere lack of response—Paul felt a sympathetically cringing sensation that he wished Erin hadn't said what she had said. Mechanically, with the lightness of bones that could move, he stood and hugged her briefly, without looking at her face.

Six hours later, when birds were chirping but it was still dark outside, Paul was sitting on his mattress watching what he'd recorded in Calvin's room. He noticed that he hadn't been in Calvin's room—he didn't remember where he'd gone, maybe downstairs to the kitchen—for a few minutes, during which Erin had spoken in a louder, more confident voice and openly debated if she wanted a beer. Maggie, Paul saw in the movie, had asked Erin if Paul drank alcohol and Erin had said "sometimes," then Maggie had asked what kind and Erin had said "beer, and sometimes tequila," in a subtly, complicatedly different voice like that of a shyer, less friendly version of herself. Hearing this, aware that Erin would normally attribute non-firsthand information, that she'd say she had read about him drinking tequila, Paul began crying a little.

He lay against a pile of blankets and pillows, away from his MacBook, unsure why he felt emotional. Gradually he realized he'd intuited her voice sounded different because she had probably assumed, to some degree, that only she knew—and only she would ever know—of the aberration in her behavior and, while saying "beer, and sometimes tequila," maybe had distractedly felt an uncommon nearness to herself that Paul, knowing this in secret from her, had also felt.

Two months later, in mid-July, around a week after Paul turned 28, Calvin and Maggie were in Brooklyn for five days to act in a low-budget movie. They were no longer in a relationship. They met Paul and Erin on a Friday night at Sel De Mer, where Erin gave everyone Xanax and Calvin shared a marijuana cookie with everyone and Maggie, who hadn't eaten meat in two years, ordered lobster. They confirmed to snort heroin in Paul's room after dinner, then go to the Union Square theater to "group livetweet" whatever movie fit their schedule. They would sit separately during the movie and communicate only through tweets, in service of making the experience "more fun and interesting," said Paul, who anticipated wanting to be alone in the theater.

At Paul's apartment Maggie volunteered to help Paul juice fennel, celery, cucumber, lemon while Erin showered and Calvin did something in Paul's room. Paul, who had been silent most of the night, partly because he and Erin ingested 2mg Xanax each before dinner, asked if Maggie had asked her brother about "the thing," which he was surprised he remembered.

"Shit. Yeah. I forgot to tell you."

"What did he say?"

"I don't remember," said Maggie absently.

"Are you depressed about you and Calvin?"

"Yeah. I don't want to talk to him. I feel really depressed."

Paul organized three bags of heroin into four different-size piles—Maggie only wanted a little—while Erin bought tickets for *X-Men: First Class* at 12:35 a.m. Paul drew lines connecting three names to three lines of heroin and heard Calvin say "I think I just figured out I can be happy no matter what people around me are doing" to what seemed to be himself and earnestly thought "funny" in a monotone with a neutral expression, then snorted his heroin and showered and ingested 15mg Adderall, two Advil, half a marijuana cookie. Paul vomited on the street twice before they got in a taxi with Erin in the front passenger seat and Maggie in the backseat between Paul and Calvin, who was commenting on the taxi's TV, which was talking about Shaquille O'Neal.

"You should tweet it, stop talking about it," said Paul, and opened his door at a red light to vomit, but didn't and received from someone a plastic bag, which he vomited in twice with an overall sensation of disconcern-based serenity. He tweeted "in cab to theater, 'already' vomited twice (jk re seeming to imply xmen will make me vomit)" and read a tweet that said "put hand through cab glass to pet Paul as he vomited into a bag, cabdriver looked at me in a sitcom-like way" and said "Erin, you forgot the hashtag" while staring at his own tweet. "I forgot the hashtag also. We're all just going to keep forgetting it. What're we going to do?"

"I recommend copy and pasting." said Erin.

"We're all just going to keep forgetting it," said Paul "pessimistically," he thought, and when he exited the taxi he walked into, instead of onto, the sidewalk and fell stumbling ahead in an uninhibited, loosely controlled, briefly uncontrolled manner reminiscent of childhood, when this partial to complete abandonment of body and/or limb (of rolling like a log on carpet, falling face-first onto beds, being dragged by an arm or both legs through houses or side yard, floating in swimming pools, lying upside down in headstands on sofas) was normal, allowing his unexpected momentum to naturally expend, falling horizontally for an amusingly far length. He imagined continuing forward in a pretending of momentum, transitioning into a jog, disappearing into the distance. He vomited on the street, then turned around and jogged to Maggie, who stood motionless with a preoccupied expression.

"I'm okay," said Paul. "Where are they? Calvin, Erin."

"Buying water," said Maggie.

"How do you feel?"

"Floaty," said Maggie with a neutral expression. "Good. How do you feel?"

"Good," said Paul smiling. "I just used too much."

When they entered the theater the movie had already begun. Paul sat in a stadium-seated area, above and behind everyone else in the front area. After a few minutes he went to Maggie, who was in an isolated seat, on the right side of the theater. Maggie pointed at Erin and Calvin, twenty feet away, talking to each other.

"We agreed to sit separately," said Maggie.

"I want separately also," said Paul.

"I feel upset," said Maggie.

"I'm going to see what's happening," said Paul, and crossed an aisle, past five empty seats, to Erin, as Calvin left the theater. Erin said Calvin had wanted to share her phone. Paul said Calvin "should just go charge it for like ten minutes."

"I know. That's what I said. He's doing that now."

"Calvin went to charge his phone," said Paul to Maggie, and returned to his seat. He tweeted "someone in my row is snoring #xmenlivetweet" and "kevin bacon had something like 10 hands #xmenlivetweet." Maggie tweeted she wanted more heroin. Paul tweeted "i can hear someone snoring ~8 seats to my left #xmenlivetweet" and saw Maggie leave the theater and stared absently as Kevin Bacon talked to people. Kevin Bacon walked outside, where it was snowing, then he turned around and talked to the same people as before, who had followed him. Paul tried to remember why Kevin Bacon had gone outside. He read tweets from Maggie that said "feeling lonely #xmenlivetweet" and "i am in the bathroom contemplating chugging my beer," which had no hashtag. Paul saw that Erin had left the theater. Paul cautiously entered the women's bathroom, a few minutes later, hearing Maggie's voice and movement noises from the handicapped stall.

"Excuse me, ma'am," said Paul in a loud, authoritative voice, and the movement noises stopped.

"Yes?" said Erin after a pause.

"It's me," said Paul.

"Oh, shit," said Maggie, and the door opened.

"I was scared," said Erin, partly in view.

"You're in the women's bathroom," said Maggie.

"Sorry," said Paul grinning, and left and sat on the carpeted floor near an emergency exit and tweeted "where is everyone . . . i'm sitting in darkness near the women's bathroom #xmenlivetweet" and that he was going to try to scare Erin and Maggie again. He read "just stood up, lost 'all control' of left leg and fell into an arcade game, making a loud noise and 'yelping' #xmenlivetweet" by Calvin. He read "someone just said 'we did it!' while seeming to float in an indoor 'future area' #xmenlivetweet" by Erin. He heard Maggie's voice and walked quickly to her and Erin and thrust his glass bottle of water at them but water didn't leave the bottle until, as the bottle neared himself, some splashed onto his chin and neck. Calvin was sitting on the floor by the candy machines, smiling calmly at his phone. Erin gave Paul and Maggie tea-tree toothpicks. Paul went in the theater to his seat and tweeted "why is 'beast' flying a jet plane . . . #xmenlivetweet" and "is this world war 2, i don't understand anything #xmenlivetweet" and "i'm going to stand to look at who has been snoring loudly for ~15 min. #xmenlivetweet" and "someone seems to be laying across 2 seats sleeping #xmenlivetweet." He became aware of the tea-tree toothpick's wiggling, outside his mouth, and of his intensely concentrating expression, as he worked on editing a tweet, a few minutes after credits had begun scrolling down the screen, when the white shape, of Erin in a white dress, in Paul's peripheral vision, stopped enlarging, indicating an arrival.

In the lobby, by the bathrooms, Paul said he felt nauseated. "I feel," said Erin, and was quiet for around five seconds. "Never mind." Paul asked carefully, with vague aversion toward himself, if she usually thought of what to say before speaking, or would start talking without thinking. "I think at least fifty percent of it before talking, I think," said Erin. "Why?"

Paul said it was annoying sometimes to wait for her to think, and they stopped talking—Calvin and Maggie were ahead, sometimes looking back—until they got on the L train, when Paul apologized for saying it was annoying and said he understood her behavior. Erin quietly said it was okay. Paul asked if she felt okay and she said she did, and asked if Paul did. Maggie jumped in front of them and posed with the sleeping, drooling, middle-aged man in an opposite seat. "I'm okay with everything," said Paul distractedly, with some confusion, after moving his iPhone into position and photographing only the middle-aged man because Maggie had returned to her seat.

"Are you sure?" said Erin.

"Yeah. I'm okay with everything if you are."

"I am," said Erin.

"I feel nauseated," said Paul a few minutes later. "But I'm okay with everything. If I'm not talking it's because I'm nauseated."

"Okay," said Erin. "Thank you for telling me."

In the large deli below Harry's apartment Paul walked away, at one point, from everyone else and, alone in an aisle, turned into a barrier-like display of heavily discounted tomato sauce. None fell, or seemed to have been disturbed, or affected, to any degree, and no one saw. After buying beer, fennel, celery, a plastic bag of apples, three lemons and walking six blocks Paul and Erin sat on a sidewalk waiting for Calvin and Maggie to get their sleeping bags from where they'd been staying.

"You're really quiet suddenly," said Erin.

"I'm really nauseated," said Paul, and rested the weight of his head facedown on his open palms, covering his eyes and cheeks and forehead. It began raining lightly, in a mist, as if onto produce, or probably an air conditioner was dripping condensation. Paul weakly tried to remember what month it was, stopping after a few seconds, and moved his shoulders to indicate he didn't want to be touched when Erin began rubbing his back.

Maggie was in the bathroom and Paul was sitting cross-legged on his mattress, around half an hour later, absently reading descriptions of mutants on *X-Men: First Class*'s Wikipedia page—"scientist who is transformed into a frightening-looking mutant in an effort to cure himself, but is kind at heart"—when Calvin asked if "anyone" wanted to sit with him on the front stoop while he smoked.

"Me. I will," said Erin, who had been drying her hair with a towel after showering, and Paul saw her looking at herself in the wall mirror. He clicked "Kevin Bacon" and looked at the words "Kevin Bacon (disambiguation)" without thinking anything for a vague amount of time, until Maggie entered the room, when he stood and went in the bathroom and heard Erin say "actually, I'll have a beer" and Calvin say "really?" and "cool." The thick carpet of the bathmat, folded like a soft taco, was in the bathtub, sopping and heavy. Paul thought with some confusion that Maggie must've put it there, maybe for slippage prevention. While showering he thought about what he'd done during the filming, last year, August to December, of *X-Men: First Class*: hid in his room, gone on a book tour, gotten married, visited his parents. He entered his room wearing boxer shorts—Maggie was sitting in a far corner looking at her MacBook with a serious expression—and turned around and put on a shirt, sat on his mattress, placed his MacBook on his lap, stared at the words "Bacon in 2007" with slightly unfocused eyes. Maggie said she had a stomachache and moved onto the mattress asking if Paul wanted beer, which she held toward him and which he mutely held a few seconds before moving it near Maggie, who drank some and put it on the floor and resettled herself on the mattress with the sides of their knees touching.

"Calvin and Erin have been gone so long," said Paul.

"Maybe they're watching the sunrise," said Maggie.

"I don't think you can see it from here."

"Maybe they went somewhere."

"I don't think you can see it from anywhere near here."

"I don't know where they are," said Maggie.

"Do you feel depressed still?"

"Yeah," said Maggie.

"Because of you and Calvin?"

"Yeah."

"Did you end the relationship or him?"

"It was me," said Maggie. "He didn't want it to end." She said she felt depressed because she'd been really close with Calvin, so now something in her life felt missing. Paul asked about the singer, of a punk band he listened to often in high school, who had kissed Maggie, she'd said in an email, in someone's car after a concert. Maggie said the singer didn't want to bring her in his hotel room because his friends would think it was weird she was 17 and that he wanted to perform oral sex on her but she didn't want that and he'd said they could "get naked but not have sex" and Maggie had said she didn't know what that meant. Then the singer had told intimate secrets about his ex-girlfriend. Paul had idly opened iMovie on his MacBook and they'd been absently looking at it, not recording, as they talked and he accidentally clicked—and quickly closed—one of the movies.

"That might be porn. Erin and I made a porn."

"What's that?" said Maggie pointing at "ketamine."

"A drug we used before going to Urban Outfitters."

"It seems like you and Erin have a lot of fun together. Is that true?"

Paul said they saw each other once every ten days and usually started "fighting" after one or two days. Maggie asked what they fought about. Paul vaguely remembered when, on a large dose of Xanax, alone one night in his room, he fell on his way to his mattress to sleep—pulling down his high chair and causing his shoulder, he discovered upon waking eleven hours later, to bleed heavily from two places into a dark pile on his mattress—only slightly aware that this was unrelated to Maggie's question. Paul remembered when he calculated three divided by two as three-fourths regarding an amount of heroin and vomited steadily eight to ten hours, beginning around noon. He and Erin, who'd been resilient, maybe from weeks of Percocet after her car accident, had snorted the miscalculated heroin upon waking and, after riding the L train, he'd begun vomiting—near Union Square on streets and sidewalks, in Pure Food and Wine's bathroom, while walking thirteen blocks south, in Bobst Library's bathrooms. When they left the library at night he stopped every ten to fifteen feet to vomit nothing and Erin began expressing a previously suppressed concern, insisting Paul drink water. Paul vomited repeatedly after each sip and sat—and, at one point, briefly, lay—on the sidewalk outside a New York University dorm by Washington Square Park, inaudibly mumbling that he was okay and, when Erin said she wanted to call an ambulance, barely perceptibly shaking his head no with a sensation of reluctantly imparting an ancient wisdom. In his room, an hour later, around 9:30 p.m., Erin wanted Paul, covered by his blanket on his mattress, to drink a glass of water and didn't think he should be lying with eyes closed because people in his situation died by sleeping. After an increasingly tense exchange culminating with Paul "sarcastically," he thought, chugging the large glass of water—in a display of functioning that probably seemed unlike that of a dying person—Erin, to some degree spitefully, Paul felt, had said she was driving home to Baltimore and, to Paul's surprise, had left him to sleep alone.

"Just . . . things," said Paul, and laughed a little.

Maggie was staring at his MacBook's screen.

"Different things," said Paul.

"I'm just curious," said Maggie in a frustrated voice.

"I know," said Paul staring at the cursor on the screen, repeatedly disappearing and reappearing in the same place.

"Can I watch some of a movie?"

"Yeah," said Paul. "Which one?"

"Your favorite one. Not the porn."

Paul clicked a ninety-two-minute movie beginning in his parents' apartment, when he and Erin had returned for ecstasy because he'd vomited his MDMA. Paul's mother was talking about the Flip cam she'd bought for Paul's birthday. Paul clicked near the end of the movie. Erin was describing, in "the voice," which they hadn't used in months, how salmonella was harvested, in the residential area behind McDonald's. In the movie Paul said something inaudible and Erin said "Android? You're bringing Android into this? Amateur." Paul clicked elsewhere and the movie showed solid black as Erin said "and here we have the brainchild, really, of this whole operation." When Paul described his time in Taiwan as "hellish," a month or two ago, Erin had been surprised, because she'd enjoyed Taiwan, which had surprised Paul, who had cited "overdrive" and their excessive drug use before the trip as why it had, for him, been "hellish." Descending to McDonald's first floor, in the movie, Erin looked different than she did now, Paul thought, and for maybe the eighth time in the past month considered that she had subtly denser bones or unseen scar tissue now that her face had fully healed. Paul stopped the movie and the vanished image, of Erin and the Christmas tree, reappeared instantly in his memory, looking similar, being already memory-like, on the screen, from low resolution. Taipei seemed gothic and lunar, in the movies of that night, with the spare activity and structural density of a fully colonized moon that had been abandoned and was being recolonized; its science-fictional qualities seemed less advanced than ancient, haunted, of a future dark age.

Maggie was showing Paul emails from the punk singer, after showing him writing she'd emailed to a magazine, when Erin and Calvin returned. Calvin asked what they were looking at and Maggie, closing her MacBook, said she was showing Paul writing she'd emailed to a magazine.

"You guys are still awake?" said Erin. "What have you guys been doing?"

"What were you guys doing?" said Paul in a quiet monotone, mentally stressing "you." Erin went in the bathroom and Paul heard the sink turn on and, when she exited, asked if she had smoked cigarettes. She said Calvin had but she hadn't. Paul removed his contact lenses and washed his face, and said he was going to sleep and lay facing away from Erin, who asked if he'd set his alarm. Paul said he'd set it for 2:30 p.m. (they'd agreed to be extras, in the movie Calvin and Maggie were in, tomorrow at 4:30 p.m.) and Erin asked if he was upset about something.

"No, I want to sleep. I'm putting earplugs in."

"If you're upset, tell me now instead of later."

"I want to sleep," said Paul.

"You seem upset. Can you tell me why?"

Calvin and Maggie were unrolling their sleeping bags. Paul turned toward Erin, whose expression he couldn't see without contact lenses, and loudly whispered "I feel upset you went outside for so long without talking to me first and that you kept asking me if I was okay when I told you I felt nauseated and that you keep asking me if I'm upset after I said I wasn't" and turned away.

"So you are upset," said Erin after a few seconds.

"I'm nauseated and want to sleep. I'm putting in earplugs."

Erin put an arm around him, and he stood and turned off the room's light and lay facing away. After a few minutes Erin squished an arm under his neck, wrapping it around his chest to hug him tightly with both arms. Paul thought of the monkfish he'd shown her—the light-absorbing mass of it, a silhouette of itself, Wikipedia's stock image for monkfish—and felt emotional, and committed to not moving, then woke to his alarm. He kept his eyes closed, feigning sleep. He could faintly hear Maggie saying his name. "Paul, your alarm," said Maggie louder, and touched his arm.

He turned off the alarm and covered his head with his blanket, feeling tense and uncomfortable. He removed his earplugs, went in the bathroom, showered and moved quickly to his MacBook and looked at the internet sitting cross-legged on his bed, facing away from Erin, who was waking, it seemed. Paul could feel his left eyebrow twitching. Erin, after a few minutes, sat and said "has everyone showered?" in a voice that sounded loud and sleepy, as if contented. Paul, who felt an excruciating dread of being spoken to or looked at, was startled by how Erin was calmly, unself-consciously, nonchalantly directing attention toward herself. Paul emailed Erin while she showered and, after she blow-dried her hair, Calvin and Maggie left, saying they'd see Paul and Erin in an hour. Erin sat at the foot of the bed, facing away from Paul who lay on his back with his MacBook against his thighs, and they communicated by email (they'd agreed to type, not talk, whenever one of them, currently Paul, felt unable to speak in a friendly tone) for around fifty minutes, until Erin said "it seems like you don't care about me" aloud.

"I don't," said Paul. "I don't right now."

"It seems that way."

"I know. I don't care right now."

They were quiet a few seconds.

"I'm going to Think Coffee," said Erin, and went in the bathroom, then back in Paul's room, then into the kitchen and out of the apartment. Paul slept three hours, then texted "how's Think Coffee." Erin responded she'd been wandering aimlessly on Xanax and hadn't gotten there yet. Paul rode the L train to Union Square and walked toward the library, ten blocks south, to meet Erin for dinner, beneath a membranous and vaguely patterned sky like a faded, inconsistently worn red-and-blue blanket lit from the other side.

If it were a blanket, Paul thought, beneath which existed only his imagination, he wouldn't want to throw it off and be obliterated by the brightness of a child's bedroom in daytime, or even peek outside, letting in the substrate of another world. Realizing this, as a medium dose of Xanax began taking effect, he felt a kind of safety in being where he was—inside the confines of what, to him, was everything—instead of "out there."

In Paul's room, around 3:30 a.m., after ordering a lot of food at Lodge but eating only a little and talking calmly, then working on things a few hours on Adderall, they decided to eat psilocybin mushrooms Paul had bought a few weeks ago from Peanut. The light was off and they were on Paul's mattress, forty minutes later, when Paul began asking what Erin, who seemed reluctant to answer, was thinking. She stood and turned on the light and asked where the "bag" of mushrooms was and, because she thought she was feeling it more than Paul, fed him the remaining amount and turned off the light.

"We're choosing to not talk, which itself is a communication, which seems good," thought Paul holding Erin. "I'll continue communicating in this manner, by not." His steady, controlled petting of one of Erin's vertebra with the cuticle of his right index finger gradually felt like his only method of remaining in concrete reality, where he and Erin, and other people, shared a world. Sometimes, forgetting what he was doing, his finger would slow or stop and he would become aware of a drifting sensation and realize he was being absorbed—from an indiscernible distance, beyond which he wouldn't know how to return—and, with some urgency, move his body or open his eyes, seeing grid-like overlays on the walls and holograms of graph paper in the air, to interrupt his being taken. The effort became gradually smaller and more unconscious and, as if for something to do, in place of what was now automatic, Paul began to discern his rhythmic petting as a continuous striving to elicit certain information from Erin by responding or not responding to her rhythms, in a cycle whose goal was to produce momentary equilibriums. He felt increasingly attuned to the speed and quality of her breathing and heart rate, until he felt able to instantly discern changes in her physiology, which in entirety began to seem like an inconstant unit of unique, irreducible information (an ever-changing display of only prime numbers) that was continuously expressed and that bypassed the parts of them that allowed for deliberation or perception or intuition, beginning and ending in the only place where they were exactly together, undifferentiated and unknowable, but couldn't, in their present form, ever reach, like a thing communicating directly with itself, rendering them both irrelevant.

Paul began to sometimes laugh uncontrollably, with his face at the back of Erin's neck, unsure what was funny. When he saw her frowning, a few minutes later, she burrowed her head against his chest and he said "what are you thinking about?" and she didn't answer and, in an increasingly incredulous voice, like he mostly wanted to express how amazingly difficult it was to know—sometimes pausing after each word for emphasis—he repeatedly stated the question. "This isn't what I expected at all," he heard himself say, at some point, without knowing what he was referencing. He'd obviously wanted something good to happen, but what was happening wasn't expected, based on what he'd said, therefore it must be bad. He was yawning, so was factually bored of Erin. "I feel like I can't breathe," he said, and suddenly stood and felt confused and unreal. He repeatedly fell onto his mattress, which every time seemed much less substantial than expected, dropping his body with increasing force and desperation, then lay on his back, unsatisfied and worried. "Sleeping, waking," he said frustratedly. "Is there a difference? Am I dead?"

"You're not dead," said Erin.

"I think I'm dead," said Paul distractedly, and covered

his face with a blanket. He was thinking of how people say that when you die you experience your last moments for an eternity, when Erin yanked away the blanket and began tickling him and pulling him from the mattress as he giggled and intensely struggled, with confusion and frustration, to hide beneath the blanket. After succeeding, facedown with Erin sitting on his back, he seemed, while hidden, to not be thinking anything, then when he absently shifted to expose his face, to breathe, he believed he was insane. He asked if he was and Erin said no, which proved he was, because if he were he would ask and Erin would say he was not. He would never be sane, now that he was insane, he knew, then moved directly past that conclusion—unable to stop there, or anywhere—and believed again that he was dead and remembered hearing the word "bag" and thought of heroin and said "did we overdose?" He realized he would be alone if he was dead, even if Erin had also died—death would seal them into their own private afterlives—and, in idle correction, quietly said "did I overdose?"

"I just have to deal with it," he said in reference to being permanently alone, with only his weak projections of Erin and his room—requiring an amount of effort to sustain that was immense and debilitating, which was probably why, he realized, he couldn't sate his breath, feel comfortable, think coherently—to occupy himself forever. "It's okay," he said, to begin some process of consolation, but felt only more despair and a panicked suspicion that he'd barely comprehended the terribleness of his situation. "This will go on for twenty years," he said vaguely, and stood and slapped his thighs with both hands, then held the bathroom door's frame with his arms in a V and his head hung down and repeatedly said "oh my god" while thinking "I can't believe I OD'd" and failing to view his death—the horrible, inexcusable mistake of it—as interestingly absurd or blackly comic or anything except profoundly troubling. He fell facedown on a mound of blankets and pillows and rolled onto his back, suddenly contemplative. "I don't remember that at all," he said of the months, or years, when their drug use increased and they began injecting heroin, crudely visualizing a stereotypical montage of downward-spiraling drug use. "I don't remember . . . that. But it must have happened . . . I just can't believe I overdosed."

"You can't overdose on mushrooms," said Erin meekly.

"I forgot we used mushrooms," said Paul in a curious voice, but didn't consider the information and immediately forgot again. "I think I am where you were twenty minutes ago, so you need to console me," he said while thinking "that's exactly what I would tell a projection to do if I were dead." He tried to fondly recall a memory of his life, of life generally—he would need to learn to be satisfied with his memories, which was all he had now—and said "kissing is good" and "remember Las Vegas?" He said "Taiwan was good" knowing it hadn't been, aware he was openly trying to deceive himself, then thought of tracing back his life to determine what caused the sequence of events leading to his overdose. "The book tour . . . after the summer. Two trips to Taiwan. Remember Arby's? In Florida?" He heard Erin say they never went to Florida and realized he was talking to himself while sustaining an imaginary companion and that he wasn't saying what he was thinking. "Why do I keep thinking about RBIs, runs batted in? And something about Hank Aaron?" Paul believed again, at some point, that he was in the prolonged seconds before death, in which he had the opportunity to return to life—by discerning some code or pattern of connections in his memory, or remembering some of what had happened with a degree of chronology sufficient to re-enter the shape of his life, or sustaining a certain variety of memories in his consciousness long enough to be noticed as living and relocated accordingly. Lying on his back, on his mattress, he uncertainly thought he'd written books to tell people how to reach him, to describe the particular geography of the area of otherworld in which he'd been secluded.

Paul was on his back on his mattress thinking "faces are circles," and of cutting a face into four parts, as his room slowly brightened with indirect sunlight. Erin held his hand and he stood and went with her to the window and focused on the metaphysical area where he anticipated hearing her voice, wanting to be surprised, or to hear something consoling— apportioned from himself to his projection, to ventriloquize back to himself—about death. Erin was pointing at the sky, asking if Paul saw "that thing"—a pale, logo-like silhouette of antennae, or leafless plant, rising from a sixth-floor roof's corner, foregrounding a pink sky. Paul said he did, and that it looked pretty, he felt like a sleepy child willingly distracted from worries about a lost pet by a mother pointing at a star saying "everything will be okay, just focus on the twinkling— that's where we came from and where we'll be again, no matter what happens here, yes, I promise."

He held Erin's hand and wandered somewhat aimlessly into the bathroom and picked up a tongue scraper. "You bought me this," he said with dull, unfocused eyes. "I never used it. But I really appreciated it. I liked getting it. I never told you." He put it down and disinterestedly thought "it's not going to work," as his hand idly turned a knob, and was surprised by the rupture and crackling of water, its instantaneous column of binary variations. He moved his hand into the water and was surprised again. "I didn't expect that . . . to feel like that," he said with a serious expression. "That's really weird." Realizing he had no concept of what water felt like until he touched it—cold, grasping, meticulous, aware—he felt self-conscious and said he wanted to pee alone. Sitting on the toilet, with the door closed, Paul realized he felt less discomfort and could breathe easier and that the surface of things was shinier and more dimensional from greater pixilation, all of which he viewed as evidence he was successfully convincing himself—through an increasingly elaborate, skillful, unconscious projection of a reality he would eventually believe he was exploring—that he wasn't dead. With an eternity to practice, he realized, he would forget everything he had thought or felt while dead, including his current thoughts and feelings; he would only believe, as he once had, that he was alive.

He was startled, entering his room, to see Erin already moving, as if independent of his perception. He briefly discerned her movement as incremental—not continuous, but in frames per second—and, like with insects or large predators, unpredictable and dangerous. He wanted to move backward and close the door and be alone again, in the bathroom, but Erin had already noticed him and, after a pause, distracted by her attention, he reciprocated her approach. They hugged a little, near the center of the room, then he turned around and moved toward the kitchen—dimly aware of the existence of other places, on Earth, where he could go—and was surprised when he heard himself, looking at his feet stepping into black sandals, say that he felt "grateful to be alive."

ACKNOWLEDGMENTS

Thank you to my editor, Tim O'Connell, and my agent, Bill Clegg.